In a rainy town where nothing ever happens, a sardonic yet bubbly potions witch on the outs with her family after a failed Valentine's Day love potion has her entire life turned upside down. With her shop being raided by people seeking out her love-potion-turned-accidental-hallucinogen, she is forced to put everything on hold to face what is quickly becoming an ordeal worse than anything the town has ever seen.

When bad turns to worse, she is attacked on a dark road after her car is sabotaged, saved by a dragon that looks far too much like a sexy version of Dracula, and thrown into a world of fae mafia and an omnipotent being that appears to be en-tangled in it all with her.

Storm Carlisle must try to juggle a budding relationship with a man who is more beast than human, struggle with a family who is far too involved in her business, and stop the enemies who are hell-bent on recruiting her to join their side while cor-rupting every inch of the three worlds they can get their hands on.

Once Upon A Dragon
Copyright © 2019 Ellise Valentine
ISBN: 978-1-4874-2677-4
Cover art by Martine Jardin

Published by eXtasy Books Inc or
Devine Destinies, an imprint of eXtasy Books Inc

Look for us online at:
www.eXtasybooks.com or www.devinedestinies.com

Once Upon A Dragon Witches-Brew Cove

By

Ellise Valentine

DEDICATION

To all the dreamers.
Never be afraid to try.

CHAPTER ONE

"What do you mean we are out of nightshade? I just went on a run to collect some yesterday!" one very angry she-wolf exclaimed from the back of my shop.

I let out a harsh exhale, slumping my shoulders down defeatedly to rest on the counter before me. "You saw how many people have been demanding the new *love potion*. We are lucky we have been able to keep them from busting down our doors every morning, Jessica."

It had gotten to the point where every joint in my exhausted body ached from the stress of using far too much magic these last few days. Normally my cutesy little potion shop sold anything from hair growth formula to energy drinks, but when my loveable yet batshit crazy aunt flew into town on her cherry-red broom she'd labeled the *Cupid's Stick*, she changed all of that with a single idea.

An idea I would later regret.

She waltzed right into my shop with a half-baked scheme of a small partnership between our two shops, mine being a potion shop named Pills and Potions and hers being a sex shop named Wands and Whips. She claimed to have just happened to have the crazy idea to come out with a potion named *Love Potion* on the wild ride that was the week before Valentine's Day.

It took getting me smashed with a two-hundred-dollar bottle of champagne for me to agree, and three more days for me to perfect it. The idea? A potion with effects strong enough to have a couple do it like rabbits for at least the entire night.

The outcome? A hallucinogen strong enough to make a person's wildest fantasy come to life and screw them into oblivion.

Well, they didn't really come to life. It was just a vision so strong that it felt real in every way. Within twenty-four hours after it hit my shelves, dozens of couples were ranting and raving about how suddenly they were having foursomes with the movie stars of their dreams.

Which brings me to now. My entire shop had been ransacked by rabid customers hell-bent on getting their hands on the miracle potion. People even came in from other towns to get their hands on the cursed thing.

It was like a sea of needy people of all shapes and races crashing into my small, homey shop. At worst, it was a severe fire hazard. There was simply no way a building could handle that many heated bodies rubbing against each other in one place with tempers boiling hotter than the sun once they realized they couldn't get their paws on what they had come for.

At best? It got my business out there, just like my aunt claimed it would.

"I thought you already announced you were discontinuing Love Potion," Jessica griped as she walked out from the back cradling a basket of smelling salts. "Why won't they leave you alone?"

"I discontinued it two days ago. I already told them I wouldn't be selling it anymore because the potions are immoral and I don't want my shop associating with that kind of practice, but they keep coming. They had some other witches pinpoint the ingredients, but nobody else has been able to get it right. That's why we are out of every ingredient I used in that god-awful brew," I whined, pointing toward the empty shelves of ingredients to prove my claim.

In all my days, I had never had to deal with a catastrophe of this degree. My shop was open for the residents, a small exchange shop for people to get little magic cures instead of heading up to a doctor or healer. It was never meant for commercial success like this.

If you had told anyone ten days ago any one of our stores would bring in crowds like this, you would be laughed out of town.

Witches-Brew Cove is the typical melting pot of a small American town. We have our hicks, our upper-class, our townspeople, werewolves, vampires, fae, and witches. Lovingly named by the coven that founded this town, Witches-Brew Cove was one of the many towns in America that perfectly settled into a slow non-dramatic existence after the outing of the paranormals that had always resided secretly in society.

About a hundred years ago when the human population had officially dipped to become the minority around the world, it had been decided that the secret of the other races that crowded this world just couldn't be kept a secret anymore. A huge surprise to everyone involved was that it all went completely fine.

No riots, no earth-shattering consequences, the world just accepted the fact that it had changed. Though it might have helped that a good deal of the human population had already functioned normally while already knowing about the other half of the population, but that's neither here nor there.

Of course, my family had been the first to open the gates of their closed-off little chunk of the woods and founded a nice little nowhere town where everyone could exist together. Since then it had been just that, a slow, drama-free town.

Until now everything was fine and dandy, with most people sharing a street with any number of paranormals. Being a witch myself I was more than happy to be born in this new generation, especially since I could now sell my potions on the main strip of Witches-Brew Cove without worrying about being burned at the stake.

Unfortunately, due to my familial connections in this town it meant now I had to face the consequences of my actions. If I had a choice, I might have ditched the place by way of an overgrown path in the woods during the night while cackling at the top of my lungs like my ancestors would have. I'd like to think that's how I'd do it.

"So I take it work is going to be hectic for the next few days?" Jessica looked distraught by the idea and didn't even bother hiding her disappointment.

One thing I knew from working with the wolf was that she loved working for the shop but hated the people to an insane degree. The less she had to deal with customers, the better.

If I had my way as of right now, I would ban everyone from coming into the shop who wanted to ask about the potions and let Jessica continue her work, but I didn't see that working. From what I could tell, the more I poked at the stewing crowd, the worse they got.

That was when an idea had come to mind. A good idea. One that might be able to solve both of our problems.

With a victorious grin, I snapped right back to attention, no doubt startling the she-wolf with my sudden change in mood. I was in no mood to care, however, because I just singlehandedly knocked out both of our problems at once with a brilliant plan.

"Nope," I sang, hopping excitedly around the counter to the front of the shop, "because Pills and Potions is officially closed!"

She did not greet my declaration with even a fraction of my happiness — quite the opposite.

"Closed?" she shrieked. "You can't just close up shop when things get tough! Remember, you aren't just some boner factory, Storm. We have customers that rely on our products!"

I rolled my eyes at her dramatics. "First of all, don't pretend we both don't realize you would freak out if your pay suddenly got cut off and didn't get your weekly collection of comics, so don't act the selfless concerned heroine. Secondly, that's why we aren't actually closing. Just the store is."

Jessica rounded the wide collection of shelves to watch in utter disbelief as I flipped the open sign to closed, cocking one hip. With her dark hair spilling around her shoulders and those wicked blue eyes, you could almost imagine her wolf itself staring you down with its beastly gaze. Compared to my red-haired, pale-skinned self, she won the battle of bad-ass beauty.

Not that I was complaining, I was still a cute-ass witch. I didn't hold that sort of warrior woman physique other women had.

"What does that even mean? How are we going to close the store but magically not close the business? All of our transactions come directly from over the counter sales."

My grin widened even further, and with an excited spin in place that allowed for a moment of dramatic pause, I declared, "We are going to deliver!"

Somehow my dramatic reveal didn't do anything to change Jessica's sour mood, and in fact, she appeared only to get more exasperated. Honestly, if it weren't for my absolute lack of self-awareness at all times, I would suspect she thought I was stupid.

It hurt a little, thinking she thought of me that way. After all, I had done a lot to try and assume that sort of older role-model behavior for her I had admired in other women, despite the fact I was barely older than her myself.

"You are really running away from this? I thought you were the type to, and I am quoting you here, *take a wolf by the fangs*," Jessica said slowly, as if that would lessen the blow in any way whatsoever.

"I am not running away! I am solving the problem in a non-face-to-face manner," I insisted, coming across almost pleading.

I knew she was probably right. It wasn't a good idea to solve any of your problems in a moment of weakness, but I genuinely couldn't see any other avenue out of this situation. I could continue working and grit my teeth through the customers demanding I give them what they wanted, or I could do this and allow it to blow over naturally.

Considering just allowing things to happen and hoping nothing goes wrong was how this all happened in the first place, I wasn't going to entertain that route.

That was why I had even entertained my aunt when she showed up on my porch, blitzed out of her mind and ranting about her very own potion idea. Sure, I may or may not have been drunk out of my mind as well, but I should have known it would amount to nothing good.

I would have to remind myself never to entertain long lost family members blowing into town with scandalous ideas in the future. Though other people might be able to figure that out themselves with the use of their brains.

Jessica turned to face the back—a firm set to her jaw, as though what she was about to endure was going to be worse than torture. I had to bite my lip not to laugh at the petulant look, reminded once more that my employee was still little more than a moody teenager.

"Go ahead and tell me just how you are going to attempt this."

It took some time to smooth out some of the details in order to get Jessica to agree that this was the best idea, considering all of the factors rooting against the shop.

She had been hesitant, probably rightfully so, considering it was her job I was changing up out of nowhere. However, once I explained she would be able to do her job without interacting with the new crazies while I still made customers happy, she was more than happy to oblige the idea.

We both knew the shop wouldn't suffer from the lack of traffic. I didn't need the money from the open shop. The shop itself was no more than something to do instead of wallowing away in my home like a hermit. I could close it for the next two weeks, and I would still be running smoothly without dipping into my resources.

Overall, everyone was happy, including the customers now getting free delivery.

Of course, my one good idea had to come with a dozen other really bad ones, like deciding that I would take a long way home instead of driving straight home like a normal person. After the last few days, being alone with my thoughts on an empty road had seemed like a great idea.

Of course, the fates just couldn't let my attempt to escape my punishment go unpunished, so that meant that I got stuck in the middle of the backwoods when my *Subaru's* gas mysteriously emptied onto the road. It was at times like this I cursed myself for being the only witch who chose to drive instead of flying.

"No! No! No!" I cried, banging my hands onto the still-warm hood of my car.

My baby girl was still as a rock, completely dead. Even her lights switched off, leaving me in the gloomy light of dusk. It only took a quick look to figure out that the hanging tubes under my car were my newly severed gas-line.

Somehow between this morning and now, some monster had fucked with my car, and of course, my dumbass had to choose this day to go through the backwoods. I was a sitting duck, miles away from a gas station or mechanic, equally as far from a house that would answer when I knocked.

I'm sure that if whatever douche fucked with my car could

see me now, they'd be cackling. I essentially gave the person exactly what they had been aiming for.

Lucky for me, it was 2120, and no witch in her right mind went around without a pocket mirror — no apps and games, but 100 percent reliability. If you're in a pinch, the pocket mirror will send your messages and emails without fail, no service required, as long as you have the power to wield it.

Unfortunately, that meant I now had to sit and wait for not only a tow truck but a cop car to come and drive me home. Apparently, things like a severed gas-line are *signs of malice towards an individual* and *need to be taken seriously*. As if.

It was probably some disgruntled customer wanting their share of love juice. Sure, it was concerning, and the person better hope I never catch who did it, but I wasn't too concerned about it. With creatures capable of summoning a league of zombies to surround your house at any point in the day, things like a car being compromised was a drop in the bucket.

The waiting might have been a blessing in disguise, though, because breathing in the sharp air of the night calmed me more than anything else had in the last few weeks.

It had been rough. The potion was barely half of it. Whoever said living in a small town where everybody knows you was simple was a liar.

First, my sister up and packs all of her stuff and decides to go on a *spiritual journey* into the fae realm for no reason other than she felt like it. Secondly, my youngest sister still attends high school and makes a point never to interact with any other living being on earth, so dealing with breaking out of her shell was a nightmare. It wasn't even that she was a bad kid. Valentine is a dream. It was just concerning.

Then there's my aunt, the out of her mind crazy one who disappeared for around ten years. My life was quickly devolving into a bad soap opera, like the old ones from before paranormals had announced their existence.

I wasn't going to say my life was a wreck. I could eventually smooth things over and be just fine, but it was stressful. Working my own business turned out to be a hell of a lot harder than I ever thought it would be. People in town talked and would be talking long after this all blew over.

The only thing I had that was stable was knowing my great-grandmother was fine. She was the one thing in my life that was immovable. She had raised us since we were thrown into her arms after a fire burned down our house when we were all fairly young, taking a good portion of our existing family with it.

I might be at odds with her right now, but at least I had that.

Putting all of that aside, getting some fresh air out there might be just the thing to take my mind off of it all. Sometimes all it took to take a little bit of the weight off of your shoulders was as simple as standing still and letting yourself sink into a cool evening night. I never got to sit and enjoy myself anymore, and even though this was forced upon me by some twist of fate, I was going to enjoy the small bit of peace.

It was about thirty minutes later when I grew tired of smelling the roses.

Maybe it was me, but those trees were starting to look less scenic and more like they were harboring some kind of monster in their depths. I knew I tended to see the worst things in the dark once the sun set, thanks to my urge to freak out at the slightest bump in the night, but this time it didn't feel like I was irrational.

I tried to ignore the feeling as I snuggled deeper into the inky cab of my car, but the woods seemed to grow bigger and louder around me. Every second the sound of crickets and rustling leaves grew until it was an overwhelming symphony in my ears.

I closed my eyes, closing off the world around me, trying to focus just on myself.

Crack.

I jolted up in my seat, eyes flying open. The sound came from the top of my car, the sound of protesting metal. I tried to look around my dark windows, but whatever it was couldn't be seen from where I sat. I could only see the desolate roads long overdue for an update that would never come.

Absentmindedly my hand snuck to the switch to lock my doors, even though I already knew the car was locked up tight.

The hair on the backs of my arms stood straight, the first sign of my instinct sensing something very off. No other sound came, and I was left with nothing but the ringing in my ears and the feeling deep in the pit of my stomach that something was wrong.

I tried telling myself it must have been a fluke, something falling from the trees. I remembered this fat little squirrel used to love pummeling my sister with acorns from his perch in my great-grandmother's bat tree when I was younger, so maybe it was something like that.

It didn't help with my tension in the slightest. My nerves were wound so tight I swore they would snap if even the slightest sound came from outside my car.

Another loud crack right above my head made me shriek and jump, almost sliding right into the steering wheel. I barely had time to react before the sound came again, closer to where I sat in the car.

Then another, and another. The sound was growing louder and louder, accompanied by the unmistakable sound of metal creaking. I felt a tremor run through me, and I had to will my trembling body to look up at where the noise was now coming from. Deep welts were beginning to pierce the metal, and each new sound was mirrored by a large indent being punched right into the thick metal of the car roof.

It looked like claw marks, jagged and uneven. The marks of a hungry beast.

I wasn't screaming anymore. Instead, I sat very still trying not to draw attention to myself. I knew if it kept up the noise, whatever it was, it was going to kill me.

I knew now this was no coincidence. Whoever stranded me out here wanted to leave me for this thing, and I was too terrified to care.

Even though I could barely move, I tried looking around for a sign of what the creature might be, looking for anything that could help me try and figure out how to stop it. I only caught a glimpse of an impossibly pale limb, skeletal thin, as it shot above me out of sight.

I tried to comb my mind for any scrap of information that might match what little I saw, but the little glimpse was too fast to identify anything important. It was too brief, too little. It could be any number of creatures.

It was clear that whatever was shaking my car was no human, however, and definitely not a zombie, though its pallid color did match that of one. As each indent above me grew deeper and shook the car harder, I knew I had no time to play the identifying card.

My potions weren't an option. Since I couldn't identify what it was, I had no chance of landing a blow that would harm it, but my only other option was my Witch's Fire. I didn't even know that I could call upon it. Every time I had tried in the past, the spell was weak, and I knew the idea was not an option.

I couldn't get out and try my luck fighting the thing. My mind rebelled at the idea of getting out of the safety of my car, even if it was currently turning into a mess of scraps above my head. It was a miracle the windows hadn't blown out yet.

As if the fates themselves were on my side, a flash of gold

in the dark drew my gaze, and I was met with the shiny gold badge of the Witches-Brew Cove police.

The cops had finally come. Or rather, the cop. A single man in civilian clothes stood at the foot of my car, and at that moment I couldn't care less. Anything could have appeared in the dark wearing a badge, and I would be jumping for joy.

I was so distracted by my relief at his sudden appearance that I nearly missed the dark fog of shadowy magic engulfing his body. The sounds on the hood of my car halted, and whatever it was made an angry keening cry at the growing shadow. It sounded like a child's cry mixed with that of a screeching cat, a sound that came straight from the depths of a nightmare.

I clutched my ears, trying to protect myself against the piercing sound, but it bounced around in my skull with dizzying force.

The fog had just begun to clear as the man launched himself over my car hood in a single bound, thudding against the creature and revealing strong scaled animal legs. I immediately recognized that whatever my savior was had to be some kind of shifter, and I thanked the fates for granting me luck once more.

I watched through my back window as the two slammed to the ground just behind my car, getting a glimpse at the pale skeletal creature clutched in the former police officer's scaled grasp.

"Please let him win," I begged. "Please let him win."

From what little I could see, I knew that what was taking place behind my car was no mere brawl. It was a full-blown vicious fight accompanied by the glint of golden scales and a set of dark claws slashing. A bright red splash of blood struck my window, blurring my vision and making me flinch back as if it would come through the window right at me. The whole ordeal could have been five minutes or five hours, for all I knew. Each second I sat paralyzed in my front seat felt like an eternity.

After endless tense minutes, there was a loud hissing sound before all movement ceased behind the car. The only thing left that I could see through the gory window was the golden back of a dragon lying motionless on the ground.

I felt a tendril of cold fear curl low in the pit of my stomach.

Surely he wasn't dead. There was no way. The man was a police officer. They couldn't die. That didn't happen in the movies.

There was no sign of the other creature, not even the continued sounds of it trying to pry its way into my car. If I had to guess, the golden beast had scared it away.

I didn't trust the quiet, even if my senses told me the creature was gone.

I debated whether or not to leave my car and find out, trying to calculate my chances of survival once I left the safety of the cab of my car. Caution fought to win out, coming up with a thousand reasons why leaving my car was a bad idea, but worry for the beast won out.

I wasn't going to let the man who possibly saved my life bleed out on the sidewalk just because I was too much of a coward to try and save him.

Moving quickly, I flung open my door and made my way slowly to the beast, taking care to make enough noise so as not to startle him. I didn't want him to think I might be the creature coming to finish him off. My best bet was to be as loud as possible in order to avoid being diced by his claws. Once I reached the beast, all fears of startling him escaped right out the window.

In the place of the golden form of what I assumed to be a dragon was the man I had seen before his change, his clothes bloodied and his body limp. His chest heaved in labored breaths that were visible from where I stood, clearly indicating immense pain. I dropped to my knees beside him, carefully getting closer in order to assess his wounds.

Claw marks were littered all over his exposed skin, and there were some indications of lacerations concealed by his clothing.

Despite his ragged state, I could see that he was incredibly handsome. It felt wrong to acknowledge that now, but it was the first thing that came to mind upon seeing him up close.

He looked exactly like one those romantic movie versions of Vlad the Impaler, waving dark hair, thick dark brows and a face that reminded you of a stalking panther. Plus he was big, too, like he had giant's blood somewhere in his line big. I was never big on tall guys — compared to things like being employed and not being misogynistic height came in second place — but I had to admit it was very attractive. Images of climbing him like a tree flashed in my mind, immediately batted away by my self-disgust at even thinking of something like that in a time like this.

"Back to the present. The dragon is bleeding out, no time for fantasies," I hissed under my breath, slapping the sides of my face to wake myself up.

Getting back to business, I immediately looked around for the man's car, assuming he'd brought one since he appeared before my car as a human. There was no way I wouldn't have seen a glittering golden dragon flying toward me in the sky, dark or not. Granted, I should have seen his car coming down the road, too, but that was something for me to scold myself for not seeing later.

Sure enough, about a hundred feet away was a sleek black *BMW* sitting almost invisible by the side of the road, an odd choice of car for a small-town cop. Perhaps since he was in civilian clothing he was off duty. It wasn't the first time the Witches-Brew Cove PD was understaffed and had to call in someone off the clock.

It was still odd, however, because I didn't see a small-town cop having a wage large enough for a luxury car. He could be from out of town. We did get the occasional stray cop looking to settle down in a quieter place. Either way, I fished the keys out of the man's pocket and rushed to pull the car forward.

Logically, I knew I should call the police again and report the officer down, but my mind was only focused on getting the man to the closest healer to make sure he didn't bleed out on the concrete. Lucky for him, I just happened to have all the tools I needed to heal him back at home. Waiting another hour for an ambulance would for sure be the death of this man, so it was only logical to choose the shorter route.

Also, I wasn't turning down the opportunity to drive a *BMW*, even if it was to rush its owner to my home before he died. I wasn't looking this gift horse in the mouth.

CHAPTER TWO

I awoke to the sound of rain. Outside the wind gusted against the house, which protested with the low creaks of wood. I stayed in bed for a long while staring out at the tempest beyond my window, allowing myself to bask in the comfort of the familiar storm.

Rain and wind were common in Witches-Brew even before my great-grandmother, Polly Carlisle, an obscenely powerful storm witch, was born. Not as common as other portions of Washington state, but still enough for it to be rare to go without it.

Something nagged in the back of my mind, but I couldn't quite recall what it was trying to remind me of. My brain remained foggy, even as I forced myself to stop watching the weather outside my window and get myself dressed for the day.

It was days like this when the air was cool and the world outside was flooded that made it difficult to do anything.

I decided the best idea would be to warm myself with an overdose of caffeine and sleepily headed into my kitchen to brew myself a cup of coffee. It wasn't until I looked up from my pot that I remembered what it was my brain was trying to remind me of.

A giant dark-haired man stood blocking the doorway, staring at me with unblinking amber eyes. I barely stopped myself from shrieking and jumping fifty feet in the air, just barely catching myself as I remembered the man from the night before.

"You scared me!" I laughed airily, hand glued to my chest as to try and calm my racing heart.

The man, looking a lot more intimidating than the night before, watched me from less than a few feet away, half-dressed in my biggest pair of pink sweats and a huge fuzzy black robe. One might think that the man might seem a little less scary in an outfit like that, but he didn't seem to be bothered by his attire at all. In fact, he wore the ridiculous outfit like a second skin.

He took me in from head to toe, his gaze lazily predatory. It felt like I was being sized up by a wild animal.

"You are the witch in the car, yes?" His voice was a low timber, an unidentifiable accent rolling off of his tongue.

I'd like to think of all of the questions to ask, that definitely wouldn't be my first. Maybe a *Who are you?* or *Where am I?* but not an *Are you the chick I saw in the car?*

"Yes, the one you saved from whatever that creature was last night," I said with a grateful smile, before gesturing toward my kitchen. "Why don't you come sit down? I'll make you something to properly thank you."

Nothing said thank you for almost dying for me like a nice fresh cup of coffee and some eggs.

The dragon nodded, walking over to sit at the table, then watched as I worked quickly to pump out some breakfast.

I knew that after all of that healing last night, he would be more than peckish. Hell, I made myself double for how much magic I'd used to save him.

Once the food was all cleared off the table and I was working on how to begin questioning the man, he finally spoke. "It was a pixie."

"What?" I asked, taken aback by his sudden confession. "A pixie? What on earth would one of those be doing in the mountains in Washington? I thought they couldn't leave Faerie."

17

The idea was baffling, and the only thing that stopped me from throwing it completely out the window was the sheer fact that he had no reason to lie to me about it. A pixie on earth was unheard of.

It took legitimate magic to be able to cross the barriers between worlds without dying, the magic which lesser creatures rarely had. Pixies were not one of those creatures, even if they possessed nightmarish powers.

Instead of answering my clear question, the dragon stared blankly at his empty plate, looking as if he was going to pass out right on the counter. I considered brewing him another cup of coffee but was stopped as the man seemed to snap right back into focus.

The healing magic tended to do that to a person. It was one of the drawbacks to healing in a non-natural way.

"What is your name, witch?" he asked after managing to snap himself back into the present.

I felt my cheeks heat at the realization we hadn't yet introduced ourselves, and even though I wanted to question his earlier proclamation, I figured I would allow him a moment of normalcy while he collected himself.

"Storm, Storm Carlisle. I own the shop *Pills and Potions* downtown," I said, my tone tinged in embarrassment. "And you are?"

"Gold." His tone was deadpan, not an ounce of humor in his voice.

"Your name is Gold? Is it because your dragon is gold?" I laughed. "It's definitely a unique name, don't think I'm trying to insult you."

Gold raised one dark brow. "And being named Storm is completely normal?"

I walked right into that one.

"I suppose you have a point," I said haughtily, turning my nose from the male. "Well, I am happy to at least know your name. It felt weird to not even know the name of the guy who saved me."

Gold remained silent for a long beat, as if thinking over my words. It got on my nerves just the slightest bit how easily he seemed to be evading my questions.

I decided not to think anything of it. The way I saw it, he wouldn't even be here answering my questions if I hadn't brought him here after he saved me, so he didn't owe me an answer. It did get on my nerves, though.

I had to admit, seeing such an attractive man dressed in practically nothing in my kitchen was a sight I hadn't known I was missing in my life. Normally I didn't have anyone in my house for the night, let alone a man, so it almost felt like an alien experience.

No doubt my neighbors, as few as there were out here in the sticks, would be having a heyday gossiping about the shiny *BMW* out front. I couldn't wait to hear just how tall a tale the old bat next door would weave.

"Do you know why the pixie was attacking your car?" Gold finally asked, pulling me from my reverie.

Truthfully, I had no idea, other than the feeling it might have had something to do with me getting stuck out on the long road in the middle of the night. There was just no way it was a coincidence that the attack happened on the same night I happened to get stranded out on the road.

Nothing ever happened in Witches-Brew, especially twice in one night.

"Unless the pixie was a fan of my newest potion, I have no idea. I would have noticed if I sold one of my love potions to a pixie, I think," I joked. Though if I were sure I wouldn't, I wasn't too sure Jessica would have.

She'd sell root beer to an Imp and never ask for an ID.

He made a humming sound, brows knitting in concentration.

Of course, his frustration bothered me more than I'd like to admit. I wanted to try and help him piece this together as much as I could, but I couldn't help feeling like I was useless in this situation.

If he was even the person assigned to my case, of course. I didn't know how it worked, but I would assume he would be, right? He was after all the first responder on the scene and happened to see the creature himself.

"I forgot to ask, how are you feeling?" I hadn't even thought to ask him after being startled by him moments before. "I spent almost an hour patching up your wounds, but I couldn't predict how they would heal. I had never really healed anyone like yourself, so it was a new experience for me."

Gold's eyes flicked down to take in his freshly healed torso, where not a single scar marred his brawny chest. "You did very well. Even with my dragon's healing, those cuts would have taken a day. You must be fairly skilled."

I tried not to preen at his compliment, feeling a happy little warming in my chest. I shouldn't care as much as I did, but some part of me wanted my work to be praised by such a strong male.

I was as much of a feminist as the next woman, but a hot man is a hot man.

"I would be lying if I said I wasn't good at what I do. You should stop by my shop in town sometime when it's open. I'll give him a discount." I gave him a sly wink.

He watched me with a heated gaze, slowly nodding in confirmation, "I will remind myself to go see it. However, my first stop might not be recreational. I'm going to need to check out that potion you mentioned. The *Love Potion* was it?"

Something about the way he said it made a bit of heat rise in my cheeks, feeling embarrassed at him knowing about my little failed experiment. For some reason, I didn't want him to think I was some desperate witch concocting potions to lure in unsuspecting men.

I could get me a man of my own at the drop of a hat, and I didn't need any magical roofie to do it.

"Yeah . . ." I sighed. "It was for Valentine's Day. My aunt's idea. I don't have any leftover samples, but I would be happy to tell you all about it if it will help you with your investigation."

A confused look finally chased away the residual heat in his gaze. "Investigation?"

I laughed, equally confused by his question. "Are you not going to investigate? I thought it was illegal for a cop not to report a crime, especially when he was harmed during it. You were on the clock, right?"

Gold's face morphed into a look of sudden realization, and as he opened his mouth to answer, the familiar ring of the doorbell chimed across the house.

We both stared in the direction of the front door, silent for a beat until it rang once more. I was glad I wasn't the only person overly cautious after the night before, Gold looked as if he was considering ducking behind the counter to hide.

"Hmm," I said, quickly abandoning the dragon to rush and open the door. "I wasn't expecting anyone."

I left him in the kitchen, not wanting to trouble him if it was just a package. The last thing I wanted was to startle my poor mailman who already had to trek up the side of the mountain in his worn-down mail van. He might only look twenty years old, but that boy had seen more things on his job than any paranormal saw in years.

Nobody was more surprised than I was when I opened the door to see none other than Shannon Grigsby, the town sheriff, standing in full uniform at my door.

Mrs. Grigsby was six-feet-four-inches of pure were-bear brawn packed into the body of a slightly aged Amazonian woman. Add onto that bronze skin and luxurious brown locks pinned into the tight bun she always wore while on duty and you could almost imagine the terror she must inflict on anyone she charged at.

"Good morning!" I cried, trying not to sound shocked at seeing the elusive woman standing right on my doorstep. "I haven't seen you since you came into the shop last year. You're looking fit as ever."

Mrs. Grigsby smiled a tight-lipped smile, looking like she'd rather be anywhere than here talking to me at the crack of dawn. "Ms. Carlisle, always a pleasure."

What a liar you are, Sheriff Shannon.

Everyone in town knew she viewed me as everything but a pleasure, but I was never going to acknowledge that out loud. It was far more fun to torture her by acting like she was among one of my favorite people to see at any point in the day.

The two of us had a long history, ranging back to when I was fourteen and *accidentally* ran a golf cart right through the main street and into the side of my ex-boyfriend's car. At the time, she didn't believe I was so distracted by the sight of him making out with his *cousin* in the back of his car that I ran full speed into the unsuspecting lovebirds.

It didn't help that I might have accidentally done it four times. What can I say? I'm just terrible at driving automatics.

"What are you doing here so early? I thought nobody could get you out of the office until after twelve." I made sure to add an extra cheeriness to my questions.

The sheriff's eyes hardened a little, either annoyed or pissed off. I couldn't tell which.

"I was checking up on you. After last night when you called the station saying you got stuck out on the road and my boys found your car empty and beat up on the road, they thought something might have happened to you," she ground out.

She must not have gotten a call from Gold yet, which might be a good thing. I might have a chance to convince him to leave out the part where I took him and his car to my place instead of calling an ambulance. Technically it wasn't illegal to try and save a man, but I didn't know if that would fall under some obstruction of justice law.

This woman wouldn't hesitate to take me in over something so trivial.

"Well, here I am." I gestured toward my body, which was altogether in one piece. "Alive as ever. Thank you for worrying, though."

The woman exhaled a harsh breath, letting out a quiet. "Shame."

"What was that? I didn't quite hear you?"

Her look remained amused as she carefully observed me with her blank brown eyes. "It was nothing."

There was a long silence where we stared nearly blankly between each other, waiting for the other to speak.

Shannon decided after a moment to step away, turning without another word to leave. Only, out of the blue, something appeared to force her to stop abruptly and turn to assess me once more.

"Did you happen to see a dragon in your shop yesterday?"

If I was any different person, I might have gone stiff at her question. My mind immediately thought of Gold, the man currently in my kitchen and one of the very few dragons currently residing in the town. I would have to be a fool not to recognize it was him she'd asked about.

If he hadn't informed her of where he was yet, I wasn't going to.

I channeled my inner actress and forced my eyes to go wide. "A dragon? You don't mean Sammy, do you? He only stops by very rarely, so I'm afraid you're out of luck. I can give you his number, though."

Shannon's eyes went sharp, immediately sensing deception, and I forced myself to remain wide-eyed and innocent. I knew she could tell I was lying, but I wasn't going to give in and rat out my house guest savior.

"Oh, really?" she asked slowly, her voice going low and growly. "How did you get home again? I realize I never even thought to ask."

Her sudden questioning didn't faze me. "My aunt sent me a broom. Why do you ask? Is there something I should be worried about?"

She shook her head, eyes remaining trained on every little facial movement. "Not really, unless you are worried about thieves."

That was surprising. I hadn't thought anything about thieves. "Thieves? Is that why you are asking about dragons? Surely Sammy hasn't done anything, has he? He has only ever stolen one thing in this town, and you know it was because he had a rough day. I would have taken that car, too, if it was me."

My diversion must have worked, because any suspicion was immediately replaced with that familiar annoyance.

Shannon looked about three seconds away from strangling me right there, "No. The dragon I'm asking about isn't Sammy. The one I am asking about is a thief, plain and simple. He stole the badge right off one of my officers last night after opening a portal in the town square and tearing off in the shiny new car he stole from the mayor."

I tried not to let my shock show, puzzle pieces slowly clicking into place in my mind. So Gold wasn't a police officer at all, not that he ever claimed to be. Surprisingly, I didn't feel scared at the news that the man in question was undoubtedly sitting at my island counter mere feet away, but I did feel a bit let down.

All my fantasies of saving an officer and nursing him to

health went right out the window. Now my fantasy version of him where he settled into town and pined after the woman who saved him for years was for nothing.

Instead, I just had a sexy half-naked thief. *Now that's criminal.*

My eyes flicked to my driveway, where I had parked the shiny *BMW* the night before, only the car was gone. Somehow it had been moved, probably by the dragon himself, if he was smart. It did make me wonder just when he'd had the time to do that without waking me.

"Sounds like a strong entrance," I said with a laugh that sounded constricted even to my ears. "I'm sad I missed it."

"Yeah . . ." the woman muttered, finally giving up and turning to leave. "Call me if you see anything."

With that she was off, driving away without so much as a wave, always the heart breaker.

The man had disappeared. Gone, poof, nothing left but his clothes and random belongings on my coffee table. He even left the car, which he had hidden in the woods behind my house. I was exasperated and relieved all at once.

I hadn't been anticipating confronting him, but I also hadn't wanted him just to disappear out of nowhere. He was the only one other than my great-grandmother who might know anything about this, thief or not.

Since he was gone, I was able to gather myself enough to push my worries of him aside and deal with the problem at hand. I had to figure out just what I was going to do about yesterday. After the sheriff left, I had forgotten that I never reported being attacked to the authorities, and though I'd been saved, I still needed to make sure the people in charge kept this from happening to other people.

I knew I should have told the sheriff when she showed up at my door, but at the time, I had only been concerned with not getting the dragon arrested.

What did I even have to tell? The one thing I knew was that Gold said the thing was a pixie, a creature infamous in fairy tales and feared in real life. Where kids came away from pixie encounters with tales of small sparkling creatures, very few adults survived encounters to tell the tale of the ravenous decaying zombie-thing that despised adult humans and fae.

I had yet to see one, thankfully. Though it terrified me to think that if the thief hadn't been there to scare it away, I might have been pixie food. It baffled me even more to think that this thing was loose out on earthen soil. Most fae creatures couldn't survive on earth due to its wilder magic. They suffocated in some of the more magically dense areas of the world.

The fae themselves, both the Summer fae and the Dark Fae, had to adjust to our world slowly bit by bit. That was why you never saw the fae creatures roaming Earth like you did with the other creatures that flooded in after they all came out at once to the human population back in the twenty-first century.

With all of that considered, I decided to call the police and inform them of the pixie. I knew it was the most obvious option, but there was no reason I could think of not to do it.

The last thing I wanted was to get someone else eaten by that thing. Even if it didn't help me, I had other ways to get information. Which is why right after the call, I made my way to my great grandmother's house. If anyone had the answers, it would be that old bat.

Polly Carlisle had resided in her beautiful glass and log cabin out in the woods since our old family home burned down years ago. Everyone had thought the house to be too modern for the hundred-year-old woman, but nobody was enough of a fool to try and predict what Polly Carlisle was going to like or dislike.

Now the cabin looked just as chic as the day we moved in,

only the rows and rows of singed lightning rods scattered strategically around the yard giving you a warning of its storm witch inhabitant. Polly had been working on her collection a lot since I moved out, it seemed. Since I'd got my place, it had gone from a circle of lightning rods surrounding the main house to a cemetery of crisp burned iron acting like an ancient medieval battle trap.

"Well, well, if it isn't the love guru herself," the familiar too-young voice of the woman in question called.

Out of the doorway stepped a tall leggy white-blonde bombshell, cherry red gloss gleaming in the dull light of the Washington afternoon. Now, when people called my great-grandmother an old lady, it was their way of reminding themselves just how old the ancient witch truly was. Physically Polly was barely older than me, her magic slowing down her aging process to a snail's pace while she matured like a fine wine.

It was the way of us witches. Living to such unbelievable ages was probably the only reason we ever survived the dark ages. Even back in the good old days, having a slammin' bod could save your family line.

Hell, Polly's probably still could. Her youth and looks were part of the reason we all called her Polly instead of Gran or one of those other nicknames for the elderly. Well, that and she'd probably curse us forever for calling her something so aging. She even preferred Grandma to Great-Grandmother. Polly was anything but traditional.

"You say that like I was the one who decided you would ban me from visiting you more than twice a year," I called to her, weaving my way through the maze of metal to greet her at the door. "I told you months ago when I moved out I wouldn't be stopping by until I settled in."

She flipped her glossy locks over one shoulder, looking more petulant than a child. "I didn't mean it. You know how

I am when I'm upset. I say things I don't mean."

Instead of responding, I finally managed my way to the door and took her in a tight hug, pushing a wave of calming magic right into the agitated woman. She hated it when I did that, but it was the only way I could make her calm without two days of talking her through her densely tangled emotions.

After a minute she pulled away and begrudgingly invited me inside, trying to make it seem as if she couldn't care less if I was there or not. We both knew she had missed me just as much as I had missed her.

The inside of the house was still the perfect balance of messy and immaculate in the way where everything was where it needed to be. There was still a bit too much of it, but I hadn't expected any less of the two women that lived here. I would have to make a mental note to stop by once a month from now on to cut down on some of the mess before she ruined this house like the impulsive hoarder she pretended not to be.

She seated me in a little cove area she used for mixing her herbs, giving me a cozy rocking chair next to the window. It had always been my favorite place to sit in the whole house, and I was happy that she remembered.

I shouldn't be so shocked. It wasn't as if we hadn't talked for years. It was only a couple of months, but it felt a lot longer.

"I had to close the shop." I decided to start with the least important detail, reaching out to take the iced coffee she handed me.

I couldn't start this conversation with the big guns. If I did, I wouldn't be able to talk about anything else other than the attack.

I didn't need to see her face to know she wore a smug look. "Let me guess, it has something to do with that potion your aunt, Carmin, convinced you to make."

I felt the urge to grit my teeth, but just barely managed to quell it. "Yes."

Her look morphed into a satisfied grin, and she swung herself up on the counter to get a better look at me. "I'm not surprised, but I already know that's not why you're here. Though I will admit, I am looking forward to whacking that overgrown toddler for messing with your shop."

I knew Polly wasn't kidding with her threat. The next time Aunt Carmin stepped foot on this property, she would be lucky to leave in one piece. I had witnessed Polly smite one too many people on the front lawn back in the day.

Storm witches were some of the scariest witches out there.

"Call me when you do. I'd like to watch."

Polly let out a little harrumph. "Don't distract me, little girl. Get to the real reason you showed up out of nowhere."

I sighed, absentmindedly twiddling with a stray herb "I take it you probably have already heard what happened last night. The portal in town?"

"Yep, Valentine was out with her friend and got caught in the middle of the mess. It's not often a big dragon bursts through a portal out of nowhere. I about lost it when I heard the thing stole the mayor's car." The way she said it was unbothered like she didn't care that much at all.

It was odd that Valentine was the one to tell Polly about the portal. Being the youngest of us three sisters, she still lived with Polly, so it would make sense that she would call Polly first thing if something happened, but what was odd was the fact she was out.

Valentine rarely went outside. Most days we had to force her to go to school.

"What was she doing in town?"

Polly dismissed my question. "That's unimportant. What's important is what this has to do with you. You didn't come here to ask about your sister."

I was getting annoyed by how many people were dismissing my questions. "Fine. Last night my gas line got cut on the back road up to my house. I got stuck out there for an hour or so. It was fine for a while, but then after I got back in my car it was attacked. This guy saved me, and now I'm here." I was so annoyed I didn't even bother to fluff up the statements, boiling them down to simple sentences.

Polly flew off the counter, an electric whipping current in the air. "You were attacked? And you didn't call me?"

"Polly," I soothed, layering another wave of calming magic right into her, "I was going to call you after I got back home, but I got caught up on something important. I was healing the man that saved me from the thing attacking me."

Her anger clashed with my magic, but my magic prevailed, and the spark in the air from her storm magic slowly fizzled out. Polly still looked pissed, maybe even more so now that I'd used my magic to force her to calm down.

I was used to calming her like this, so it wasn't much of a struggle. Ever since the accident that burned down our family home, Polly had had a problem healthily expressing her feelings, and I had learned quickly to work around some of her quirks. We never blamed her, though. It was hard losing that many people all at once.

It was part of the reason the remaining five women of the Carlisle family were as weird as they were. She had lost not only a husband but her children and grandchildren, including my mother, who she considered one of her own, all in one night. It was natural she'd be more than a little protective of the few she had left, hence the anger at finding out about my attack.

"Who was it? I swear if it's one of those creeps stalking your shop for that potion I will strangle Carmin for ever convincing you to shelf that filth," she spat.

"Aunt Carmin had nothing to do with the attack. I wasn't attacked by a person at all. The man I saved said it was a pixie."

Polly's look of confusion must have mirrored my own from this morning. "You can't be serious. If a pixie were roaming this town I wouldn't be hearing about dragons in the town square. I'd be hearing about bodies being recovered."

She was right, which was why the radio silence from the cops was a bit off. One pixie could and should have done a lot of damage in twelve hours.

"I know, I don't get it either. If that dragon hadn't come out of nowhere, I would have been pixie food. I only regret not telling everybody sooner."

"The dragon from the town square? Is that why you brought that up?"

"Yes," I answered, "his name is Gold, and I spent the better part of last night healing him. I would have brought him here, but he ditched me after the sheriff showed up at my place."

That wasn't true. There was no way I would have brought the dragon up here to her cabin, but she would be a little less angry if she thought I was planning to. The last time I'd brought a man up to this cabin it had been my high school boyfriend, and I got dumped the next day. Apparently, no guy wanted to hang around the girl with the insanely hot great-grandmother who could strike you with lightning.

Boys just weren't built like they use to be.

She crossed her arms petulantly, looking as if she didn't believe me for one second. "Do you and the dragon think it had something to do with your car being tampered with?"

I shrugged. "Probably not, I couldn't imagine a reason why someone would go through the lengths to obtain a pixie and hunt me down with it. Let's face it. If someone were determined to kill me, it would take a lot less effort than that."

"You don't really think that, do you? It's too much of a co-incidence not to have something to do with you." She looked puzzled for a moment, working over something in her mind. "Or maybe that dragon. It can't be a coincidence he popped up at the same time as the thing."

It wasn't a bad idea. I hadn't even considered that until now. "Maybe you're right. I doubt he unleashed the thing, but maybe he's chasing it? It would explain why he went out of his way to fight it. I'll have to ask him when I see him again."

"That's probably your best available option right now, but be careful, Storm. You don't know the man." Polly looked concerned, giving her a look more in harmony with her real age.

I agreed with her and decided to put the topic aside for the time being. I didn't want to trouble her anymore with a con-versation neither of us knew enough about to come up with any real resolutions. Instead, we talked for a while after that, a lot of catching up, until the time came to leave and handle other business with the shop.

Leaving was hard, but I felt happy knowing that I at least had a better idea of how to handle the next couple of days. Polly had brought up a good point about how I had no reason not to believe the dragon didn't have something to do with this. Even if he wasn't in town when my gas was slashed, it would be a bad idea not to pursue all available leads.

I didn't want to accuse the man, but I didn't have much room to budge. Anyone could be the culprit, and since learn-ing about his entrance into town, I couldn't claim not to be a little suspicious of him.

I couldn't help feeling it was a dead end, though. Some-thing about this nagged at something hidden in the back of my mind. For now, I would keep walking forward, taking things in stride as they happened.

CHAPTER THREE

The shop was uninteresting, which was a nice change of pace. Jessica made it her mission to let me know the deliveries were a nightmare, and that trying to convince a centuries-old vampire she wasn't trying to poison him was something she wasn't paid to do. While that might seem like a bit of a red flag, the deliveries were going a lot better than I thought they would.

Closing down the shop hadn't completely gotten rid of our visitors, however. We still had plenty come and knock on the door to try and get us to answer, but we waved them away.

At least they weren't trying to break in.

I also didn't have a car they could tamper with anymore. After I'd left my car out on the road, I had finally decided to express order myself a broom — pure ebony with gold accents, very expensive yet so worth it. When it came to brooms, the more rare and powerful the wood, the better. Think of it like driving a plastic car versus a steel one.

It was time I went Eco-friendly anyways — one less car, one more broom. It's not like I wanted to pay out money to install a whole new roof on that old clunker anyway.

After filling out the orders and sending Jess with the deliveries, I decided to close up and go stop by the police station to check up on the sheriff. I needed to know if they had made any discoveries hunting down that pixie, since I didn't hear anything about it in town.

To my annoyance, the minute I stepped out of the shop, an

annoyingly familiar summer fae hailed me. The man practically bulldozed me the second he caught me outside of the building. I had to catch myself on the door not to go toppling headfirst onto the pavement below me.

Dressed in the familiar black suit and shoes, the luminous skinned fae stood tall and arrogant before me, his shoulders back so far one would be forgiven for thinking he had some posture problem. Being a summer fae, he was almost painfully beautiful, but in that way where it just made his whole face look kind of off. Just a little too *Ken doll* to be a real boy.

"I know I've asked too many times, and your dog in there threatened to kick me off the property if she ever saw me again, but I need that potion," he begged, somehow still snotty even as he pleaded.

I looked him up and down for a long moment, trying to make sure I was really seeing what I was seeing. Sure enough, it was real. The proudest member of Witches-Brew Cove, or WBC for short, was standing before my shop looking properly disheveled. His slicked-back hair was messy, his suit rumpled. If not for the fact I was seeing him with my own eyes, I might not have believed it.

"No. I've already told you a million times, no." I pushed him out of my way as I rushed out my reply, trying to hop onto my broom before he could reach out to stop me.

"Come on, Storm," another cried, this time one of the town's most popular cougars — as in the man-eater, not the shifter.

Another person rushed forward and nearly snatched me right off my broom before I shot myself directly up in the air. The jolt nearly sent me tumbling, but luckily the broom itself swerved to correct my balance.

In seconds the area below me was filled with a small gathering of people that had previously been hidden out of sight of the shop, clearly having waited for one of us to come out and lock up to swarm. It was shocking seeing how truly desperate this small grouping of people was for a stupid potion.

I didn't waste any time zipping right out of there, not wanting to have to look at the desperate faces of my neighbors for a moment longer. It was bad enough I was the cause of this. I didn't need to have the image burned into the back of my brain.

I managed to collect myself by the time I reached the police station on the opposite side of town. It was hardly busy, which normally would be a welcome sight, only it felt very off, considering there should currently be a search for the pixie on the loose out there in the woods.

Something about this left a sour taste in my mouth.

After talking with the secretary in front, I was directed to the back office, led by one of the recruits who looked bored out of his mind. They put me in the sheriff's office, which to nobody's surprise was decorated like a hunting lodge.

I was sure having that many decorated deer heads and a fur rug had to be against some protocol, but I wasn't going to be the one to rat out Sheriff Grigsby. I'm sure even if I had the guts nobody with the power to punish her would be stupid enough to do so.

She wasn't in yet, but that didn't stop the young shifter from leaving me completely unsupervised in the big office. It was a stupid move, but I didn't doubt the shifter thought little ol' me wouldn't dare try anything in the woman's office.

I hadn't been planning on doing anything anyway. I wasn't the type to snoop through peoples belongs. However, as time stretched, it seemed almost like the fates were offering me the opportunity on a silver platter. I would never have a chance to search Grigsby's office ever again. The beady glassy eyes of the animal heads seemed to be daring me to do something.

I didn't even notice I was shaking my knee nervously until I realized I was vibrating my entire chair. As time passed, I was steadily getting more annoyed. I knew I had no reason to be mad, considering I hadn't called in to reserve an appointment, but she sure was taking her sweet time meeting up with me.

Just as I reached the end of my patience, the door flew open and in stormed the sheriff, fresh as a daisy with a steaming cup of coffee in her fist. I let out an audible sigh of relief, to which she rolled her eyes and propped the door open behind her.

Never before had I been relieved to see this woman's face, but it seemed that this last week had been a week of new experiences.

"Good afternoon, Ms. Carlisle," Shannon Grigsby grumbled, sounding every inch the sleepy werebear she was. "Why have you stopped by my cave this morning?"

I wasted no time jumping right into my concerns, deciding my politeness had no place in this conversation. "I was concerned about whether or not you found the pixie yet. I didn't see any hunting parties on my flight out, and I haven't heard any bad news."

Shannon slid slowly into her comfy swivel chair, sliding her cup onto her desk and booting up the computer on her desk. She had yet to make eye contact with me since entering the office.

"That's because when my boys went out to examine your car, the only thing they found was the scent of a dragon, no pixie," she said dully, typing away at her computer.

I almost couldn't believe what I had just heard.

Had they found nothing?

"What? You've got to be kidding me. That thing turned my car into a pincushion, and you're telling me you found nothing?"

She slowly looked up from the computer, her eyes looking completely flat. "Ms. Carlisle, those claw marks on top of your car could have belonged to anything."

"Then how come you couldn't scent anything but the dragon?" I growled, feeling anger bubble up, "Because a dragon's claws sure as hell wouldn't leave small marks like the pixie did. It would have torn off my roof."

Shannon didn't appear moved by my outburst. "My boys did scent a cougar out there. In fact, they found a claw embedded into the roof of your car, along with its body carried out into the woods not far from your car."

A cougar. This lady thought what happened that night was caused by a cougar. I don't care if she found its body lying on my car with an *I did it* sign. There was no way the thing that caused that much damage to a dragon in full prime was a cougar.

"You don't believe me." It was more of a statement than a question, my voice barely audible. "You really think I'm out here trying to trick you."

Mrs. Grigsby raised a single, perfectly arched brow. "What I am having trouble believing is that somehow you, after causing one of the biggest media firestorms, managed to not only get attacked by a pixie but saved by the very dragon that stormed through the town not hours before. It just seems really convenient to me."

It dawned on me just what she was trying to get at.

"I don't understand, Sheriff," I slowly said as if saying the world slower would add any meaning to them. "Are you trying to insinuate I planned this?"

"What I am saying is that it seems to draw even more attention to you and your shop," she answered sharply, "which seems to be booming with business these days. I can only imagine what a story like the one you're brewing would affect that."

I had no reply, just sitting there staring at the woman with my mouth agape. Even my brain refused to accept what she was saying. She couldn't be serious. I had never done anything to make her think I was that kind of a person.

Sure, I did some things when I was a kid, but that was years ago. She couldn't seriously write me off as a nut trying to get attention.

She was an officer of the law, sworn to protect the people of Witches-Brew Cove, and yet now when I was warning her there was a dangerous creature out there in the woods, she chose to believe in whatever lie her men had spun?

I didn't believe for a second that the cops had only found a cougar. Even if someone had spent the entire last twelve hours cleaning up that scene, there would still be pixie blood soaked into the pavement.

Somebody was covering this up. I didn't know who, or why they would do it, but someone was trying to write me off as untrustworthy.

Whoever it was had done a good job, because the way Sheriff Grigsby glared at me from across her desk spoke volumes. Even if I came in with the pixie in a cage, my word was no longer viable to this woman. Probably to the whole police station.

Instead of yelling, allowing rage to power my next moves, I emptily grabbed my broom and stood to leave.

"You're making a mistake," I said to her, not expecting a reply as I turned and walked right out of the station.

My car looked a lot more mangled than I remembered leaving it the night before. The driver side door had been completely ripped off its hinges, my seats were cut to shreds, and somebody had left every single door open, exposing the interior to the moody Washington weather.

In other words, my car was trashed. I had half a mind to finish the job and stretch my rarely used destructive magic right on the useless hunk of mangled metal.

However, the whole point of coming back down to the crime scene wasn't to cry over my destroyed car. I was here to go over the evidence myself. If the cops were going to write this off as some attention grab, I wasn't going to fail my town.

I would do the investigating, even if it might count as tampering with evidence. Though let's be honest, I was long past that at this point.

My thorough scope of the car turned out to be a dud, which was no surprise to me. I hadn't had anything but some potions and supplies for the store in the back, which had no doubt been confiscated by the police as evidence. The only thing that was left was my registration and insurance information, which I bagged.

Despite the fact I was playing detective, I still had to be a grown up after all. Identification cost money to replace, and I needed to cancel my car insurance.

Something big had changed though, and that was the roof where the pixie had been beating on it. Besides the dents and indentations from where its claws had attempted to rend through the metal, there were thin claw-like gouges crisscrossing the entire length of the car.

It was almost as if somebody came in and went at it with a sword strong enough to cut through metal. The lines barely even tapered.

It was so blatantly man-made I had to laugh at the idea of the cops looking at it and agreeing a wild animal made it. Any doubts I had about the cops covering this up were quelled just by that.

I got out and checked from the top to be sure of my findings, and sure enough, it was clean on top as well. The marks were not organic, far from it. Some kind of tool made them.

There was no question in my mind what they were, but the cops would never believe me if I told them now. They would probably pass it off as more evidence I had staged the whole ordeal.

Quite frankly, it pissed me off. To think somebody could come that close to death and the very next day have that fact denied to their very face was the most comical thing I had ever heard.

I tried to cool my temper by leaning against the ruin of my car and allowing myself to contemplate my findings for a while, staring deep into the surrounding woods. My mind was in tangles, processing a thousand things all at once. I wished I could go back to two weeks ago when my worst problem was restocking the erectile dysfunction shelf, which potions required five minutes of sexual energy each.

To my surprise, I was drawn out of my mind by the appearance of a familiar golden scaled dragon suddenly flitting through the trees in the distance. I didn't need a pair of binoculars to know just what that was.

What on earth was the dragon doing here of all places?

CHAPTER FOUR

I probably hit my head on about a thousand tree branches trying to catch up to the overgrown lizard currently loping across the entire mountain. Managing to weave a broom through thick evergreens and piles of thickets was hard enough without going as fast as magically possible, but of course, since I was Miss Detective, I had to make sure not to be spotted while stalking the beast.

I had to admit. It was impressive. The sheer amount of muscle it took to run a mile a second was astounding. I was always told that a shifter's animal was never far off from their human form, but the dragons were on a different level.

It made me wonder what he was capable of in his human form.

Occasionally he would completely stop and examine something on the forest floor, and I had to physically stop myself from flying right off the end of my broom to avoid flying smack into his line of sight or a tree or just launching myself right into his backside.

Silently I cursed to myself, righting myself on the broom for the fifteenth time and questioning why I was even following him. Sure, it was a good idea to try and follow him to see if he was doing something suspicious, but I should have cut it off the minute he went into hyperdrive and started sprinting.

Of course, I was long past that now. I had already chased the fucker down for the last hundred miles. There was no way I was stopping now.

Luckily for me though, this time he appeared to be fixated on whatever he'd found. I decided to take a chance and slowly edge toward the dragon, taking advantage of his distraction to fly forward enough to hide a couple of trees away.

If luck was on my side, I could hopefully maintain this distance and make out whatever he appeared to be messing with while remaining hidden.

I thanked myself for wearing all black today, not that it was a rarity, but it helped conceal me from where I dangled up in the trees. Even if he were looking for me he would probably miss me among the darkness of the evergreen canopy.

It was a better camouflage than bright gold scales. I suppose dragons didn't care much for disguise when they were breeding. Otherwise, Gold's golden form would never have made it past the first couple of generations.

Despite being as close as I could manage without blatantly hovering above the dragon, I found myself leaning forward to get a better look.

Whatever he was sniffing around looked to be a campsite. There was a blackened fire, the remnants of a tent, and an unidentified bag lying out in the grass. It looked to be barely a day old and completely wrecked, if the tent was anything to judge by. It was barely held together by thin straps.

The fire was still an ashen gray instead of the coal black of a fire long abandoned.

I was curious as to why he had to lead me here. To my knowledge, he should have no business still being in town at all, so finding him snooping around in the same area I had just been investigating aroused many questions.

Did this have anything to do with last night? Or did this have something to do with why he even arrived in this town?

It could be both. The sheriff was right about it being an odd coincidence that he'd appeared in town just hours before I was attacked.

I had been so engrossed in watching the dragon's moves that I hadn't even noticed how far I was riding up on the broom until I slipped right over the handle. The only sound I could manage was a quiet gasp as I plummet a hundred feet, just barely managing to grasp my broom and pull myself back up onto it a few feet before I broke every bone in my body on the forest floor.

Thank the fates the broom had followed me at least. Otherwise, I'd have broken every bone in my body. Without the presence of magic, all things were subject to gravity after all.

Even as my heart was still racing from my dance with death, I knew my little stalking charade was over. My field of vision was filled with the giant head of the dragon, now crowding me where I dangled six feet from the forest floor.

There was something to be said about the sheer size of a dragon. It was nothing like what was depicted in the old medieval tales, but they were huge — like semi-truck huge. The head of this thing itself was the size of my entire body.

Its pupils widened and contracted to a slit several times as if analyzing every part of me before he snorted and nudged my torso. The move almost knocked me right back off of the broom.

"Yeah, fuck you, too, buddy," I said as I slowly allowed the broom to lower me to the ground. "You caught me."

By the time my feet touched the ground, he had shifted back to his human form, fully dressed and looking far better than I had seen him hours before. He had this whole timeless pirate-king look to him that normally I would have scoffed at any other time but somehow fit on him.

His collar even had ruffles. Where did you even get a top with ruffles?

"Why did you follow me, Witch?" Gold asked, looking at me through narrowed eyes.

"I'm trying to figure that out myself. My original intention was just to get a look at my car, but I spotted your ass in the woods and decided to give chase."

The dragon nodded, clearly believing my statement. "I'm sorry for my sudden disappearance. I had to find some clothing and decided to track down the creature. I would have been done by now, but I had to wait a while for the men in blue to disappear."

The cops. He must have been out here while they were investigating the car themselves. That is if you can call what they did *investigate*.

"Those were the police, and I would recommend you avoid them," I informed him. "At least until I can figure out some way to fix the mess you caused yesterday."

The dragon grinned slyly. "You mean my entrance? I thought I did well. After arriving, so many people were entranced by me I had to take the shiny black car to escape the people trying to chase me." He stopped to throw me a fiery look. "Much like yourself today."

"First of all, I assume they were chasing you because you stole the police badge. The shiny gold star you pinned to your coat last night." I paused long enough to watch his eyes widen in realization. "And secondly, I was following you to see if you were up to something. Not because I just couldn't wait to jump on your scaley ass."

Gold's smile turned wolfish. "My apologies, Witch."

I rolled my eyes, shouldering past him to walk into the campground. "Well, since you found me out, I might as well accompany you on your search. Why were you out here anyway? I followed you for miles, just watching you sniff the trees. I'm sick of just watching. You weren't looking for that pixie were you?"

I led him back to the campground, snatching up the cloth satchel in the grass I had been fixated on since seeing Gold sniff at it. It was a simple brown bag, empty and torn. Its only distinguishing feature was the buckle, which was the shape of a blooming rose—an interesting design feature, one that probably cost a pretty penny.

Clearly whoever owned it had enough money to buy a bag with a solid gold rose buckle. Personally, I wouldn't touch the bag with a twelve-foot pole, even before it was ripped up, but now it proved to be a pretty good piece of evidence.

"No. I knew the pixie would be long gone. What I am looking for is where it came from," the dragon finally answered, moving past me to check out the other items scattered in the dewy grass.

I dropped the bag and turned to look up at the man. "Where it came from? Do you mean like a fae portal? Those are only open in the traveling stations, so I don't think you'll have any luck there. No pixie has ever successfully been transferred through one of those and lasted longer than a day."

Gold shook his head and gestured for me to get up. "Follow me. I think you'll sing a different tune once you've seen this."

He led me into a small clearing of grass behind the camp that I hadn't been able to spot from the trees. In the center was a small and perfectly circular patch of dull green grass only interrupted by a second, smaller and brighter circle of grass in the center. Mushrooms of many different breeds and colors dotted all over the circles, growing tighter and tighter together the closer to the center they were.

I had never seen anything like it in my life.

Even the air felt different, thick, and syrupy. Radiating with indescribable magic that coated my skin, it was the kind of magic that clung to portals.

"What is that?" I asked, looking over to Gold for answers.

"A fae circle. They show up when a creature of faerie has been summoned into another world." He moved further into the clearing to stand just outside the circle. "A rather hasty one at that. A fully prepared circle would be sunken further into the ground. My guess would be that someone from your land was in a rush to summon the creature."

I had no idea what he was talking about, mostly because I had never familiarized myself with fae magic. I did know portal magic, even if I could never summon it myself. It took lots of practice to be able to pull off by itself, and even more to accomplish it in a small amount of time.

"A creature of fae? You mean the pixie?"

"Yes," he returned. "Back on Eerie, my homeworld, there were many cases of scorned fae summoning beasts from there world to slaughter unsuspecting victims. I had thought that might have been the case with your pixie last night."

A dark shudder of fear and realization struck through me all at once. This wasn't a coincidence. If Gold had tracked this thing down to this summoning circle, then there was no doubt about its origins.

Somebody had brought this creature to this town.

Why would somebody go through the trouble? Unless they were aiming for someone else and I just happened to get in the way, it didn't even make any sense.

There was no clue to tie this all together. No neat little handwritten note confessing the villain's purpose had been left for me to find. No clue as to who the person even was — just the remains of a destroyed camp and a summoning portal.

"Who do you think did this? Did you get any hint from the camp?"

"No."

He sounded just as disappointed as I was. "Whoever it was must have completely wiped all scent from the surrounding woods or used something to conceal their scent. From what I can tell, they even attempted to get rid of the pixie's scent, but something that foul just couldn't fully be cleansed."

I nodded grimly, looking over the circle once more and allowing myself to take in the magic. If I could make out a clear imprint of the caster's magic in the land around us, I could probably trace it back to them, but I came up with nothing.

I hadn't expected to find anything anyway. It would be too easy.

At least following the dragon hadn't been for nothing. Now I knew just how the pixie came to be, and that someone had summoned it on purpose. As far as I was concerned, that was more than enough to start building a case.

Now all I needed was to gather some things from the camp and see if my great-grandmother might be able to get an imprint off of them.

There wasn't a thing Polly couldn't do, and if she couldn't, she knew someone who could.

After turning to gather the bag and some scraps from the tent, Gold and I were left standing back in the clearing, staring at the fae portal as if it would spring open at any moment and more creatures would pour out. Luckily it remained just as still as it had been since we arrived.

Gold stood just a few feet away, his tall, bulky frame seeming to radiate the same intense energy he had been putting out since starting the search. A bigger mystery to me was why he seemed to be genuinely focused on searching with me.

He didn't even owe me a favor, considering helping heal him was more than enough thanks for saving me from that thing last night. There was no reason for him to feel the need to help me find out who attacked me.

Yet there he was.

I was happy to have somebody out here with me. I would never have been able to find this without him, but I couldn't help feeling like I was missing something.

"Why are you helping me? You don't have to thank me, you know. You already helped me enough last night," I asked him earnestly.

He looked down at me for a long moment. His amber eyes shone with an unidentifiable look that strayed too close to possessiveness for my comfort. I felt like squirming under his intense stare.

"Because you're mine."

It took a second for me to realize his meaning.

"Hold on, what?" I worked over each word slowly, as if it would make my question sound any less shocked. "What do you mean I'm yours?"

The dragon's mouth quirked into a boyish half-smile, as if what he was saying was obvious.

"You're my mate. I could tell from the minute I scented you in the town last night. That's why I caught up to you in time to save you from that pixie. After hopping in that car, I caught it just on the edge of town. I knew right then anyone who smelled that good had to be my mate."

My eyebrows must have hit my hairline. He couldn't be serious.

So many things had happened in the last few days I genuinely couldn't comprehend what the fuck he was saying.

"Are you fucking with me?" I laughed. "Because if you're not, I don't know how the hell to respond to that."

His smile only grew wider. "Oh, I'm not playing with you little witch. I knew without a doubt you were mine the minute I saw you from across that road. I don't play games when it comes to things that are mine."

He stopped only long enough to cock his head and look me up and down. "Maybe I can make an exception for other games."

His playfulness didn't even register.

In the last twenty-four hours, I had been attacked, saved, told I was lying and found out that the very dragon standing before me thought I was his. On top of all of that, there was someone in this town psycho enough to summon a blood-thirsty pixie to attack the townsfolk.

I didn't have the energy to process this right now.

I should be at least intrigued. A handsome man shows up out of nowhere and claims to be my mate? What girl wouldn't want that?

However, this was just a wrong place wrong time kind of situation. I was 100 percent certain if I even entertained that conversation, my head would explode from stress right then and there.

So instead of talking this out like the mature adult I pretended to be, I turned around and walked away.

I was cursed. It was the only way to explain it. I was seriously considering checking in with a voodoo priestess to see if someone had hexed me because nobody's luck was this bad.

"Hello, dearie," the throaty voice of the witch that had just breezed through my front door crooned. "Been a while."

I didn't fight back the aggravated sob that broke forth as I let my head fall into my hands. I had thought seeing my great-grandmother this morning would be the last time I would see my family for at least a week, but I was mistaken.

I just wanted to make my dinner and pretend everything was normal for two minutes. I'd made it all the way home without any single thing going wrong, so why did this have to happen now? I would never be able to calm my nerves.

The six-foot-tall witchy version of Jessica Rabbit didn't even fully walk in my front door. Instead, she draped herself right in the entryway, catching the perfect angle for the afternoon light to dance on her perfectly made-up features. Dark red curls, fire red lips, crimson lashes, dark red eyebrows, she had sex appeal in spades.

People may say what they like, but Aunt Carmin never did anything in her life halfheartedly. It was as if some fertility goddess up in the stars had blessed her with the perfect vessel for her chaotic, sexually charged energy.

"You could have shown up ten years from now, and it would be ten years too soon," I groaned.

She laughed, low and purring. "Oh, come on, Storm. You know you love me. I'm your favorite aunt."

She's my only aunt. "You are the reason for all of my current problems. Sure, I love you, but you are not a welcome sight right now."

She had the nerve to look puzzled. "What are you on about? The potion was a huge success! Sure, it had its problems, but in two years it will be as if nothing ever happened. The point of the thing was to boost sales during Valentines anyway."

"Had its problems?" I hissed, "Carmin. People have been ransacking my shop and camping outside for the last week."

"All the better, now you have fans!" She giggled

She was getting close to seeing me snap. After everything I had gone through today, it was going to be her simple appearance that was going to send me right over the edge.

Just the way she was able to completely brush off everything she did wrong got on my nerves. Even when she reappeared after being completely off the map for over a decade, she acted as if nothing had ever happened.

When I didn't reply, she sobered. "What's wrong, babes? You look a little tense. I know you can't still be that wound up over the potion, even you can't hold a grudge that long, so tell me what's wrong?'

I felt annoyance well up at the fact that I could never get anything past my family. When it came to our coven, we might as well be an open book to one another.

Trying to get anything past my family was a lesson in failure.

"I take it you have already heard about the attack from

Polly?" I asked, knowing that was probably the reason she had showed up in the first place.

She shot up straight, looking genuinely shocked. "You were attacked? I had no idea. I just came back after checking up on my warehouses. I thought I'd stop by to check up on you since I saw your shop was closed for the next couple weeks."

I didn't want to spend the next twenty minutes filling in yet another person on the drama, but I knew it would be better to get it out of the way. It would only cause more problems if I made her go hunt down the answers from Polly.

If there was one thing I didn't want to happen, it was those two coming within twenty feet of each other if it wasn't necessary.

Twenty minutes later, with some interludes for preparing my dinner, I had completely caught her up to date on everything that had been going on with me the last couple of days. She no longer held the wide-eyed playfully seductive look that was so fitted to her normal personality but had slowly morphed into a more serious and concerned version of herself.

It was like looking at a completely different woman.

In all of my life, I had never seen her look so . . . human. The personality she wore like armor had melted away and revealed a far more approachable woman underneath.

"Storm, you do understand there is no way that thing wasn't summoned to attack you, right? From what you told me, the summoning circle was halfway across the mountain. There is no way that thing traveled that far without attacking anything only to come upon you on a back road out in nowhere." She insisted, "Coincidences happen, but this is not one of them."

I had already come to that conclusion myself, but I hadn't wanted to say it out loud. I thought maybe if I didn't say it, then it would somehow not be true.

"That would mean someone is out to get me, Carmin. I just can't think of a reason why someone would be willing to go through the effort." I waved my hands around wildly, gesturing toward myself. "I mean, look at me. I am the last person someone would try to kill."

Carmin gave me a long look. "Oh, come on, Storm. I can think of a couple of reasons. A jealous potions witch concerned with how strong your power is. A scorned customer. It could even be a stalker. The longer you spend trying to work out the reason behind all of this is the longer you go without figuring out who the hell this is. Stop focusing on the why and focus on the who."

She had a point. I had been so feverishly trying to come up with elaborate answers to a question I didn't even know that finding the person behind this hadn't even crossed my mind. Perhaps I was going about this all wrong, trying to solve this case from the bottom down instead of stepping back and assessing it as a whole.

Lucky, I already had the keys to solving that very issue.

All I had to do was bring my evidence up to Great-Grandma Polly, and I would be a couple of steps closer to hunting down at least one lead. From there, I could focus on everything step by step instead of wallowing in my thoughts as I had been this whole time.

"So what do you think I should do in the meantime? If someone is trying to kill me, then I'm completely vulnerable," I asked. "Sure, I can have fun playing detective, but if somebody is determined enough to summon a fae beast I don't think finding out who they are will keep me from becoming a snack for another fae beast."

She raised one perfectly painted brow, making me feel two feet tall under her unforgiving gaze. "For one thing, invite that hunky dragon you have pouting out there inside. I can smell his pheromones from here. That boy is convinced you're his mate, and I know for a fact you are just keeping him out there because you don't trust yourself around him."

I winced at the reminder of where I had left the dragon after he followed me all the way home. I hadn't meant to be so heartless and leave him out in the cold, but Carmin was completely right. I wasn't keeping him out there because I thought it would be less stressful. I was just terrified I'd make a stupid decision while I was vulnerable like this.

I felt a flush rise in my cheeks as I turned to face away from the witch. "You can smell that? I thought that was just something he said to try and seduce me."

Her laugh was low and throaty. "Oh yes, there isn't a thing I don't know about the mating habits of the paranormal, love. One thing I definitely do know from studying those overgrown reptiles a couple of years back is that boy would protect you with his life right now. Stop pushing him away because you feel like playing the damsel."

"I'm not going to seduce him for protection," I mutter under my breath, feeling a sort of childish anger at being so thoroughly talked down to.

"Oh no," she said with a wave of her hand. "You don't have to sleep with him, just give him a chance. He can protect you, and you can take that time you spend together and see if what he's claiming is actually true. Two birds, one stone."

I knew she had a point, but I wasn't going to give in just because she was telling me to.

Carmin had a thing for trying to force romance on every person she came in contact with, and I wasn't going to give her the satisfaction of seeing me give in.

A sudden chime filled the air, and Carmin pulled her phone from her bag, glancing at her messages. Whatever she read must have irritated her, because, with a roll of her eyes, she pushed away from where she had leaned against the counter and moved over to give me a large hug.

"Sorry, Storm. I was planning on staying for a bit longer, but work just called. There was a problem with the new batch of lube," she said with a frown. "I have to fly out there and help hose down some werewolves."

The way she said something as ridiculous as that without a hint of humor made me bite back a laugh and the humor was a nice change of pace after the last couple of days. I could always count on her to lift my spirits with her sex shop misadventures.

"Okay, Carmin, go get 'em," I said as I pushed her towards the door with a teasing smack on her ass.

She tossed me a fleeting grin, turning on her heels to storm right out, only to stop and take a notepad out of her bag and hastily scribble a couple of lines. "I almost forgot, but here are some barrier spells I picked up on my travels. I know you already know plenty of your own, but I'm sure you could learn a few things from these. Follow the steps, and you should be a little better protected."

I was grateful for her thoughtfulness and tucked the note in my back pocket to remember later. I hadn't even thought about putting up a barrier, which was a little ridiculous, considering I spent a good year of my life studying them.

"Thanks, I'll send you something to thank you later."

She nodded, clearly satisfied with my answer. "Just remember, I'm a size eight in dresses and a ten in shoes. Also, I think diamonds are tacky."

I snorted, waving her away dismissively. "Right, I'll be sure to remember."

With that she was gone, disappearing as quickly as she appeared, leaving me alone once more in the quiet of my own home.

Chapter Five

"You hungry, dragon man?"

Gold looked up from where he had been sitting against the house for the last few hours. He looked tired and weary, and yet his entire demeanor brightened at my sudden invitation. I was glad he chose not to ask any questions. Instead, he silently got up and quickly made his way into the warmth of the house, barely brushing past me on his way in. He was so quick to seat himself that by the time I closed the door behind us, he was already perched at the dining room table like an excited little boy.

Deciding not to make him wait any longer after making him sit outside all night, I quickly served us both, happy for the grateful smile he threw my way. I was going to feed him anyway, so giving in to my aunt and allowing him inside wasn't too far of a step for me to make. Besides, it was cruel of me to make him stay outside anyway.

I had overreacted out in that clearing earlier today, and this was the only way I could think to apologize for it.

At least now I wouldn't feel guilty leaving him out in the cold.

"It's very good," he somehow managed to say between hulking bites of the burger. "On Eerie we rarely have earthen meals like this. With this and your breakfast this morning, I am afraid I'm going to become spoiled."

"Thank you, it's a family recipe," I told him, knowing Polly would be ecstatic to hear he enjoyed her work. "I'm happy you can eat food from Earth. From what I know of Faerie, the fae can't stomach some of our meals, I hadn't known if your people couldn't either."

Gold's brows rose in surprise. "You know nothing of my people? I could have sworn I scented a dragon nearby in town when I arrived."

"No, not really. We do have one dragon, but he's not very open when it comes to sharing information about his people, not that I blame him." I could imagine constant questions about a life you had left behind might be irritating. "You should meet him sometime, he might be able to help you figure out these lands."

Gold made a noncommittal noise as if telling me that was unlikely, and he went back to attacking his second burger.

That was interesting. Until now, I had barely been able to get any sort of sense around his emotions toward anything other than our investigation. Mostly he had seemed aloof and elusive, evading questions like it was his job to do so.

It made me very curious as to why the mention of talking with others of his kind elicited such a telling response.

"You don't want to seek out other people from Eerie?" I asked, trying not to sound as curious as I was. "I thought maybe you could learn how to fit in a little easier on Earth from somebody who went through it themselves."

"I am fine with you."

Another hard shutdown. This time it was accompanied by the complete erasure of emotion from his face. He almost sounded robotic.

"Gold, I'm being serious," I said, mirroring his sudden seriousness. "I know you're convinced about this mate thing, but you should seriously seek out somebody who can help you settle down here. You know, get an ID, Social Security Card, etc. I can help you with as much of it as I can, but you might want to seek someone who knows the right people to talk to."

When he didn't respond, I grew coy. "That is if you were planning on trying to mate with me. It would suck to have you kicked off Earth before we could even begin our relationship."

"It's not that, little witch. I assure you I would reach out if I knew I would be welcome," he growled. "Unfortunately, I am not very welcome anywhere right now."

My interest levels just went through the roof. What in the world could he have done to get himself shunned by his people? From what I knew nobody was laxer when it came to judgment than the people of Eerie.

They had entire kingdoms fitted strictly towards maintaining a wilder state of life. I might not know much about the world, but I knew it took more than a couple of quick stunts to get someone banned from an entire world.

"And why is that? Did you sleep with a queen or something?" I tried a more humorous approach. Finding the right way to pry information out of this man would be essential for future questionings.

Gold nearly choked around a large bite in an attempt to laugh. "Not quite."

"Oh come on, Gold. No need to be shy, I won't judge," I insisted. "You've done more to help me than anybody else in this town. You can at least trust me not to rat you out."

Polishing off the last of his burger, he pushed the plate away, leveling an intense stare on me.

I didn't expect the slight jolt of interest that shuddered through my core at the sudden realization that we less than a foot away from one another. He could reach out right now and slam me on the table, and there would be little I could do to stop him.

Since meeting him, I hadn't allowed myself to view him as a man. Sure, I appreciated his beauty, but seeing him as an actual man was a-whole-nother thing. Now, after his literal declaration of his interest in me, I was forced to face the truth this large virile man wanted me.

This might have been an inappropriate time to size him up as a male, but any woman worth her salt would have a very hard time denying their interest in connecting with this man.

"I managed to get myself thrown out of every kingdom on the planet," he finally admitted, pulling me from my thoughts. "My family has always been a part of the Thieves Guild that has always resided in Eerie, so that might explain where my youthful days as a thief came from. However, it was this last stunt that really put me over the edge."

Remembering the tales of his entrance into this world, I wasn't surprised by the news. However, I was surprised to hear he was a part of the Thieves Guild. They were infamous across all of the three worlds as some of the most brilliant con artist and thieves to have ever existed.

Recently they seemed to have calmed down, or at least gone under the radar, but for a while, they were target number one for most of the three worlds' governments. There were probably still people that would pay a pretty penny to get any knowledge about where any of the members of the guild were located.

It was weird to think one of those men was sitting across the table from me, talking to me about himself as if all he had was a bit of an odd life.

"What did you do that put you over the edge?"

There was no way I was going to let him not tell me about whatever monumental feat that made all the people of Eerie mad at his presence.

"I took the crown from the high king's head after a particularly drunken night at the tavern."

I had to put a hand to my mouth to stop myself from nearly spewed the water I had been drinking all over the man. "You're kidding."

Gold shook his head. "Nope."

I threw back my head and cackled, more than amused by the image of a smashed dragon trying to steal a crown from a king's head. I could have been given a million chances to guess the reasoning behind his exile, and never once would I even have come close to that answer.

It was so off the walls and out there that I just knew it had to be true, which made it all the more hilarious. I had to grip my sides to keep from hurting myself cackling so hard.

"If you think that was good, you should hear about some of my stunts from my teen years. My family put me to work fairly early." He sounded a little less nervous, and I guessed he had thought I would react poorly at hearing about his troublesome past.

Lucky for him, I didn't care in the slightest. I mean, if we were going to be an item, I would hope he'd think before doing anything like that again, but as long as he wasn't hurting anybody, it was fine in my eyes.

Everybody had to make a living somehow.

He then amused me by telling me some equally profound stories about how he built his hoard when he was younger, and to my surprise, I wasn't put off even a little bit. In fact, it only made him all the more attractive.

With each new story, he grew more and more animated, until he became so expressive I had to lean back to avoid his more passionate arm movements.

"You really don't care about my past?" he asked sometime later after we had both sobered.

He seemed to be earnestly seeking my opinion, clearly caring whether or not his stories had tainted me on him as a person. It brought a vulnerability to the dragon that melted the ice around my heart more and more.

"Nope," I said without hesitation. "My family consists entirely of people who should spend at least fifty years in jail.

Each. You'll fit right in."

If Gold was taken aback by my confession, he did not show it. "So then you've decided you're not going to keep walking away from me like you did this afternoon?"

It was a good question. One I had been chewing over in my mind for some time now. I couldn't just say yes. After all, the dragon was still little more than an acquaintance, but for some reason, I also couldn't outright deny him.

There was a pull between the two of us, an underlying sensual promise that drew me towards the dragon. I was never one to believe in love at first sight, and this wasn't that, but there might have been something that clicked between the two of us in the last day or so.

I would be a fool to turn away from that.

"I'm still considering," I said as I got up from the table. "In the meantime, you can sleep in my spare room. It's a lot more comfortable than my couch."

His smile could have lit up my entire house. "You won't regret it, little witch."

I hadn't initially planned on taking Gold with me on my trip the next day, but trying to say no to this man was a more than impossible task. It was like feeding a stray dog. Once you do, they will never leave you alone.

Lucky for him, I wasn't too opposed to being the new owner of a smoking hot dragon, even if he was a delusional thief from another world.

However, even if I didn't protest his presence, the real problem was still going to be finding a way to get him through town without people recognizing him. He was a person of interest as of right now as far as the town's concerned, so I couldn't just allow him to waltz around with me in his full glory.

Instead, I had to spend the better part of the morning whipping up an illusion potion out of what little I had in my kitchen after fulfilling all of my backorders for the store. The result was that Gold now looked like prince charming, if prince charming was a lumberjack.

Sure, it would raise suspicion, but with results like that, I couldn't care less. I was sure my deepest darkest fantasies couldn't whip up a blond man that hot. Of course, it didn't hold a candle to Gold in his normal form.

I had always had a thing for the dark-haired medieval king look, so I might be biased. *Dracula Untold* may be bad, but the actor sure wasn't.

It was dark by the time Gold and I had managed to fly over to Great-Grandma Polly's place, which put a little bit of a hitch in my plans to go and check on my shop earlier that afternoon. Juggling a pack of evidence and the huge dragon suctioned to my back as we flew being the most major cause for us being so late.

Usually, I could easily jam someone like him in the back of my car and take off, but the universe just seemed to hate me recently. With my car in ruins and my only legal transport being the broom, there was no other option available to me.

As it was, I still needed to wipe down the *BMW* and transport it into town where someone could return it to the mayor — if I felt like it.

Still, I had managed to squeeze both Gold and me onto the broom and take off in time to hit up her place before the witching hours.

It was funny, though. I would rather fly for hours on a cramped broom with a dragon who forgot to balance himself every two seconds than go through the process of bringing a man home to meet Polly.

Unfortunately, being a coward and turning around to hide

back at my place wasn't an option, as I found both of us confronted by the witch the minute we landed.

"Who's this tall drink of water?" she purred as soon as the door swung open.

For some reason, the look my centuries-old great-grandmother was leveling on Gold made my skin itch in irritation. I knew it was irrational, but I had to close my eyes and take a deep breath to get rid of the uncomfortable feeling.

"The name is Gold," the dragon said in greeting, sounding as polite as his prince-charming looks made him seem. "It's a pleasure to meet you, Polly Carlisle. Your Storm has told me much about you on the way here."

It was a lie. I only told him not to say anything he might regret later. I didn't have time to inform him just who my great-grandmother is and also manage to warn him to stay away from anything metal once she got angry.

It was one or the other, and I chose the safe route.

"Who's here?" the familiar voice of my youngest sister called.

Polly broke her gaze from the newcomer for the first time since opening the door to allow us inside, managing to slide me a wink past Gold's shoulder as she gestured for us to come in. If I was any other woman, I might have blushed at her look of pure feminine approval.

A woman over one hundred should not be as active and rowdy as this woman was at the worst of times, but at this point all of us three sisters had just accepted it for what it was.

She never hurt anybody, except for the men whose hearts she had broken, so it didn't bother me much.

Sure, it had been upsetting to hear boys talk about your hot grandmother in high school, but we had managed just fine. Occasionally I did wonder if I might have turned out differently if my elders didn't look eternally youthful for thousands of years.

Probably not.

We were ushered quickly into the dining room, where we were greeted with Valentine cleaning the last of the dishes off the table from whatever meal they had that night. The pink-haired teen's face immediately burst into a wide grin upon spotting me, and she quickly whirled around to drop the dishes to the counter.

"Sis!" she cried. "Oh my god, I haven't seen you in so long."

I had to physically brace myself to keep from being knocked backward by the force at which she propelled herself at me, taking me in a hug so tight the air wheezed from my lungs. For such a scrawny thing she sure did pack a punch.

Letting out a small cough, I speedily tapped her back to let her know to let go before she strangled me. Luckily, just as my vision began to spot, she pulled back and took me in from head to toe.

"You look amazing!" she continued babbling. "I thought for sure you wouldn't show up on your own for at least another month. I was going to go see you tomorrow!"

"Okay, Valentine, calm down." I chuckled, lifting a hand to brush her unruly hair from her face,

"I would have come seen you sooner, but I had business. You look good, too, by the way."

Valentine grinned brightly, doing a brisk twirl to show off her cute black sundress. "Thank you. I've been working on establishing my style."

It was cute, and the kind of thing I had thought the youngest of the three of us would be up to. Out of all of us, Valentine was the artist through and through and showed that with her constant changing of styles in a bid to find the one that fit her best.

Terry and I joked that Valentine's true power was never being able to settle on any one thing. It would be all or nothing with this one.

"Valentine, I don't think they came here to admire your style," Polly said as she blew into the room, arms filled with a stack of old-looking books.

"They?" Val looked puzzled before her eyes finally landed on Gold as she truly hadn't noticed he was there. "Oh! Hello."

Gold looked amused, greeting Valentine with the full force of his feigned charm. She looked about ready to melt through the floor in embarrassment.

The girl then proceeded to babble an apology to the dragon, but my attention was drawn away from the two as Polly briskly splayed out the books over the entire surface of her table, briefly glancing up to meet my eyes. She looked tired, something I wasn't used to from her.

Ever since I'd moved in with her after my parents died, she had always had the same cool controlled woman persona, maybe at first more cold than she would have normally been. Nobody had been okay after that, but she managed to hold on for all of us, becoming the rock the family needed at the time. So for her to be tired now, it meant something was wearing on her.

"You okay, Polly?" I whispered so as not to be overheard by the other two.

She seemed startled by my question, her eyes going wide as she looked up from her books. Our gazes locked for a long worried moment before finally, she seemed to release all of her tension with a long weary exhale.

"I could never get anything past you girls," she said with a soft laugh. "But yes, I'm fine. I was just worried is all."

"Worried? Over the attack? I told you I'm fine," I told her, giving her a small reassuring smile.

"Aunt Carmin stopped by last night and gave me some barrier spells to protect my house. My place is locked up tighter than a bank vault."

Polly scoffed, "My no-good granddaughter took time out of her busy day to visit you? Here I was thinking she had nothing better to do than bother everyone in town."

I clenched my jaw to keep from defending her, knowing it would only upset Polly further. No one was more affected by Carmin's disappearing act after the accident than Polly. She not only had to deal with the death of her family, but taking care of three children, and the disappearance of the remaining grandchild all at once.

In her eyes, there was little anyone but Carmin could do to fix that. It was hardly my place to get involved in either of their business anyway.

"Anyway, this is the dragon who helped me with the pixie," I said, changing the subject. "I have him under an illusion spell while we are out doing some investigating in town. It should last another couple of hours."

Gold looked up from his conversation at the mention of his name, giving us both his brilliant fanged smile. "To be fair, she helped me as much as I did her."

If Polly had anything to say about that, she didn't voice it.

"Don't call me Mrs. Carlisle, Prince Charming," she told the dragon, rolling her eyes as if he should have known this already. "I hate being called Mrs. Carlisle. It makes me feel old."

She was old, but I wasn't going to tell her that. I liked my ass alive.

After hearing her pet name for the man, I knew what she must be thinking.

We both knew damn well why Gold's illusion came out the way it did. Sexual magic was potent and overwhelming, and if a witch was even slightly aroused when casting, it meant for a whole mess of changes for the outcome of the spell, including making the already sexy Gold into a sexy prince-lumberjack.

I was just happy she wasn't all out teasing me for it.

"Well, then it's a pleasure, Polly," Gold replied with a regal bow, and I had half a mind to shove him over while I had the chance.

Luckily all of our attentions were grabbed rather quickly as Polly nodded and gestured for us to sit, to which all of us gathered obediently around her at the table. Gold deliberately grabbed his chair and pulled it right next to mine, so we sat flush at the table. The entire length of his hard body brushed mine as he lazily sat back in the old wooden chairs.

I might have said the proximity made me uncomfortable, but what I was feeling now was far from discomfort. In fact, the feel of his strong thighs brushing my own brought images to mind of them brushing my thighs in a whole different way.

Polly only raised an eyebrow at the move, and I diverted my gaze from meeting her hawkishone. I could feel the curious look even without seeing her. I knew she could see right through the move to the surprisingly possessive dragon waiting at my heels for a moment of weakness to pounce.

She let out a long exhale that sounded suspiciously like a laugh before turning her attention to the bag I had dropped on the table. "What is it you brought for me, Storm?"

I attempted to push aside my R-rated thoughts and focus on the situation before us before I embarrassed myself in front of everyone in the room. "Um, I brought some evidence we gathered from where we tracked down the pixie. There was this campground and a summoning circle, which is like this portal to Faerie where people can just call forth beasts from there onto Earth."

My explanation was jerky and left out a few details, but Polly didn't seem to be bothered by that. "I've heard of it, though that process is quite difficult. I suppose I should have thought of that, though I was under the illusion only high fae could cast that kind of spell."

"You mean the summer fae," Gold corrected as his hand lightly dropped onto my thigh. "There is no high fae. That's propaganda spread by the royal summer fae in order to put down the wilder dark fae kingdom. I had heard that myself, but I didn't want to limit myself before thinking of all the possible subjects."

I felt a bit stupefied by the ease at which these two revealed information to each other that they didn't have the mind to tell me beforehand. I never knew of any fae summoning circle before today, and Gold sure as hell didn't tell me he already had a wealth of knowledge about it when we were there.

Though maybe he never got the chance to tell me anything, since I did storm away in a rage after only five or ten minutes.

Whatever thoughts filled my mind quickly fled as his heavy male hand splayed across my thigh began to trace lazy circles up and down my sensitive skin. My whole body shivered, and I could feel each rasping circle through the thin fabric of my skirt like it was barely there at all.

I glanced over at Gold, trying to see if he was toying with me, only to see him completely absorbed in his conversation with Polly. His face betrayed nothing, remaining a cool, polite mask even as his hands drew wicked patterns along my inner thigh. Did he not even realize what he was doing?

I should at least attempt to move away or something. We were at the dinner table, and his hand was playing between my legs like he was a teenager trying to cop a feel at the movies.

I couldn't find it in me to move, though. It was like all the muscles in my body refused to comply with my orders. I found myself inching my thighs apart to encourage the movements before I realized just where I was and caught myself partway through.

"Either way, it seems a bit overboard. Why summon a pixie when it can be so easily traced? Wouldn't it be easier to just kill the person they sicced the creature on?" Valentine nonchalantly asked, as if I wasn't that person.

The wickedness of this situation dawned on me as my younger sister spoke, and alarm bells went off in my mind warning me of just how wrong it was to allow myself to be felt up in front of my family. What was even worse was this wasn't just some normal family meeting but a meeting talking about the people who attacked me days before.

There must be something seriously wrong with me to enjoy something like this.

"That's what we want to find out," the dragon said as he reached for my bag.

Moving his distracting hand, he splayed out the contents over the table, pushing them towards Polly in order to reveal all of our evidence. She didn't seem bothered in the least by the scraps of junk and the worn brown bag no doubt making her freshly cleaned table filthy.

"You want me to do a tracking spell?" she asked after a quick survey of the junk. "You know I can't give you names or anything like that. No one in our family has that level of skill when it comes to tracking magic."

"I know," I managed to say as Gold slipped his hand further up my thigh. "We just need a locator charm. I have quartz you can channel it into, if you need."

The charm would work like a game of hot and cold, lighting up gradually if we were getting closer and vibrating once we were within a half-mile of the person. Polly had used it several times to hunt down people who owed her money back in the days when she was leasing out most of the buildings in town when our family invited otherworlders into our secret little cove. Only back then my great-grandfather had been the go-to source of the tracking spells.

He had been hunting and tracking ever since his youth on the reservations before marrying Polly and moving to

Witches-Brew with the entire Carlisle family. During that time it had been tense for witches, so the help of someone as rough-hewn as him had helped our family establish a nice stronghold in the town they were opening to new residents.

I often wondered if she still missed him. I had been too young to get to know the man, but his wild spirit still shone in every building he helped construct. I found myself wishing at the worst times that the fire had never happened.

It was a tragedy to have a man die in the house he built with him and his family inside. Polly always said only chaos could breed something as tragic as that.

At least we still had the knowledge he left behind. Polly was more than well versed in tracking spells thanks to him, and even though she was no master, she would still be able to help me out with our newest problem before any more trage-dies could arise from the figurative ashes.

Once we got the person's location, it would be as easy as jumping on the guy. Or girl. Or whatever. Anybody could summon murderous pixies regardless of titles.

Polly let out a long sigh, reaching out to grab the satchel. "This will do, then. It was most likely worn on the person for longer than this other junk, so isolating their essence imprint will be easier."

While she began her work, Valentine excused herself to her room and left Gold and me at the table. Gold barely waited for her to leave the room before pulling me even closer to his side, opening me further to his wicked fingers. Any attempts to ignore the dragon went right out the window at that mo-ment because trying to ignore as he practically kneaded my soft thigh was like trying to ignore a vibrator zeroing right in on your clit.

"You are very tense, little witch," he purred in my ear as soon as my great-grandmother was out of earshot. "I can fix that for you."

Even as I felt every organ in my body flip in excitement at the dark promise in his words. I knew he was telling the truth. Just looking at the man was enough to tell he could ruin a girl for other men.

I halfheartedly batted him on the arm. "You dickhead, you can't just feel me up while talking to my family! We are at the dinner table."

His eyes grew hotter than molten amber, twinkling with humor. "Yet, I see no food. Apart from the nectar, I can smell between your thighs."

The breath in my chest hitched at his words. I cursed myself for not going another round with my toys last night. That way I wouldn't be so excited just by some dirty talk and a warm hand.

My family was barely a room away, and I was allowing this to happen. This level of sexual tension should not have been illegal here!

I didn't even want to think about the implication of the smelling comment, either. Everybody knew shifters could smell a woman going into heat a mile away, and dragons were no different in this. No doubt he was drowning in my scent as I squirmed beneath his attention.

"Fuck you."

He grinned devilishly, but before he could retort, Polly swiveled back in the room, a glowing blue stone in her right hand.

"Here it is, easy as pie," she chirped, carelessly tossing it to me across the table. "Consider yourself in my favor."

Gold's hand disappeared from my leg as I jerked guiltily up from my seat. Her sudden reappearance was just the bucket of ice water I needed to bring me right back to where I needed to be.

With this stone, I was one step closer to finding the person who most likely wanted to kill me, and I didn't have time to entertain heated heavy petting with dragons at dinner tables.

I quickly rounded the table to take her in a tight hug. "Thank you. I'll make sure to pay you back as soon as I can."

She waved a dismissing hand. "Don't worry about it until after you deal with the guy. We will be waiting here for updates, so don't forget to mirror us."

CHAPTER SIX

It was almost midnight, and the damn stone had been losing its shit in my pocket for the last hour. I knew that the half-mile radius restriction was a terrible way of narrowing down somebody's location, but I hadn't thought at the moment that whoever it was we were searching for might be in the middle of town.

The culprit could be any number of people on this street alone. It was the middle of spring, which meant people were starting to come out more and litter the streets at the worst of times. I had probably seen at least half of the residents of our town stumbling down the street in the last couple of hours.

In other words, we were doomed.

Gold had spent the better half of the hour sniffing every new gust of wind, as if the freshly rained upon streets would give away even the slightest hint of somebody's scent. He was thinking the same thing I was. We were going to have to find this person the old-fashioned way by using practical methods instead of the tracking spell.

We had gotten this far and were so close to finding the person. We couldn't give up now just because of a few minor setbacks—if you could call every resident in town a minor setback.

People around us were looking at him like he was crazy. It probably wasn't too far from the truth. However, most of the residents of Witches-Brew Cove were more than used to things worse than a hot guy sniffing at buildings around these parts, so most of them looked the other way or didn't even flinch when we passed.

Mostly it was the town gossips that watched us with hawk eyes as we stumble down the entirety of the main streets. Even a blind person couldn't miss them with their phones in hand, ready to record at the drop of a hat.

No doubt the town spectacle with a brand new man at her hip would breed a lot of tall tales in the coming days.

"The people here are odd," Gold said out of nowhere.

I couldn't stop the startled snort of laughter. "Wait. What?"

"The people," he answered, the smile carrying through his tone. "They are odd. They watch and talk as if unafraid of the people they talk about."

I gave him an assessing look, intrigued by his wording. "Why would they be afraid? They are just gossiping. It's harmless. Wouldn't you talk if the current person of interest in town showed up with a hot new friend?"

Gold looked bewildered by my question, and I was reminded once more that his homeworld of Eerie was in no way Earth. It would make sense for him not being used to such open judgment when he came from a place that housed dragons, gargoyles, wyverns, and an assortment of other creatures that could kill you with a look just for pissing them off.

"On Eerie if someone caught you talking about them in a bad way, it would be grounds for a fight," he said wistfully. "I remember many times being scolded as a youngling for nearly getting my father into a brawl with the drunken townsfolk."

I liked the idea of a young, mischievous version of the man beside me. I had no problem picturing a tiny Gold terrorizing the people around him on a daily basis.

Gold and I brushed shoulders as we walked, and I couldn't help but give him a playful nudge. "So you were a little drama starter, too, huh? I once was the cause of a fistfight between my great-grandmother and my ex-friend's mom back in the day."

He let out an amused laugh, loud and hard. It was a nice sound, one that shook everyone in the surrounding area with its power, and I felt a slight giddiness at being the one to have caused it.

If it hadn't been for me being absorbed by his laughter, I might have missed the shadow darting through the street just in front of us. It had been so fast that my gaze didn't even catch up before it rounded the corner and disappeared.

I didn't need the stone currently going off in my pocket to know that had to be the person we were here for. My witch's intuition screamed to give chase, even as my mind screamed for me to turn and run.

It was that damn fear again, rising to choke me in the last moment, but I wasn't going to let it win this time — no more waiting to be eaten in a car like a fearful damsel. I owed myself more than that.

"The alleyway," I hissed, taking off after the shadow in a sudden burst of speed.

Gold was faster, sprinting in the direction I pointed, eating up the space between us and the shadow in large bounds. I tried to keep up with the two, but my powers didn't constitute a body athletic enough to keep up with two creatures who could move far faster than any human. By the time I rounded the corner into the alley, I had found I was seconds late as I watched the coattails of Gold's black jacket disappearing into a large glowing blue and purple wall of energy pulsating in the center of the normally barren alley.

Everybody in existence knew what that was — a portal.

"What the hell?" I asked, muttering, as I skidded to a halt.

Portals did not just appear in dark alleys in seconds. This shouldn't be possible. Even the strongest of witches took at least a minute to call forth one of these, especially big enough to transport people.

That meant whoever opened it was either as powerful as a god, or had illegally obtained a portal key. I was hoping it was the latter.

I was frozen for no longer than a second before a dark arm reached out from the portal and dragged me in headfirst. I had no time to process the owner of the arm before I was plunged into the thick of the magic, swallowed entirely in seconds.

It felt like I was in a wind tunnel, suspended in midair with nothing but the bright pulsing fingers of magic absorbing into every inch of my body, unbothered by my clothes. I felt the hand on my shirt, pulling me forward, but saw nothing but the eerie expanse of pure, unfiltered magic.

Around me, there was nothing, yet everything all at once. I was completely alone, absent of any other form of life, yet the air around me danced in its own imitation of the very force the endless abyss lacked.

The longer I looked, the more I felt pulled to leave the path I was being pulled along. The abyss seemed to beckon me, calling me forth to be swallowed into the never-ending void. I felt my limbs go numb and my mind go blank, yet just as I felt myself reach down to release the hand holding me to the path, it was over.

In a blink, I emerged on the other side, rebirthed into the real world as I gulped in air too sweet to be real. My feet hit the hard stone of a cobbled street, eyes registering nothing as they tried to adjust to the sudden change of light. The too-familiar feel of the man holding me to him was the smallest comfort allowed to my mind as it struggled to gather itself after that experience.

"Breathe," Gold whispered in my ear, holding me tighter to himself. "It was just a portal. The first time is always the worst. You'll get used to it in time."

"Where are we?" I asked, looking around us wildly even

though I knew I could see nothing. "Where's the man?"

"Gone. The portals take a lot longer than you'd think. By the time I got spit out he was gone, but I got a good look at him before he went into the portal," he answered, much to my disappointment.

Some part of me had hoped that would be it, and we'd have the man in our grasp ready to question, but of course, it wasn't as easy as that.

I blinked slowly in an attempt to refocus my eyes, which were slowly but surely beginning to register the beginnings of dark shapes around me. "Who is he? Did you recognize him?"

"No. It was just some fae male, long blond hair and pale skin. I can track him by smell, though, since it's fresh, so we need to get moving before he goes too far," he urged, steadying me back onto my feet.

His face finally came into focus, and I could barely make out his worried expression. Whether he was concerned over me or the thought of the fae escaping I did not know, but I did know he was trying to help me out as much as he could, even though at this point I had only been dragging him down. Deciding to push through my delirium, I gave him a tight smile and righted myself, taking in our surroundings with a quick blurry once over.

Our surroundings looked both old and modern, with elegantly cobbled streets and smooth black iron streetlights right off of one of those modern city magazines. The buildings themselves were mostly wood and stone, with a similar look to my great-grandmother's cabin—both old-fashioned and modern in a clash of several different styles all woven into one franken-building.

What gave me a clue as to where we were was the brightly colored luminescent mushrooms sprouting out of every available patch of grass. They weren't overwhelming, making up only about one-sixteenth of the percentage of greenery, but the type of thing you would only see on a world as infamous as Faerie.

Even though I had never been to the world in person, nearly everyone and their mother knew about how amusingly storybook the place looked. The world of the summer and dark fae was filled with just about everything you thought it might be, including forests where the sunlight couldn't breach the canopies, bogs that hid the most dangerous of the beasts in the three worlds, and vast amounts of bio-luminescent plant life that made up for the world's lack of moons.

It was a children's story authors' wet dream, and their residents were hell-bent on keeping the place looking that way no matter the cost. You couldn't build a house on the summer side of Faerie without a permit from several of their government leaders these days.

Not that I could judge, people on earth seemed to be doing the exact opposite most days. Our people were still trying to recover the destroyed forests from the century before for the more exotic otherworldlers that wanted to set up homes on Earth.

Being in Faerie was unfortunate, however, because that meant my locator charm was as good as dead. The portal to Faerie destroyed petty spells like that on the way through due to its high magic potency.

I had half a mind to curse and toss the stupid stone in the grass for all the good it had done until now. I knew it was going to be weak, but I hadn't thought it would be this bad.

"First time through a portal?" Gold asked as he began to pull me down the dark streets, keeping a strong hand at my hip in case I lost my strength once more.

I nodded bashfully, embarrassed to admit I had never traveled off of my homeworld before. "Yeah, I was always too afraid to try it myself. Plus traveling alone seemed weird."

We as a family had never been much for traveling at all, favoring to stay at home since Polly had pretty uncontrollable magic at times. You couldn't burn down houses with unexpected lightning strikes if you didn't leave your hometown.

That was partially the reason I never left either. Even though my flame magic wasn't my strongest, I had always held onto the fear I would end up hurting somebody with it one of these days. I knew firsthand the kind of damage something like that could do to a person.

"It's not so bad. I've done it for centuries."

"Centuries?" I scoffed, "You didn't tell me you're an old man. I'm only twenty-four myself. Maybe twenty-five, I lost count. Are you a cradle robber, as well as an actual one, Gold?"

"I'm no cradle robber, unless you're not the full-grown sassy witch I've been thinking you were." He chuckled, adding, "And I'm only four hundred. The years go by fast after your youth."

I threw him a coy grin. "That's all right, old man. As long as you're hot, it doesn't matter. Being rich helps, too."

Before I could react, he laid a hard smack on my ass, jolting me forward. As much as I was enjoying how we teased one another, we both knew we still had a job to do and couldn't afford to lose our trail to play.

I tried my best to focus on the places he leads me past, carefully watching as we passed a line of shops with intricately calligraphic names on the front, ranging anywhere from clothing stores to simple bakeries. Though it wasn't important at the moment, one of the shops caught my interest.

It was a bookstore advertising Fae related spellbooks. I knew spell shops were everywhere, and it was of no importance to our current investigation, but the sight of it made me miss my shop.

What was weird was, until now I hadn't even thought of it.

Before today that shop had been the only thing I thought about most of the time, and yet now that I was away from it, I found myself barely even thinking about it.

Something in the back of my mind nagged that it hadn't been my passion in the first place. I knew that was partially right—I never set out to work in the shop business, but it felt like a bit of a betrayal to the business I had built.

I had started it in some desperate bid to feed the part of my soul that yearned to help people, and yet as I spent more and more time cooped up at my brewing station making hair growth potions, I felt myself descending into madness. This recent ordeal had been a huge eye-opener, because it showed me how stupid the things I was investing my time in really were.

Maybe I should have come here sooner. I should have sated my yearning to travel and see things before doing something as binding as starting a shop and buying a house. I might feel a bit different about things if I had.

My younger sister, Terry, had done just that about a year ago, disappearing into the blue with nothing but some money and a lust for life. For all I knew she was still here in Faerie, living her life among the wilds of the fae wilderness. Though that was another thing entirely.

I couldn't find her if I wanted to, so wondering about her was just a waste of brain cells.

"Is Faerie all this . . . pretty?" I asked, growing distracted by the looks of the shops around us.

"No," he answered, waving his hands towards the shops around us. "Outside of the cities and tourist towns it calms down a lot. This town in specific is one of the more decorated ones. The castle that houses The Summer Queen is only a few miles away, so they focus on making these parts as pretty as possible to lure in people with money."

The Summer Queen, the aging queen of all of Faerie. Some

said she was the most beautiful woman to grace any of the three worlds. Most called her the cruelest.

Though she didn't rule anymore, back in the Victorian age, there was a huge civil war that completely wiped out the royal line except for the queen and a few of the more humble families. The queen had been overthrown by her people, who were starving because of her taxation. In the end, the person who took advantage of the poor had paid the dearest price.

Her mind.

It was rumored the queen was no better than a child in the mind. Whatever spell the people had inflicted on her had taken away the very thing that had kept her on top.

A sad story all around, turned into a cautionary tale that had been passed around in school as a warning against repeating histories. A lot of people were trying to calculate the exact year to see if it happened around the same time as something similar that happened on Earth back in the late 1700s, but the fae didn't keep time as humans did.

"Do you think it's going to be hard to track this guy through the summer kingdom? He must know his way around here, he at least has that advantage," I pointed out.

Gold cocked one brow, giving me a judging look. "Assuming a fae knows his way around Faerie just because he is a fae is a bit presumptuous, don't you think? Most Earth fae rarely even visit Faerie."

I winced, not even realizing how my words might have sounded. "All assumptions aside, then, do you think it's going to be hard?"

He grinned, spinning me around to face a blank building with only a single set of double doors on the front. "Nope, because I think we've just found his hiding place."

I had never visited many bars, even back in my heyday. Truthfully I was always too put off by the sheer amount of inebriated people crammed into one room like a ticking time bomb of people smashed out of their mind. It's not that I looked down on drinking, but when you had so many people of different magically inclined species in one place without a working thought process, it added up to something very dangerous.

That being said, this place was completely different from what I was used to seeing back on Earth. The dark cozy cabin interior of what was clearly the Faerie equivalent of a tavern was crowded yet calm. The endless sea of fae, a mixture of both the pale-skinned summer fae and grey-skinned dark fae, was only interrupted by the occasional otherworlder mingled among their ranks.

Besides the few unique outliers, Gold and I were very much the minority among the crowded tavern. Despite not sensing any traps, the acknowledgment made my skin itch with the need to turn and run.

The few nearest us barely glanced up from their conversations as we entered, turning their backs to us as if to say our appearance was nothing out of the normal for them. It didn't bother me much, but I was amused at the idea of a witch and a dragon being nothing to these people.

Gold seemed equally unbothered as the people around us, barley surveying the crowd before he wrapped one strong arm casually around my waist to swing me through the crowd with surprising ease. We stopped at the large dark wood counter in the back, littered with several half-empty glasses of deep purple and red liquids I could only assume were the famed fae elixirs. No doubt, their ingredients remained a secret to the human world.

Down one of those bad boys and a human would be out of their mind drunk, but several steps closer to death. Luckily witches had a much higher tolerance for magically potent items, but I wasn't here to sample the products anyway.

"What can I get 'cha," the bartender asked as he appeared from nowhere.

The summer fae was tall and willowy, wearing nothing but tight leather pants and a tight black mesh shirt complementing his perfect dark makeup to a tee. He looked like one of those unearthly beautiful men that decorated fashion magazines in the big otherworld cities nowadays.

"We are looking for a fae who came in here a bit before we did," I told the man before Gold had the chance to speak.

Gold slid me a look that told me he wasn't pleased with me talking for him, but I ignored it. I wasn't going to let him drag me along on my hunt.

"Sorry, sweetheart, I'm going to need a bit more information than that," he said with a twinkling laugh, giving me a wink as he turned to service another customer.

Behind me, I felt Gold stiffen, his arm constricting around my waist so tight it was borderline squeezing me. The grip was possessive, one of jealous ownership. The tension leaked from him in waves, yet the fae in front of us didn't even blink. Instead, he just continued to look between the two of us with a heavy-lidded amused gaze.

I had to give it to the fae for not even flinching at the dangerous look Gold was leveling on him.

"A tall male fae with short white hair, wearing a black and gold colored human suit, should look like he just got done running a marathon," Gold growled through gritted teeth.

Something must have clicked in the man's head because his face fell into a blank mask. It was like his whole personality clicked off as he refocused on where he now dusted the counter. "Doesn't ring a bell. You're welcome to ask any of the guests, though."

You would have to be blind to miss the complete ice-out the man just gave us. Gold and I shared a short look before nodding and pushing away from the counter.

"You won't get anything from him," Gold said into my ear just loud enough to be heard over the still buzzing crowd.

"I know that," I hissed. "Are you sure we can't just go back and grill him to make him tell us what he knows? You know, mafia-style? There's no way he reacted like that and didn't know something."

Gold snorted. "I'm sure if I knew what that meant it wouldn't work. I would rather not get in trouble with the fae law if we don't need to, so we have to find another option."

He had a point. Fae law was one of the more harsh forms of government, mostly because they had yet to fully meet the human world when it came to rational forms of punishment. In some towns tying a man to a pole to be humiliated for a week was still a form of punishment for petty thievery.

I had done a bit of research into Faerie following one sleepless night worrying about my sister. It hadn't helped.

Luckily we had barely even begun looking around the joint for our next victim before somebody called out from the crowd.

"Hey, Goldie!" a gruff voice croaked from the booth to our right.

Splayed out across the entirety of one side of the leather booth was the pudgy bright red body of an imp. Barely taller than two feet, with the legs of a goat, dark horns curled tightly into his thick feathery hair, and skin the color of a cooked lobster, he looked straight out of one of those old Christian Victorian paintings depicting the cherub versions of demons.

"Yeah, you, why don't you take a seat," he called, waving drunkenly toward the seat opposite of him.

He sounded like a creepy Italian PE teacher and looked vaguely like it, too, but it didn't stop me from taking him up on his offer, even if he hadn't offered it to me directly. I wasn't going to turn down the opportunity to question somebody who clearly had familiar ties with Gold, who slid into the booth beside me. His large muscly frame almost pinned me against the wood paneling of the wall.

"What do you want, Sebastian?" Gold asked indignantly, looking down on the imp with indifferent eyes.

The Imp beamed at the dragon, exposing a straight line of yellowed fangs. "Good to see you, too, Buddy. I was beginning to think I'd never see the likes of you again."

It had already been clear to me the two knew each other, though Gold's look at seeing him didn't speak of a close relationship. The longer I watched the hot and cold exchange between the two, the more curious I was as to how Gold would know an Imp from Faerie. I mean, I knew he traveled through the portals before, but I hadn't thought he would know the locals.

"I finally got kicked out of Eerie. Did that crown thing I had been playing around with," Gold said with a bored shrug. "How've you been?"

"Good, business is booming, despite some deserters leaving the Fae realm recently." The imp's blood-red gaze finally flicked to me. "Who's the hottie?"

Despite being jealous of only a wink from the bartender, Gold didn't even blink at the Imp's remark.

"My mate, Storm," Gold proudly declared, sliding his clawed hand onto my leg in a fashion that was I was growing to like far too much. "She and I are here on business."

I decided not to mention the fact that we were not in fact mates yet, mostly because I didn't want him to move his hand from my thigh. If he wanted to show off to his little imp friend, then who was I to ruin his fun?

The Imp slammed one red fist down on the table, letting out a loud disbelieving laugh. "No way, lucky man. I thought for sure you'd never see a mate, let alone the likes of this broad. What, was she one of your targets when you found her and she just let you stay out of pity?"

The imp didn't give Gold the chance to respond before he leaned over the table and extended one hand to me. "The names Sebastian, by the way. Sebastian Lovestick."

Lovestick. You had to be kidding me.

As if reading my mind, the Imp threw his head back and cackled. "Believe it or not, it's a family name."

Knowing as little as I did about imps and their lineages, I would have to take his word for it. It sounded about right anyway.

If Sebastian knew just how Gold and I had gotten together, it might blow his mind. Clearly, the imp still thought of the dragon next to me as a partner in crime, and judging by the tense set of Gold's jaw, the feeling was not mutual.

The dragon didn't want me hearing too much about his past selves antics from the imp, who seemed hell-bent on ignoring any of the signals Gold seemed to be sending him. I knew why he was doing it. He wanted to seem like an angel sent to save me so I would be more likely to accept him as a mate, but little did he know I could care less.

I'd take a man with a past and character over a vanilla good boy any day.

"It's nice to meet you, Mr. Lovestick. You're the first friend of Gold's I've met." I gave the imp a firm shake in return, making sure to slide him my most brilliant smile.

The imp only got more excited with my bright greeting. "You don't say! It's a pleasure I was the first. I guess I got lucky once again, and am the first to see Goldie's beautiful new girl myself before any of the guild."

Gold looked about two seconds away from blowing his brains out in frustration. "Listen, Sebastian. It's not a good time. We are looking for a fae, and time is ticking."

"I heard. Saw the bartender turn you away," Sebastian said with a drunken nod. "Chances were you were talking about the man who went out the back an hour ago."

"You saw the guy?" Gold sounded disinterested, yet I was almost coming off my seat at the information. If the imp happened to know something, we wouldn't have to question anyone else in the bar.

Not that we'd get anywhere. Since being turned away by the bartender, everyone had been giving us a major evil eye, and it wasn't just the haughty look the fae normally wore. If looks could kill, all three of us would be long dead.

"Nope, heard him. He was asking directions for the mayor's manor. Sounded like an out of towner to me." Sebastian shrugged, cursed by a sudden bought of hiccups.

"The mayor's house?" I couldn't hide the confusion in my question. "What business would he have at the mayor's house?"

"Don't ask me, lady," the imp said with a loud belch.

This chain of events was making no sense. What would the pixie-summoner have to do with the mayor of a fae town? I barely even talked to any fae. There was no way this could have something to do with me if it went so deep as to get fae politics involved.

Again the question of whether I wasn't the target at all crossed my mind. There was still the possibility I had nothing to do with this and was getting both Gold and me in a lot more trouble than we were ever meant to be in.

Though it just didn't make sense. If that were the case, then whoever the person was wouldn't go through the effort of making my car look like an animal attack. It was far too much effort for what little payoff it afforded.

Pieces were still missing, floating around in the air just waiting for me to find the common edge that connected them all.

"You didn't hear anything else did you?" Gold asked as he hastily slid out of the booth, pulling me to follow.

Apparently, Gold was done with feigning disinterest and

had decided now was the moment to rush out of there before the fae could get any more distance between us. I didn't blame him. As it was, the fae could be already done with whatever business he had with the mayor and have ducked Faerie by now.

"No," the imp said dully. Only then did he realize the dragon was leaving and cried out, "Hey, you guys just got here! You can't leave now!"

"No time," Gold urged, reaching into his pocket and tossing a small golden coin onto the table,

"That's for the information. If you want to catch up, look or ask for my mate in Witches-Brew Cove on earth."

Gold took my hand and helped me out of the booth, and I just managed to give the imp a parting wave before Gold and I began to slink right back through the same crowd we had cut through minutes before.

This night was going to give me whiplash if we didn't stop rushing from place to place so fast. I was sure I had never gone this many places in my entire life, and yet now I was about to flounce through the upper-class suburbs of fae town to hunt down a beast summoner.

I would have to look into investing in some running shoes.

CHAPTER SEVEN

The residential area of Faerie was a wonderland of rich gardens and dirt roads, a harsh difference from the cobbled streets and authentic shops of the town.

Everything, from intricate hedge designs to the beautiful metal beasts serving as the Faerie equivalent to gargoyles on top of wrought iron gates, was far too perfect to be accidental. With every few feet of vibrant natural grass, there seemed to be some art piece hiding amongst the lot, as if to signal the owner's wealth like the rest of their property wasn't already a sign.

Instead of feeling natural and artistic, it felt like I was in one of those twilight zone episodes where the main characters were the size of a doll and made to walk through a man-made *Barbie* world. I wouldn't be surprised if a host came out of nowhere and looked directly into the camera while lecturing the audience on how you should always be cautious of too-perfect things.

Gold walked forward without care, unmoved by the oddities in the scenery around him. It made me feel slightly less out of my element being led through another world with someone who knew his way around the other worlds. I knew I should be cautious. After all, it was clear from meeting his friend back at the tavern that his knowledge didn't come from an innocent adventuring past, yet I didn't care.

Maybe my sister was right all those years ago. I might have a taste for the wilder men. Though I also shouldn't take advice from the woman who threw a hissy fit on her twentieth birthday and ran away to this very realm.

"This is the place," Gold quietly murmured as we pulled up to a large dirt drive nearly identical to the ones around it.

I shadowed him as he slunk through the wide bars of the fence, making sure to watch out for the wards he pointed out so we didn't trip some fae alarm. I would have been able to spot them myself, but I didn't tell him that. If he wanted to flex his skills from his thieving past, I wasn't going to stop him.

It was clear as we grew closer to the manor that it was nothing special. It had the same boring bland glass and metal house rich people of every realm decided to make their staple. It was like everybody with money joined some bland-ass homeowners association.

Admittedly, the exotic gardens were incredibly scenic, though.

The wildness of the foliage and rosebushes complimented the house just enough to give it the hint of something that might be beautiful to someone's eyes. It was just a shame whoever planned the garden did it around a house as uninspired as this.

He led me quietly along the outside of the property, so we could barely avoid being seen from the inside of the house. Almost immediately after rounding the first corner, it became clear we were not the only people roaming the property at this time, and a couple of guards positioned at the front door served as our first obstacle.

"What's the plan? Find another way in?" I asked the dragon, practically glued to his side to avoid having to talk loud and risk being overheard in the silent night.

"We aren't going in at all," he explained. "This is a politician's house in Faerie. You couldn't get in if you wanted to, at least not the breaking and entering kind of way. Instead, we are going to figure out where exactly the fae we are looking for is."

I looked over his shoulder to see if he was joking, but the dragon's face remained smooth and unreadable. "You think you can track him from the outside?"

Gold flashed his fangs in a smug smile. "Yes, because he is outside."

I didn't need to ask him what he meant, because as soon as we came into view of the backyard, I wished I had never set foot on that property.

A fae, naked from head to toe, was splayed out across a glass table in the center of the back garden, head thrown back in the throes of what might be passion or pain. Two other fae stood a ways away, their backs to where we crouched, staring at the man thrashing around on the table.

Even from behind, I recognized the fae watching the man on the table. It was the man from outside my shop the other day, the one I'd had to flee from to get to the police station. He was even wearing the same rumpled outfit.

If I hadn't been so distracted after the police station, I would have remembered him long before now. I couldn't help feeling disappointed in myself for not putting two and two together after hearing Gold's description of him. It was like my mind had just blanked for the last two days, deserting me when I needed it most.

Beside the man was a tall willowy fae dressed in what ap peared to be a cross between a nightdress and a toga, billow- ing white fabric dancing around her bare ankles playfully in the soft breeze. From behind, she looked like the picture of fae elegance, right down to her golden flowing hair.

The two appeared to be deeply engrossed in a conversation that couldn't be heard over the trickling of a man-made pond placed conveniently between us and them. I cursed at our luck, knowing getting any closer to the group would be a risk we didn't want to take as of yet. However, if we didn't learn why the man was here, the whole mission would be a bust.

On top of the table, the man continued to groan and squirm, fighting the throes of whatever spell had caught him. I felt a pang of empathy watching him, knowing without a doubt that he was not there of his own accord. Obvious restraints were holding him firmly in place that looked to be some form of metal shackles.

This was no kink show. This was real legitimate torture.

I shifted in place, restlessly debating approaching them further and leaving the safety of our hideout alongside the house. Gold seemed to sense my thought and shook his head.

"Something's off," he mouthed, gaze darting to survey the garden.

I followed his movements as if my witch eyes could see any better than a dragon's in the dark, only to come up with nothing. The garden was eerily still, not even the crickets sang in the dark of the greenery. There was a feeling in the air, clinging heavy and damp—like the feeling of walking into a room that hadn't been opened in months.

The longer I spent dwelling on the feeling, the more a strong scent of rot began to overwhelm us. It was strong and putrid and made me want to lose my lunch all over the grass. I tried to find the source of the smell, only nothing had changed since I looked last. Gold and I were still crouched in the bushes with nothing surrounding us but more greenery, only the tree in the back garden showing any signs of movement.

There was the soft hissing sound of something sticky giving way from a smooth surface above us, and my gaze snapped upwards to be greeted with the milky blue eyes of the most horrifying monster I had seen in my life.

"You've got to be fucking kidding me," I gasped.

I barely had time to launch myself backward before the

thing's gangly decayed limbs ate up the space I had been standing in, clambering from where it had been perched on the roof of the house. All at once, the horror before me realized it had missed its target and swung its head up to let out an ear-splitting shriek of fury. Rows and rows of sharpened putrid fangs snapped at me, and in a primal response, I felt the magic in my veins begin to well in preparations of a life or death fight.

My fingertips burned with the beginning of fire just as Gold's newly changed dragon form dived onto the beast, sinking his claws into the papery flesh of the creature. The two went tumbling, slamming into the side of the glass house. All I could see was the flash of gold and red as the two began to hack and slash at one another, neither caring for any of their surroundings.

Any relief I felt at not being the target of the beast was lost the second I realized that if I did not intervene Gold would be torn to shreds just as he had two nights ago. As fast as I could, I began to summon the flames from within me, waiting for the moment I could get a clear sight of the creature before flinging them, only to be distracted by the sight of the two fae quickly striding towards us.

It was the two in the garden, watching the torture of that fae on the table. They must have been drawn by the sounds of the two colliding with the glass and made their way to the chaos to serve as reinforcements.

Realizing Gold would have even less of a chance against the beast if paired with two more distractions, I jumped out of the bushes, stopping the two in their tracks before they reached the fight. I wasn't going to let this be a pile onto the one person who'd had the guts to defend me against what I was sure had to be the infamously nightmarish pixie.

"Take another step, and I will burn you where you stand," I growled, the flames growing so high they consumed nearly the entirety of my arms.

I could hear the battle behind me, but I couldn't afford even the slightest peek to make sure Gold was all right. I had no idea what these two were capable of, and I wasn't going to bet my life on the slightest slip-up. I instead kept my gaze on the two now standing stock-still before me, staring at me with their too-calm faces.

The female fae was beautiful beyond words, but her thick aura of darkness tainted that beauty. As she saw me her too-perfect face bloomed into a coy smile, her hands rising to clasp before her face. "My, my, Adam, you were right. She is quite a sight."

She didn't even seem to register my flames, not even sparing them a glance as she beamed over at me from where she stood. She was all smiles and gumdrops, not an ounce of it seeming fake as she looked at me as if I was the biggest Christmas present under the Christmas tree.

The other fae didn't listen to the woman's words. Instead, he grew wide-eyed and terrified once he recognized who the woman behind the flames was. The man I remembered from in front of my shop was replaced with the scared disheveled man cowering in a dark garden with an expression looking too close to crying.

"What are you talking about?" I spat out, the intensity of my flames adding power to my voice that had previously not been there.

The woman smiled slow and catlike, as if I had just stepped right into her trap. "I think it's what I want that would concern you more, Storm Carlisle," she intoned.

My name on the woman's lips made me flinch and yearn to tear her tongue out all at once. There was a certain level of sliminess this woman emitted from just a few feet away, and it tainted everything it touched. It was the bratty I-get-everything-I-want voice that came with a face as beautiful as hers.

Whoever this woman was, she thought she had power and lots of it.

"And just what's that?" I humored her, knowing the longer I waited to fight, the more power my fire would have.

If I could buy some time and manage to weasel some information out of her, we might be able to escape before the guard arrived. As it was, I was growing more and more nervous for the dragon as the fight behind me grew in chorus.

"Oh, come on," she tsked. "I want you, Storm. Why else would I send Adam to try and retrieve you?"

If that was what the man had been trying to do by sicking a pixie on me and begging for my attention outside of a crowded shop, then she didn't have the brain to hire someone who knew what they were doing. Now that I knew that was what he was trying to accomplish I was even more glad I hadn't taken him up on his request.

If she had hired someone even a little more competent, I might have been the one these two had been watching on that table.

"I don't know anything about you, lady," I said, the words clipped and biting. "Let alone enough to know why the hell you would need me."

"Oh come on, Storm." She spoke teasingly. "I'm sure if you put your mind to it, you could come up with something."

I could, but I didn't like any of the ideas I was coming up with. I knew exactly what a little rich girl like herself would want with my most recent potion, and the man currently writhing in pain on the table proved it. In the wrong hands, a discovery like mine could do major damage.

Behind us, I heard a wet cracking sound, then that unearthly shriek again, and I watched as the woman's gaze followed the battle behind me. Her eyes furiously narrowed as she watched, lip curling as she spat a curse under her breath.

I felt a slight glimmer of relief, knowing that anything that would upset her must be good for us. I sent out a mental cheer for Gold, hoping somehow it would reach out and give him the power he needed to finish his side of the fight while I held off the two fae before me.

"Call off the beast, and I won't kill you," I warned, using all of the power in my voice I could manage to try and intimidate the woman.

The woman's violet eyes snapped from anger to a deep glimmering amusement. "No, I think I will enjoy watching my pixie tear your dragon into bite-sized pieces."

With a frustrated growl, I hurled the first bolt of fire right where she stood. She raised one palm, a thin barrier of magic ricocheting the flame right into the bushes, setting them aflame in an instant.

In an instant, her humor faded replaced by a cold snarl that curled her perfect mouth. "Do you have any idea how long it takes to repair a garden like this?"

That was my only warning as her hand lifted, and a blast of wind knocked me right off my feet. I swiveled my body to fall into a roll, righting myself on my knee as I flung the second firebolt right into the lady's now unprotected chest.

It caught with an audible whoosh, consuming her dress almost immediately in the blaze of magic. That's what she got for wearing something as impractical as a slip dress into a battle.

All of her tough charades were gone in an instant as she turned on her heels with a high-pitched squeal, arms desperately flailing at the flames as the fae formerly frozen in fear rushed to her side to help her put out the fire. It was like watching a person change personalities. She flipped that quick into the squealing little girl under all those layers of bravado.

"You bitch!" she shrieked, her voice high and piercing. "You have no idea who you're messing with. Eris will have your head!"

I was shocked that my flames had worked as well as they did, especially on the second swing, and had no time to process her words as the two meaty guards flew around the corner. It seemed my excitement from the small success had come a moment too soon.

These two meant business, and almost immediately began to summon their magic as they ate up the distance between us in large strides. I was working out a way to block them with one of the wards I had memorized from childhood, only to find myself snatched right from where I stood.

It was only the sight of the familiar glint of gold on the claws clenching around my waist that stopped me from engulfing the dragon clutching me in my witch's fire. I did let out an angry cry, twisting in his grip, as if that would allow me to slip right back down onto the ground. With every push of his wings as he flew, the fiery garden grew further and further away, putting more and more distance between us and the angry fae.

I wasn't even sure that there was a place to land anymore, the flames were spreading that fast, but the thought of leaving now infuriated me. That man down there was still bound to that table, and we hadn't learned anything. If we left now, all of the momentum we had gained would go right down the drain.

"Gold, we have to get back down there!" I yelled over the wind. "We were so close to getting our information!"

The dragon above me let out a long hissing growl that I took for a definite no, and I slapped at his claws despite knowing the struggle was fruitless. No matter what I did, he was taking me out of there.

I tried in vain to get the dragon's attention once more, but he was already calling forth a portal in the sky before him, and in no time we were right back in Witches-Brew with Faerie long behind us.

It wasn't until the dragon dropped me off onto the porch that I caught the reason why he hadn't been listening to me. His back was a patchwork of exposed meat and claw marks, so bad he collapsed onto the grass with a shuddering gasp and passed right out.

He was so wounded he could barely shift back into his human form, and I felt a deep stab of guilt at being the reason he was once again wounded and unconscious on the front lawn of my property.

Gold hadn't pulled me out of there because he thought I couldn't handle taking on the guards, but because in trying to protect me from the beast, he had nearly gotten himself killed once again.

After this, I would owe him big time. Even if the dragon insisted he didn't want payment back. If I wasn't convinced he was serious about protecting me before, I sure was now. No man would go through something like that again and again if he weren't invested in your protection.

I felt the backlash of my magic all at once then, slamming into me with a dizzying weakness. All of the magic I had used these last few days left me almost magically crippled, and I had no doubt I wouldn't even be able to fly my broom for the next couple of days.

I was exhausted, my dragon was wounded, and all I had to show for it was a slightly better grasp on the situation unfolding around me.

With a resigned sigh, I began to drag the dragon back inside for the second time that week, praying to whatever deity that he healed as quickly as the other night. I was hoping after all of this he would find it in him to be smart and run away screaming, so I didn't have to feel bad about him getting hurt for me anymore.

CHAPTER EIGHT

"So, you set the lady on fire."

Jessica Glare sat across from me for the first time in weeks, looking as disheveled as I had ever seen her. Apparently, the change in her work these last few days had been as hard on her as it had been for me.

"The details hardly matter," I said dismissively, but Jessica wasn't going to let it go that easily.

"What do you mean it hardly matters?" she asked, scoffing. "You set a politician's evil daughter on fire, and there's a wounded dragon in your backroom! I mean, what does your family think of all of this?"

"My family already knows all about it," I told her. "You don't need to worry about that. I have everything under control. What I'm worried about here is you. For the time being, I'm going to put a hold on deliveries, and the shop as a whole."

Jessica let out an outraged cry. "You can't be serious. Are you firing me?"

"No, no." I tried to conciliate, attempting to calm her with a tendril of magic, only to have it bounce right off of the raging wolf. "I'm just taking some safety precautions until my family and I can sort things out. In the meantime, I want to give you a paid vacation."

"So that's it then." She looked enraged, her eyes turning yellow as her wolf pushed for control. "You're just putting everything on hold for this? Storm, you can't think this is a good idea. The shop will go out of business."

"Jessica," I snapped. "The shop won't go out of business even if I put it on hold for a year. The whole reason I am doing this is not for the shop, anyway. I'm worried about your safety. I don't want you to get caught up in this."

"I'm a big girl. I don't need my hand held. If this fucking pixie were going to scare me off I would have quit a while ago."

She wasn't going to let this go easily, despite not having a choice in all of this. I had already come to this conclusion long before I called her over to talk this out face to face, and we both knew there was little she could do to change my mind.

I knew I was fucking her over. She was my employee, and I was taking her off the job with no warning. Even though I was still going to pay her the normal amount she would get working full time, this was still a betrayal of our professional relationship.

It hurt to think of how she must think of me after these last few days. Her anger was more than justified, but this couldn't happen any other way. If I kept her on the job, there was a very real chance someone would see her as a way to get to me, and if there was one thing I couldn't live with it was someone getting hurt because of me.

"That's my whole point, Jess," I insisted. "If I don't force you to take time off, you'll take it upon yourself to try and help. I don't want to be the reason you get hurt, even if you hate me for it."

If looks could kill, I would be six feet under. Jessica's entire demeanor radiated pure fury. If it wasn't for my knowledge that the she-wolf would rather cut off her paw than hurt me, I might have been frightened of her glare.

"Fine," she spat out, standing so fast from her chair that it shot halfway across my small dining room, "but don't call me if you end up needing a wolf."

She nearly took my front door right off the hinges with

how hard she slammed it on her way out, though I didn't have the will to care about the thing at that moment. I was far more concerned about the woman's safety than my property as she sped off in a fit down my driveway.

The whole point in this had been to make sure that nobody got in the way of my enemies and me, but I couldn't help the guilt that seemed to build with each second that passed.

I closed my eyes and allowed myself a moment of calm. I told myself it was necessary — that I would never be able to solve all of my recent problems while worrying about my job. That it would be better for everyone evolved if I put distance between me and my everyday life for the time being.

I had to get to the bottom of all of this soon before it all lead to my untimely death. At the very least, I already knew who was after me. It took no time to figure that out while I waited for Gold to heal.

The girl I had burned was Gili Willow, the daughter of the mayor of the fae town we had landed in the night before. The man with her was a resident of Witches-Brew named Adam Urvine.

I had already known the latter. However, the first hadn't been that hard to figure out the following morning.

I felt a cold chill run down my spine at the memory of that morning.

I had stepped out onto my front porch in time to witness a black van shrieking to a stop on the road just where my wards ended. It all had happened so fast. I didn't have time to react as the side door slid open and a man was kicked right out onto my property. Just as fast as it arrived the van took back off in a cloud of dust, there and gone in an instant.

The man it had left was none other than Adam Urvine, beaten to a pulp and two breaths away from death. If it wasn't for the note on his chest, I might not have even been able to recognize him.

There in bold dark ink was a simple letter, addressed to me.

We enjoyed your visit. See you soon.

A light tap from behind me startled me right back to the present. Gold's warm presence filled the room as he stepped out of the hallway from where he had been hidden, offering me a small smile.

"She took it well."

I tried to laugh softly, but it came out more like a quiet bark. "Yeah, about as well as I thought she would."

I turned my full attention to the dragon, quickly surveying his formerly bandaged form. His wounds were now no more than faint pink lines across his bare torso, all perfectly closed and quickly healed. It was a small comfort, but a welcome one. The last thing we needed was to deal with an infection from pixie inflicted wounds. I had been exhausted and pushed to my magical limits when healing him, so it was a relief to see I hadn't messed anything major up in the process.

"You look good. It doesn't look like anything is going to scar from last night," I told him, gesturing toward his chest

He nodded in agreement. "I had a good healer."

He didn't appear to be surprised at the rate of his healing, which was probably due to his genetics. I knew nothing about his kind's capabilities, but judging by how much pain he was able to handle, dragons were probably some of the most durable breeds out here.

"Do all dragons heal as fast as you? Or are you just special?"

Gold looked charmed by my question, clearly happy I was taking an interest in his kind. "Most dragons heal fast, but around you, I seem to heal a lot faster."

"That's the healing magic. When you were unconscious I held your mouth and nose closed so you would have to drink some potions of mine, then I let them do their work."

It was a crude description of the intricate process of potions work, but it wasn't like I was giving him a lecture on the things.

"I would normally be mad about somebody forcing me to drink strange liquids, but I can't seem to deny the results." He chuckled. "I suppose it helps that the witch doing so is one so skilled and knowledgeable. I might drink anything you handed me."

"You say that now, but just wait. Even my family couldn't be rid of me fast enough once I picked up my trade. In no time I'll have you be my test dummy for new potions."

It was true. Polly had threatened to evict me for making her test out some of my earlier potions. It didn't help that I barely knew what I was doing and as a result, almost succeeded in putting her in an early grave on many occasions.

"I'm certain we could work out some sort of agreement," he purred in my ear, appearing mere inches before me.

I hadn't even heard the man move. Somehow he just swooped into my line of sight in a single bound. My breath hitched in my throat at the unexpected jolt of excitement that shot through me at the feeling of his warm breath against my bare throat.

The sudden shift in mood was startling. One second I was stuck in a somber state of regret, and the next there was a sizzling heat pulling me into its grasp from out of nowhere.

I got the feeling it had been building for a while around me, but like a frog in water, I didn't notice the heat until it was boiling. Now, I was in the grasp of the very dangerous predator who was locked on to me like a hungry snake.

"Gold?" My voice was a nervous chirp as I allowed myself to be pulled further into his grasp. "You're getting awful handsy out of nowhere."

Gold wasn't moved by my nervous words, burying his nose into the hollow of my throat to take in a shuddering breath. "You smell of pleasure incarnate . . ." he murmured, a low purr. "It's a miracle I haven't eaten you whole by now."

Despite the whiplash in the change of moods, I couldn't seem to conjure the energy to push him away. In all honesty, I didn't know that I wanted to. I had long since given up the pretense of putting some distance between us, and denying the attraction would be a stupid exercise in misery.

I'd had men I had been dating for months not spark even an ounce of the heat this man had in the last few days. I had certainly never seen those men jump through the hoops this one did to be by my side.

With everything building around us quickly trapping us in a panic of danger, was indulging in a liaison with this dragon the worst idea?

I pulled back from him only far enough to meet his heated gaze, letting my eyes drift halfway closed and letting myself lean into the man's caress. He wasted no time taking full advantage of my offer, caging me in his strong arms as his lips crashed down onto my own. His grip was strong and dominant, his lips soft and rough and good all at the same time like a forbidden tempest of indulgence.

His other arm snaked around my waist, and I didn't need his guidance to press myself hard against his rigid form. We came together in a tangle of mouths and tongues, taking each other in a frenzy. His hand fisted in the hair at the nape of my neck, pulling my head back, opening my mouth further to his thorough invasion.

His other hand slid down to grip my ass as he held me in place and ground the full length of his thick erection against my core. The feeling of the rough denim of his pants through the soft fabric of my tights was orgasm worthy in and of itself, but the real MVP of the situation was the massive manhood I could feel begging to burst from his jeans.

I felt my entire body clench at the thought of that absolute monster tunneling inside me. My hands moved down to pull him harder into me, rocking myself against it in a desperate bid to calm the need building deep within myself.

"Needy little witch," he hissed after he pulled away long enough to strip my shirt over my head, almost succeeding in ripping the fabric.

I didn't respond, reaching down in a flurry of hands to make quick work of his buckle. His hand darted out to stop me just as I got the zipper of his pants down, and my gaze darted up to meet his glowing predatory gaze with a confused look.

"Hold on," he warned. "Once I'm freed, I might not have the self-control to do every little thing I've been fantasizing about since I first saw you in that car. This is my only warning, little witch."

A low keening sound escaped from deep in my chest as I gave myself over to him without a single care of his warning. He wasted no time tearing both my tights and panties from me in one strong move, throwing the ruined fabric into the dark of the hall. With a low grumbling growl, he lifted me up with one arm and cleared off my kitchen table with the other, sending the contents scattering loudly across my hardwood floors.

I gasped as the cool wood met my bare ass once he threw me onto the surface, yet the shock was immediately taken away as the man buried his face firmly between my thighs.

"By the fates!" I shrieked, clenching my legs around either side of his head as his warm tongue sought the heat between my folds. "You waste no fucking time."

His eyes met mine with a wink, and the image of being splayed across the kitchen table buck naked with a man's dark head between my thighs was a near-religious experience. The only thing that improved the experience was the skill with which this man began to lay into me with just his tongue.

He swirled it right over my clit, and only his firm grasp holding me tight to his face kept me from coming right off the table at the first contact. He was merciless, teasing and retreating with feather-light strokes before laying one punishing suck right on the center of my pleasure.

I ground myself against his face, his stubble scratching my thighs in the most delicious friction I had ever felt in my short existence. He pulled away only long enough to sink two thick fingers right into my channel without warning, heatedly watching my face as he began to slowly, tortuously, move his fingers within me.

He was uncaring of my pleading, mercilessly pleasuring me as he watched each subtle movement of mine with dark eyes. They swirled with his dragon's gold, flipping back and forth between human and reptilian.

I was desperate, clawing at his arms and tryingwildly to pull his head up so I could force him to sink every inch of himself inside of me and stop his slow torture. I didn't care about anything at that moment that didn't involve me bent over the table as he had his wicked way with me, but he remained firmly in place. It was as if he was trying to wring every ounce of pleasure he could get out of me before finally letting me down from my edge long enough to inflict that final wicked torture.

Just as I flung my head back and allowed myself to ride the waves of my first orgasm, he ripped himself away, tearing his pants off of himself in a single pull and leaving me to drown in the body-shaking pulses of my orgasm.

Through my pleasure blurred gaze, I took in all of the man with hungry eyes. I had already seen him fully naked more than once, but seeing him wounded and unconscious wasn't anything compared to the sexual promise of the fully aroused male staring down on me with an almost maddened gaze. He was strong, virile, slick with a fine layer of sweat as he prowled toward me like the predator he was.

I knew what I must look like splayed across this table, but I did not care. All I cared about at that moment was getting him inside of me.

In a display of strength I didn't know I possessed, I flipped myself over onto my stomach, allowing my legs to dangle off the table and my ass to be fully bared towards the naked beast at my back. His nostrils flared, and I swear I saw his cock jet up even higher than it had been moments before.

I allowed my voice to go husky as I met his eyes with a saucy look. "Come and get it, big boy," I teased, knowing full well I was teasing a male already on edge.

It was like poking a sleeping bear. Every ounce of color in his eyes drained to the inky slitted black of his dragon's, and in a blur, he was on top of me. He wasted no time gripping my hips and slamming myself back onto him, using my lack of balance against me as he levered my body onto his thick cock.

I gasped in a mixture of pain and excitement, my eyes going wide at the feeling of being filled after years of inattention. It was everything I could have dreamed of with an extra inch added on. The feeling of being impaled on this male was a pleasure that went bone deep.

"Wicked Witch," he growled with a sharp flex of his hips. "I'll never let you go."

With a snarl, he gripped his hands tightly around my waist as he began to thrust into me almost hard enough to shake the entire table. The only sound that came from me was a surprised gasp, I was so unprepared for the ease with which the man began to plunder my core. It was rough and hot and hard, and everything I had ever wanted from a man.

I held onto the edges of the table with what little strength I had, my hips moving against his in a primal rhythm. Our bodies moved slickly against one another as we both sought each other's heated caresses.

I had never been taken with such male intensity, surrendered to the full mastery of a man who knew exactly what he wanted. It wasn't cruel, nor sweet, but something in between that spoke to the part of myself that yearned to be at the mercy of a dragon such as himself.

His hand released my hip only long enough to land a jarring smack right onto my ass, and I screeched as the sharp pain burned a path of pleasure right to my fiery core. He quirked his mouth into a half-grin, pleased by my reaction as he continued his rough mastery of my body.

"Naughty, naughty, girl," he purred with another sharp slap. "You are gripping me so greedily right now that I'm afraid you might unman me once I make you come."

"Fuck," I gasped through my shortened breaths, "you."

"Don't mind if I do."

His other hand jerked my hips even further off the table, angling me so that his cock drove even faster and deeper into my core. I might have gasped, but my chest felt like it was collapsing under the intense pressure winding through my whole body. It felt like my torso was twisted in knots, growing tighter and tighter, moving towards a horizon I knew would destroy me.

I was in a battle with myself, pushing and pulling and begging for more and yet terrified of what it was building toward. I was frightened of the part of myself so willing to fully let go, to give myself to this male, and yet I had never wanted anything more.

With a long breathy cry, I gave myself to his masterful grip, going limp against the table as the knots of torturous pleasure that had been building deep within me snapped all at once. I writhed in abandon, vision blurring as my whole body pulsed with need as I was overcome by pleasure. Muscles I didn't know existed twisted and heated, moving me like a wild woman underneath the still relentless grip of the dragon.

I felt it as Gold's hips faltered and jerked, the womanly part of myself fascinated by the sight of the man losing himself within me. He threw back his head in a roar loud enough to shatter the kitchen windows, never once stopping his merciless pounding as he began to pulse deep inside of me.

I could feel the intense warmth of his release fill me even through the white-hot daze of my pleasure, and just as I thought it couldn't get any better, a second wave of heat burned through my chest. This was no orgasm, but an intense warmth blooming right at my heart and spreading itself lazily through my burning veins.

I closed my eyes and allowed myself to surrender to the maelstrom of sensation, giving myself to the pull even as after some time, I felt him leave my body. It could have gone on for minutes, hours, hell even days, I did not know, but I knew I would never be the same after this.

I was warm and pleasured, my chest still heaving even as the last few pulses of the combined sensations left my limp body, unknowing of how long it had been since I had last been aware of my existence.

I hadn't realized he'd moved me until I was wrapped in the warmth of my blankets, Gold's strong arm pulling me into himself as a sound akin to a catlike purr softly shook my chest. I strained my head to look up into the soft eyes of my dragon, feeling a strong ache in my chest that had nothing to do with arousal.

He looked at me like I was his world, tender and sweet. I knew at that moment that I couldn't deny my growing feelings for the man any longer. In just a few days, he had managed to worm himself not only into my life, but my heart, and I knew there was nothing I could do to stop it.

He must have seen something in my gaze, because he grinned down at me goofily and reached over to gently push the slick hair back from my flushed face. It was such a harsh contrast to the roughness of our coupling that I half wondered if this was even the same man.

"Now I'll never be rid of you," I teased, with a sleepy wink.

His laugh shook us both. "You were never going to be in the first place."

CHAPTER NINE

It was storming again — full-blown gusts of winds and pouring rains that tested the very foundation of my house. It was the perfect weather to stay at home and out of danger in.

The two of us had decided to put our outside investigation on the back burner for the time being. It probably wasn't the best idea to head out in the open while we were both recharging after our fights. Instead, we both sat in my living room combing the internet for information on the few things we could look into without risking exhausting ourselves any further.

A couple of feet away from me, Gold was splayed across my recliner, one leg thrown up over the side like a caveman. The action should annoy me, but for the most part, I just found his presence in the room with me comforting. Who was I to judge someone for how they got comfortable anyway?

In the past few days, we had fallen into this nightly routine of buzzing around each other as we went about our work. It provided us both with the perfect amount of stability to tackle each of our problems head first, mine with the closing of the shop, and his with his connections back home.

Other than a few long rendezvous on assorted hard surfaces, and one embarrassing moment on a bean bag, we were constantly absorbed in whatever we had set our mind to at that moment.

We were still waiting for Adam Urvine to recover, but considering the extent of his injuries, it wasn't likely he was going to wake anytime soon. In the meantime I had him locked up in my basement as I administered some potions I hoped would help heal him in time for him to be of some help to us.

I wouldn't bet money on it, but I was pretty sure if anyone was going to aid us in our investigation, it would be the fae who'd nearly died for some fae politician to send a message. I wasn't stupid, however, and made sure the fae couldn't get out of that room if he tried. I even set a no-magic ward on the room so he couldn't just portal out of there like he had when we caught him in town.

I doubted he would get far any other way. Gold would eat him for lunch if he even thought he heard him trying to escape.

Since the table incident, Gold had been particularly concerned about my safety, as if it was now his duty to serve as my bodyguard just because we'd decided to take our relationship to the next level. I wasn't the type of woman to particularly care if somebody wanted to protect me. As long as they didn't get in my way, pushing away free help just seemed silly, but I was concerned over the vigor with which the dragon approached my protection.

When he should have been helping me research, I found him glaring outside the front windows, or staring at the door that led to my basement. It bothered me only because I hated thinking that I was taking away from him being his own person. I thought overprotectiveness was cute, but I'd prefer having Gold's mind focused on helping me prepare for whatever was coming rather than worry over the thing we wouldn't notice until it was too late anyway.

I couldn't help feeling like somehow I was dragging the man into something he should never have been a part of, even though he insisted he wanted to be here helping me. For some reason, I felt like I was at fault for everything we had been through.

While Gold was distracted on a call with one of his old

friends from Eerie, I stole away onto my porch. Somehow I thought the change in scenery and the crisp rain-filled air might inspire me to drop the funk I found myself in.

We had been working on reaching out to every person we could think of in order to find a foothold in this case, but nothing was coming up. It was growing clearer and clearer that either these people weren't letting anyone in on what they were doing, or they were scary enough to have made these people not want to talk.

Either way, it was a complete bust.

In order to avoid getting frustrated, I decided to drop that method for a while and refocus on available public information to avoid blowing my brains out in frustration.

When I;d bought my house a few months ago, a couple of things drew me to it. First, the house was perfect for my needs, including enough room for a couple of kids if I ever felt breeding a few younglings. Second, but more importantly, was the location.

I was isolated at the end of a road mainly used by hikers, my cabin centered in the middle of the deepest wooded area of the town. In any direction, I could walk and be surrounded by mile after mile of forest, no interruptions or distractions.

Now more than ever, I needed the space my place allowed. Out here, alone apart from the dragon I was growing more used to by the minute, I felt safer than anywhere else. Only now I wasn't feeling that familiar pull my land allowed me.

There was something in the air that tainted my woods, calling to me from afar.

I tried clearing my head, hugging my coat in closer into myself, but the feeling remained. Something was here, disturbing the energy around my house.

Upon opening my eyes, I immediately met those of a woman standing in the middle of a thicket of thorns on the edge of my property. Eyes black as coal, skin paler than milk, she was far from beautiful, her features too sharp and bird-like. Her hair fell jagged and uneven around her head like feathers that reached her mid-back.

The woman stood there, staring at me with a blank expression, doing and saying nothing. I had never seen anything like her. It was like something that dwelled in the back of your memories, darkness recalled from a history that was not your own.

I knew, even from a distance, the being was ancient and malevolent. She radiated a darkness that tainted the brush around her, slowly bleeding the life out of everything living that dared come in contact with her.

This was no pixie—no mindless beast. This woman was the mother of things worse than that creature.

It was said a witch was reborn of the same soul over and over. That no matter how much a witch died, the soul within her retained every ounce of memory from her past lives, even if the witch was reborn anew in the world.

My soul was calling to me now, warning me of the danger before me.

The woman's smile widened to show a perfect row of pearly white teeth, and around her, a shroud of darkness began to halo her body. No, it wasn't darkness, but wings the color of pitch-black ink. They unfolded slowly, growing larger and larger until they seemed to engulf the woman standing between them.

A hand grasped my shoulder, and I let out an unearthly shriek. Gold's topaz gaze locked onto my own as I spun to face my attacker, and I just barely registered that it was him in time to catch myself before I lit him ablaze with my witch's fire.

"What are you doing out here?" he asked calmly, looking concerned as he pulled me into his warm chest in a comforting embrace.

I let out a shaky breath, ignoring his question to whip my attention back to where I had been staring, only there was nothing there. The treelined edge of the property was empty, the grass yellowed and dead.

"Storm, are you all right?"

I turned my baffled gaze back on the dragon, feeling a veil of sluggish confusion settle over me. "I thought I saw something."

Gold glanced towards the woods, even though we both knew if anything had been out there, he would have seen it long before now. Whatever I saw was gone, even in my own head. I couldn't even recall if it was a person or an animal or something in between. It was like my mind had made it up.

A breathy laugh left my chest, but the sound was hollow even to my ears. "I guess I was just daydreaming. All the stress must be adding up."

I tried to tell myself the same, but as I brushed past Gold to go back into the house, I could still feel the fear that had raised the hair on the back of my arms.

"Well, I have some good news," Gold said, distracting me from my thoughts. "I've got some information on the mayor and his daughter."

I had almost forgotten about his phone call. When I had left him in the house, I had thought he seemed a bit more engrossed in the conversation than usual. Now that I knew it had had some significance, I regretted not just staying in and listening instead of going outside to hide.

"What's that?" I asked, trying to busy my shaky hands by nervously fidgeting with a bottle I had left on the counter. "Hopefully not more duds. If I have to hear about another disgruntled ex-lover of that shady old man, I will have to off myself."

Gold snickered. "No, this time it's legitimate. I even got some videos to prove it. A couple of locals my buddies are close with had their own questions about the family, it seems. They wasted no time sending me their findings."

"Well . . . don't leave me hanging. Tell me about it."

I could tell he saw right through the cheery facade I had plastered on. The look he gave me was telling enough. He had a thing for watching people, no doubt a result of his thieving past, and it made brushing anything by him impossible. Just in the last few hours, he had called me acting too stressed out just from a sparing glance and made me go take care of myself before coming back and continuing our work.

It was a new experience, having somebody this involved in my wellbeing, and I wasn't quite sure if I hated it or not. Somehow he was even more in tune with me than my family had ever been, and we had only known each other for a few days.

"The mayor has been involved with some shady creatures these past few days. Apparently, it's been well known that he has been in league with the new rise of cultists in the fae realm," Gold informed me, turning to pick up the notepad he written all of his notes on.

A flash of something crossed my mind, but I couldn't seem to make out just what it was. The woods outside my house, the dead grass.

"Cultists?" I asked, brow crinkling. "What cultists? I thought the fae didn't get involved with gods, other than their own."

"They don't," he confirmed. "However, recently there have been rumors of something building in the darker parts of Faerie. It's been happening for a while now. The fae are just too proud to admit it, unfortunately."

"So, who then are these cultists? And what do they have to do with the mayor? Surely the fae wouldn't allow a politician to be in league with people like that."

Gold snorted. "Their queen is a woman who has the mind

of a child, and one that doesn't think much at that. The fae will do anything to protect their pride except face their problems and solve them before they become as big as this."

Gold was glaring at the notes in his hand with a fiery expression, and I got the sudden feeling he didn't like the fae that much. Or rather the higher ranking ones. I didn't blame him. They weren't well known for their politeness.

I suppose when you go get involved with those types instead of just hearing about them, you build vendettas.

"I don't know the exact details," he continued after a moment. "But I do know whatever group he is in league with is dangerous. Dangerous enough that my old partners are abandoning the fae realm entirely."

"It's that serious?"

I was having trouble coming to terms with the existence of a faceless cultist group in my mind. Before now, I hadn't even thought this went that deep. I thought at most the mayor might be in league with the fae mafia, not this.

Cults weren't typically to be feared anymore unless they were the serial killer types. I had no idea we even had any more in today's world.

The idea that my enemies were in league with something so sinister it was making top-rank thieves leave the land of riches in droves and it was after us was terrifying.

Gold nodded. "I think it is. Only I have no clue what to do with this information. I suppose it's another avenue to explore, but it just throws another wrench in all of this."

I thought for a moment, trying to come up with some reason that a mayor's daughter in league with a cult group might have to do with me. I didn't practice for any gods. My family had never been contracted to any religious group.

So what would I have that would entice a cult?

Maybe this *was* about my potion.

When I'd arrived at the mayor's house, that fae had been

tied to the table, writhing with pleasure and pain. At the moment I hadn't thought anything deeper of it, other than disgust that someone would do that to another being and the need to help the man, but now that I recalled it, I realized the man's reaction seemed familiar.

It wouldn't be hard to corrupt one of my hallucinogenic love potions, and if pushed in the right direction, it would have the potential to create a nightmarish experience. Where my potions could make a person's wildest fantasies come to life before them in an almost tangible form, it could also make a person's nightmares come true. In the wrong hands, something like that could easily be weaponized by a cult.

I hadn't even thought of that possibility before. Just the idea made my blood run cold in my veins.

If it was true, I would have helped engineer one of the worst potions known to all of the three worlds.

I relayed my realization to Gold, trying to stop myself from rambling as the guilt riddled thoughts spilled from my mouth in horrified waves.

Once I was finished, he crossed the room and took my face in his hands, silencing me with a fierce stare. "Calm down, little witch. Even if what you say is true, guilt will get you nowhere. You would not be at fault because there is no way you could have known what it would become. Besides, we won't know anything until we sort this out."

"How do you know that, though? How do we know I'm not the cause of this?" I was growing more flustered by the second. "I never should have entertained my aunt. I knew it was a stupid idea, even then."

Gold let out an exasperated breath. "Enough. If you don't stop acting hysterically, I won't hesitate to take you over my knee."

My immediate reaction was to whip my head up and glare at the man, but the serious look in his eyes told me he was all business. Despite the spike of fury I got at being told to calm down by a man, I knew he was right, and I wasn't in the mood to risk getting spanked right now to sate the part of me that wanted to argue my frustration out.

I closed my eyes and allowed myself another moment of calm as I was pressed into his strong arms. I was stuck in a torrent of emotions that whipped me around like a ragdoll, with the only solid thing in my life being the man in my arms.

I never liked to be the dependent person. I was the oldest daughter, the most mature. I had to be strong to be a good example to my sisters and to take the stress off my great-grandmother's shoulders.

Allowing myself to lean on this man felt like I was opening myself up to being weak, and I hated myself because the more I allowed myself to be vulnerable the more I craved being taken care of by this man. For some reason, I felt like I needed him here to help balance me out, even if it sounded old-fashioned.

The one thing I knew was that it did help. I felt the tension drain off me in waves, leaving me with the feeling of being warm and safe in the dragon's arms.

"If you ever threaten to spank me while I'm angry," I hissed in his ear, making sure each word was emphasized in promise, "I will cut your tail off and feed it to you."

"That's my witch." He chuckled, quickly landing one harsh smack on my ass.

I let out a startled cry, moving to push the dragon away only to be anchored in place by his arm around my waist, his other palm moving to cup the curve of my ass. A shiver of awareness shot through me, and even though I was still peeved over his threat, I felt my pussy quiver at the feeling of his large male hands all over my body.

"I will poison you in your sleep," I hissed, moving to lean in closer to his mouth.

His eyes sparked with arousal, yet he maintained the few inches of space between us, allowing our connection to simmer hotly between one another.

Even though I knew we should still be focused on trying to find more information on our new development, at that moment, all I wanted was to take his mouth with my own and fuck like rabbits. His eyes revealed the same emotion, and ever so slowly, he closed the distance between us, watching my every little expression as he descended.

Just before our mouths met and we gave in to the sexual tension we had built around us, a loud crack shook the house, the sound of a bullet being fired.

Gold and I released one another in an instant, falling to the floor to get out of the way of the windows. The sound came from a ways outside, bleeding through the walls of my home louder than a lightning strike. No windows were shattered, no sound of wood splintering accompanied the noise.

I snapped a couple of times to get Gold's attention, gesturing for him to stay down and not give us away in case the shooter was waiting for us to show ourselves again. He shook his head, pointing back towards the hallway to tell me to get to safety, but I paid no heed to his warning.

I wasn't going to go and hide while he handled all of the business. He was still a companion on my mission, and I wasn't going to play the damsel while he did all of the work. He might have taken down that pixie, but I still had to take care of my own business like a big girl.

If I was right, and I had something to do with this shitstorm, then I was going to do my part and deal with it.

Ignoring his glare, I crawled quickly to the window, keeping low and pressing my back to the wall. Taking care not to rustle the curtains too much, I just barely pushed them back enough to sneak a glimpse over to my driveway.

A large black SUV sat at the foot of my drive, just beyond

the ward line. Three men in stereotypical black suits stood at attention behind another, with a more ruffled looking fae waving a gun around as he appeared to be pacing, ranting around just at the border of my home and the road.

Immediately, I recognized him as the very man we had been researching. Brutus Willow, the mayor and the father of the girl I burned with witch's fire. He looked on edge and crazed, and the fury with which he screamed at my home made me shift nervously in place, tucking myself further out of sight.

The last thing I had been expecting was to see this man in the flesh.

Gold met me on the opposite side of the window, and I raised my finger to my mouth to silence him. "Quiet. It's Brutus Willow, and he looks beyond pissed. He can't shoot through the wards, but I don't know if I want to risk him knowing we're here."

"I think it's too late for that, Storm," he returned after sneaking a look himself. "He wouldn't be here if he didn't know exactly where you were. I doubt he'd risk his reputation to come here and scream at an empty home."

It was a good point. Brutus Willow had a crystal clear reputation online and in person, with nobody even daring to think he might do something as off the hinge as this. As far as gossip rags went, every person in Faerie either didn't know of his mob connections or was too scared to speak of them.

"You think he had someone watching the house?" I asked as I snuck another glimpse to watch as the man let loose another loud shot.

"I wouldn't doubt it." Gold answered though it sounded more like a question.

"What do we do then, go out there?" The words had just barely left my mouth before the man's voice cut through the quiet, booming far louder than it had in the last couple of minutes.

"Come out, come out, Storm Carlisle," he taunted in his aristocrat's voice. "I have business with you, and I am not leaving until it's solved. If you make me wait, I will light this entire forest on fire. I may not pierce your ward, but I will burn every living creature alive in this fucking town to get to you."

He no doubt used some amplification spell, or just a megaphone, in order to be heard throughout the house, but of course, that was the last thing of importance right now. I knew from the fury in his tone that he would live up to his words if I so much as made him wait for another second. No doubt he would think of it as a fair way to repay me for burning down his garden and maiming his daughter.

The jig was up, our little hiding game no more than that. If I stayed hidden, there was a good chance I might be risking the lives of those around me. No matter what I wasn't going to let something like what he threatened happen because I was too scared to face him. I was going to have to face him even if it meant putting myself in possible danger.

Gold was already ahead of my thinking, giving me an affirming nod before we both moved to stand. "Looks like we're meeting him after all."

CHAPTER TEN

"Y̲ou think you're awful cute, don't 'cha?" the drunken fae asked drawlingly, his words slurring together sounding almost unintelligible.

I gritted my teeth, barely restraining myself from responding to the man's mocking words. He was drunk out of his mind, looking like he was about to fall flat on his face at any moment. Just being near this man was enough to see right through his rich facade and right to exactly what kind of man he currently was.

This was not the suave politician that paraded himself and his daughter through parties and social media. He looked like he had been put through a wood chipper, and he didn't even care enough to wear something better than a rumpled tracksuit. Compared to his well put together and stoic bodyguards, he looked like a drunk they'd abducted right out of a bar and forced to play the vengeful father.

"Why are you here? You won't be able to cross my barrier, and now that I'm out in the open, there is no way I would allow a fire to spread," I said through clenched teeth, trying to instill as much power in my voice as I could. "If you're here for revenge, you're going to need far more than a couple of fae bodyguards and a drunken politician."

The man's face, a near carbon copy of his daughters, twisted into a snarl. He looked about ready to say fuck-all and try to jump at me but was coherent enough to realize there was no way he could even attempt it.

"You and that fucking reptile burned down my house," he

spat. "You burned my daughter with witch's fire. Do you have any idea how long that takes to reverse, or what kind of damage that does to a girl?"

Gold snorted at the mayor's attempt at an insult for himself, his posture looking far too relaxed for a man standing across from four men who would likely murder us without a second thought.

It was exactly the kind of thing I had been expecting the dragon to do.

As long as he remained looking unbothered, we held the psychological upper hand. If one of the people you were threatening appeared not to care in the slightest, it gave the enemy the illusion of being weak.

"I think you're forgetting the part where one of the men your daughter hired at your house summoned a pixie to attack me in my car," I said, watching him carefully to see his response. "I was simply seeking answers, and things escalated."

"What fucking proof do you have that my daughter had anything to do with any of that?" He slurred, "None, nada, zilch. Meanwhile, I have several eyewitnesses putting you in my yard just as my daughter was attacked. I could put you in a cell for life."

I flinched, not realizing just how bad the implications were on Gold and me. He was right. Even though I now knew it was true, after what Sheriff Sharon Grigsby said she thought about me, I would end up in bars before the day's end.

If I had not seen the girl torturing that fae and heard her confession, I might have questioned myself as well.

"But you won't," Gold said before I could respond.

The mayor's gaze flicked to Gold, and he bared his pearly white teeth with a growl. "You don't know a goddamn thing about what I will or won't do."

Gold leveled a cold, unfeeling smile on the man, his whole

body radiating a cat-who-ate-the-canary aura. The look sent a cold feeling even through my own body, despite the expression not being pointed towards me.

"Well, I do know one thing. We have the man who summoned that pixie in the house behind us, and I have no doubt he will sing a different story after you abandoned him on Storm's yard following beating him near to death." He spoke slowly as if conveying his point to a child. "That might be a bit of a hindrance to you if you try to bring the authorities into this. I bet that would look awful bad around election time."

The angry fire in the mayor's eyes only intensified. This was the look of a man beyond reason, with nothing but emotions and pride guiding his actions.

To my surprise, instead of spitting more insults or even defending himself, the fae's entire body suddenly drained of emotion, replacing his anger with a hollow laugh. His shoulders straightened as he righted himself, visibly sobering before our very eyes.

It was like something overtook him at that moment, removing every bit of the furious man who had been standing in his place moments before.

Immediately I went into alert, looking around for whatever caused the man to gain a sudden backbone out of nowhere, but nothing had changed. The bodyguards hadn't even reached for their guns.

"It's a shame I can't kill you." He chuckled darkly.

His words were dull and empty, an oddly sympathetic look entering his eyes.

"You couldn't if you wanted to," I snapped without thought, off-put by his sudden change in demeanor.

"I'm not saying that because your ward would stop me, witch." He paused to laugh, as dull as rusty nails. "No, your ward is the furthest thing from my mind."

I was growing sick of this conversation. Sick of the mind

games.

Nothing was gained. I felt like he was running us in circles with all of these inconclusive statements. I knew he was here for a reason, since he was going through the trouble of yanking us around like he was. He was probably hoping to anger one of us.

We surely weren't the only ones to think of using intimidation tactics.

"Why are you here? I won't ask again," I asked more firmly.

"Isn't it obvious? This is a part two to our little present the other day," the man blandly stated as if I was stupid for not concluding that already. "I'm here to send a message."

"Well? Time's a-ticking," I said snappily. "You have our attention, now do something with it."

He didn't appear to like being talked down to like that. He must have come out here expecting a sniveling witch begging not to be harmed after dropping off the near-dead fae. Clearly, he had not thought that I would put up as much of a resistance as I had.

If he expected me to play into his fear games as easy as that, then he had another thing coming to him.

Brutus Willow's aura morphed into a steely wall of resentment. "My boss is extending an invitation. She wants to arrange a meeting to discuss your potion, or rather, a version of that potion. She wants you to extend your services to her."

Surprise, surprise, I was right. All of my awful conspiracy thought until now had been right. Gold and I now knew without a shadow of a doubt their intentions.

"Let me guess. This must be the leader of that occultist group you've been spotted with in your town?" I said with a dry laugh. "You can tell her my shop is closed for business. I saw what your daughter was doing to that fae on the table, and I want no business with her."

"I don't think you understand," he said, showing his first sign of frustration. "This isn't a party invitation. This goes much deeper than one tortured fae."

I clasped my hands before me, meeting the fae's eyes for emphasis. "I. Don't. Want. Anything. To. Do. With. Your. Boss."

He bared his teeth in a thin smile, slowly reaching into his pocket and pulling out a plain white business card. He bent clumsily, nearly falling off his feet, to set it on the ground beneath a rock.

"I'm not here to convince you anyway. I'm just here to deliver the message." He snapped, "If it were up to me, I'd have you burned at the stake and your lizard turned into a purse for my daughter."

With those words, he turned on his heels to the car.

"So that's it?" I asked as he left, "You shoot into the woods like a maniac and demand my presence to deliver a business card?"

His head turned, and he leveled a murderous glare on me. "Trust me, Storm Carlisle. I will get my revenge on you eventually. The only reason I am entertaining you now is that I know if you reject Eris by the end of this. you will be dead."

Eris, that name again. His daughter had mentioned that name, too, in the fight, but I had completely forgotten. It dawned on me then just how big of a puzzle piece I had missed, perhaps the very puzzle piece that put this all together.

I watched in dumbfounded silence as the four got into their car and sped off, tearing up the grass on the way out. The dragon's arm snaked around my midsection, pulling me to him comfortingly, and I allowed myself the barest moment to relax before I pulled away and went to snatch up the card.

It simply read instructions on where to meet and had the symbol of inky black wings spread out along the entirety of the card.

They were familiar black wings.

You would never know what a witch's coven might look like until you've seen one in person.

For instance, in the pre-coming out era where humans created most magic-based media, you might see a group of women dressed in all black with dashing style walking in some sort of V formation at all times. Those were particularly funny because, in my entire life as a witch, I have never known two witches ever to coordinate an outfit.

Each witch had her style, her moods, and these were typically fitted to her personality or magic. Like how not all witches had the same powers or elemental controls, no two witches acted the same.

And that leads me to the group of three women who trudged their way out of the woods and right onto my doorstep a few minutes ago.

It was odd seeing most of the remaining Carlisles in one place. Even weirder seeing my candy red aunt next to my cool and prim great-grandmother. My youngest sister, Valentine, didn't stick out at all for some reason, despite her bubblegum pink hair and flowery pink outfit.

Looking from the outside, one might think these women were just here for a visit, but I knew far better than that. Each member of the party had arrived with their magic fully charged and ready to go off at a moment's notice. I was sure if I searched their bags, I would find many battle weapons just aching to be wielded.

"It's not safe for you here," Polly began the moment she entered earshot, tossing her overflowing bag onto the countertop.

"I feel like that goes without saying, Grams," Valentine replied, crossing the distance between the two of us to take me in a tight hug. "Glad to see you're safe, sis."

"She's about as safe as a woman with a criminal in the basement and some fae mafia after her can be." Carmin snorted before blowing me a kiss as she settled herself right on the counter next to where Polly stood.

"Welcome, make yourselves at home, I guess," I said with a laugh, giving my sister a light pat on the back before separating to stand across from the three women.

The stop by had been unexpected, and after the visit from the mayor, I didn't feel emotionally prepared for whatever confrontation they were planning. Gold was downstairs dealing with our prisoner, so I was alone facing the whole brigade.

"Yes, yes, sorry for intruding." Polly waved a dismissive hand. "We got your message."

I had almost forgotten calling to inform them about the very visit I was so caught up about, and now I was regretting letting my emotional state fuel my decisions. If I had just waited and thought out what I was going to say better, I might not have almost the whole family seated in my kitchen looking for all the world like they were considering going to war.

"We need to get you two out of Witches-Brew Cove," she continued. "It's just not safe for anyone involved."

Just what I had been expecting, a full-force confrontation.

Valentine cut in to reassure me before I could reply. "We can defend ourselves just fine. It's you that we are worried about. If we are focused on protecting you and your new scaled boyfriend, we put ourselves and our friends at risk."

It was apparent they all agreed with this. Not a single one looked ready to budge on their conclusion, watching me carefully to judge my response.

"So you just want me to leave? To run away from this." I tried to make my response as flat as possible, but the tightness in my throat gave away my frustration.

"I think that's what *you need to go* means," Carmin dead-panned.

I sent her a rude gesture. "And go where, genius? Need I remind you I would be twice as unsafe somewhere where I'm not one hundred percent familiar with and couldn't properly protect my surroundings?"

Every time people retreated from a battle in history, hey were always hunted down and overcome. There was a reason that plan was written in so many history books as a bad idea.

If I stayed here, I would at least have the upper ground. I had connections and long-standing wards, along with an area I was familiar with. It seemed like they were throwing this on me without even thinking about any of the other options.

Where would I even go? To Faerie with Terry?

"I can take you to my home," Gold said, appearing from nowhere and making Valentine shriek in shock.

The other two women appeared unfazed by his sudden appearance, nodding along with his words as if they had already thought of them themselves even though I knew they hadn't.

They had known him for an even shorter time than I had, so there was no way they thought he was a viable option when it came to hiding options.

In reality, they were going along with the best option as it came to them, which happened to be my new boyfriend. Lover? I didn't know.

Yet, as much as the idea of seeing the man in question's homeworld seemed fun, I wasn't dumb enough to believe it would be a good option. For one thing, there was no way the enemy wouldn't think to look in Eerie for a dragon—that was just a no-brainer.

Second of which was a problem I decided to be more vocal about. "You can't take me to your home. You're banned from your entire homeworld."

Polly and Carmin rolled their eyes as if this was nothing but a minor inconvenience. Even Valentine looked unbothered by the news that her sister's new man had somehow gotten himself banned from an entire world.

I don't know why, but somehow I thought that would at least warrant a gasp. Instead, they seemed eager to brush aside any problems that came in the way of their escape plans for me.

I found it funny that the two older women didn't even seem to think twice about the man's offer, just accepting it at face value. Normally it took people months to win over Carmin, and some people still had yet to win over my stingy great-grandmother.

So why now? What made them so eager to pass me off to this man?

Maybe I was just paranoid, but I had the feeling that they were hiding something from me. Something they were trying to distract me from.

"I am not banned entirely. I am still allowed to go home. I just need someone to vouch for me," he interjected. "I was planning on saving my few connections for coming home and relocating my hoard, but I would not hesitate to exhaust any connections in order to secure your Storm's safety."

I knew exactly what kind of connections this dragon would have, so I didn't doubt he could probably worm his way back through a portal. However, that wasn't my problem with the idea.

"That's cute," I said sarcastically, "but I don't know that running to an entirely new world is a necessity. As far as we know, they can't make it through my wards."

Aunt Carmin snorted. "Maybe not some fae, but we aren't dealing with the fae anymore. From what you told us over the phone, this is that new cult currently spreading through all three worlds. All it would take is a phone call, and they would come to attack your half-assed wards with the magical equivalent of a battering ram. The wards might be able to hold up against that force for a while, but they would crumble under the right amount of pressure."

I held back from reminding her that the wards were a result of her instruction, instead turning to focus on the far more reliable Polly. Polly's gaze met my own, and she shrugged, apparently finding no fault with the woman's words.

"I'm with the other two on this. Going to the dragon's homeworld would be best." She affirmed my worst suspicions. Then turning to Gold, she asked, "You live in Eerie, right?"

My mouth fell open at the realization my ex-guardian agreed with this. All my life I had known Polly to be the one person who thought through everything for days before deciding to try something as simple as a new brand of trash bags, and yet here she agreed to send me off to some foreign kingdom to hide?

There was no way she would ever agree to any of this if she wasn't completely convinced it was necessary. Either I was stupid, and the pieces hadn't clicked as they had with these four, or I was completely out of the loop.

Our family had owned this town for generations, and it had only been open to strangers for the last hundred years or so. It had been built hundreds of years ago for an occasion just like this one, to hide our family in the case of an emergency.

The thought that I would have to leave my home soil to hide from some cultists rebelled against every prideful bone in my body.

"Correct, The Mountain Kingdom, to be exact," Gold answered her.

Of course he lived in the mountains. He probably slept on a pile of gold at night as well. Gold on gold. It was just like him.

"Are you sure you can secure your place?" Polly asked.

"Yes. No one but myself has ever found my cavern. It is disguised with the most powerful wards a half a kingdom of gold can buy, and"—he puffed up his chest in an obnoxious show of strength—"it has Eerie's most successful thief and warrior protecting it."

I was happy that not a single woman's gaze lingered on the impressive show of muscle fully on display through the man's tight flannel shirt. I was disappointed in myself, however, because I couldn't seem to take my focus off the skin bared just slightly by the three undone buttons.

It almost distracted me from the fact that everyone in the room was not only teaming up on me but making decisions for me like I was a dimwitted teenager. One of them *was* a teenager in fact, which I didn't appreciate.

"Thief and warrior, huh?" Carmin purred at me, "You really can pick 'em, Storm."

A warm flush enveloped my cheeks, yet before I could come up with a snappy reply, Gold thrust me into his chest hard enough to rattle my teeth. "I am proud to be her mate, as well. We work very well together, both in work and in bed."

Valentine giggled nervously, her eyes going wide in embarrassment, while Polly and Carmin shared an amused smile. I felt like my face was going to combust. I was so embarrassed. At that moment I could strangle the dragon alive.

I tried to pull out of the dragon's grip, but his arms snuggled me closer into his chest. As much as I wanted to hate it, I did feel a sort of satisfaction from the contact. I was not used to being held so openly like this, especially in front of other people.

"Enough, you two," Valentine groaned. "Can we get back on track? We still have to deal with this visit thing from earlier."

"She's right," Polly said, returning to her more serious poise. "We still have to address that name your visitor mentioned. Eris."

It appeared I had conveniently forgotten that name until now.

Gold reluctantly let me go, giving me the space I needed to recollect my thoughts. "Right. I almost forgot about that."

"You almost forgot one of the biggest clues the man who threatened to kill everyone in town just happened to drop?" Carmin asked, sarcasm dripping from every word like venom.

Her attitude since walking in had gotten on my last nerve. I was one sly word away from abracadabra-ing her ass out the door.

I turned to face her, giving her a what-the-fuck expression. "Have I done something to you? You're acting really off right now."

Carmin seemed to check herself all at once, stiffening as if she hadn't noticed how on edge she was. After a long second, she let out a long sigh and pinched the bridge of her nose in frustration. "Sorry, love. I'm just stressed. I get that way when the people I love are being threatened, as would anyone with a heart."

She was hiding something, I just knew it. Her mood was too off character to be anything other than her way of trying to keep something from me. She had the false personality she had adapted to entice her customers turned on to a ten, and seeing her using it on us just made me plain uncomfortable.

Maybe she was stressed over this like she claimed she was, but I got the feeling it was much different than that. She had given off the same feeling since she arrived back in town.

Something about her just screamed that she was far more invested in all of this than she seemed, but for some reason, I felt the need to shrug it off. I knew for a fact she wouldn't be involved in anything that could hurt other people, especially us. So it made it easy to shove the suspicion in the back of my mind for the time being.

"All right, whatever," I returned the conversation to its path. "We haven't been able to look up anything on the person in question yet. Have you managed to find anything?"

"Have we found anything?" Valentine repeated smugly, sounding amused by my question,

"Oh, we found a couple of things."

I silently implored one of them to continue.

"Eris is the name of an ancient Greek goddess," Carmin finally said. "The ancient Greek goddess of strife and discord, most commonly well known for being the catalyst of the Trojan War back in the ancient days. We looked into the recent cult happenings in Faerie, and we believe that may be who he was talking about."

The explanation was so wild I found myself waiting for one of them to smile or something to show they were joking, yet there wasn't so much as a smirk. Surely they hadn't come all the way here to feed me a punchline like that.

"An ancient Greek goddess? You want me to believe a goddess is behind some fae mafia summoning a pixie," I asked, not bothering to hide my laughter.

The witches looked downright miffed at my complete dismissal of their declaration. From their looks of outrage, you might think I kicked a puppy.

"Is that really so hard to believe?" she asked. "I mean, we are witches, your boyfriend is a dragon, and everybody knows the gods exist. I mean, we all are aware of Thor's fighting clubs in Vegas. Besides, we wouldn't come to you if we weren't serious."

I didn't have a defense for that.

It was true, and since the outing of the paranormal, the

gods had only grown more and more comfortable in the spotlight. It was like the resurgence of the religion for them, feeding their need to be worshiped and in the spotlight. It took them barely a decade to restore their reputation as bad-ass beings. To my knowledge the goddess Aphrodite even had a dating app out, though it was pretty unsettling how you had to sign a contract in blood to get in.

It was the price of love, I guess.

"I've heard of your goddesses. They are rather scary women," Gold murmured, more to himself than anyone else. "I suppose that could be the leader behind the cultists, but how do you know it's specifically her? There could be thousands of people named Eris in Faerie."

"Only, those thousands weren't spotted on multiple occasions causing chaos around every single reported meetup of said occultists," Valentine replied.

The probability that somehow an all-powerful god was behind this was a bit discouraging. It would have been fine if it was just a cult, but a goddess tied in as well? I wasn't even sure a dragon could help us in those regards.

It didn't help that I was only slightly familiar with the one in question. Eris, to my knowledge, was more of a minor mischievous goddess — kind of the original *Maleficent*. When she wasn't invited to a marriage with the rest of her family, she decided to take it out on her three sister goddesses, Aphrodite, Athena, and Hera. She came up and offered one of them a golden apple, a big deal to the gods, saying it was for the most beautiful lady. Surprise, surprise, the goddesses took the obvious bait to start a fight and ran with it, desperately needing to assign themselves as the prettiest goddess.

By the end, a whole war was waged.

"That's why it's best for you to get out of here. Until we can gather more information on all of this, none of us are safe," Polly told me earnestly, stepping forward to take my hands in hers. "We aren't just thrusting you to the side. We think it's better if you get out of Dodge while we all find our footing in this."

A muscle in my jaw ticked, the first sign of me caving into their demands. "Fine, but I'm not happy about it. It's not like packing up and leaving your home and shop is the easiest thing to do, you know. Plus, I worry that I won't be able to be here to protect you guys if something happens."

"Honey," she deadpanned. "We can protect ourselves, and so can you. Sure, we're stronger together, but we'll do just fine alone. If anything happens, we will just mirror message you."

She said that easily, like something as simple as a mirror message would be enough to sate the desire to be here to protect my family. I knew the decision was made already, and I might as well be packed, but I couldn't help but feel I was leaving both of us vulnerable in the meantime.

Not sensing or not caring about my doubt, she released me and turned to the other two women. "As for us, we still have work to do. We need to secure Storm's shop and the cabin."

I had already secured the shop myself while closing it for good, but I knew Polly would go in and triple check even if I told her I had.

I knew no matter what I said, the outcome wouldn't change. It wouldn't even matter if Gold changed his mind on bringing me to his home — my great-grandmother wouldn't allow anything else. Somehow, even though they had just talked once, she trusted the man to have my back.

If only she trusted me that quick. I was still sure she put tracking spells on me any time I left town. Not because she was a helicopter parent or anything, She would still let me do whatever I wanted. She just didn't trust me not to get lost or kill myself in the meantime.

After briefly instructing us on how to protect ourselves on the road there, the three women begrudgingly made their way out of the house. I made sure to hug each of them extra tight in case I didn't see them for a while.

Gold had escorted them out of the house, offering to take them home, but Polly simply got up on her toes and whispered something in the dragon's ear that made him jerk back in surprise. Polly then turned on her heels with a cackle, rejoining her quickly retreating family with one final wave of her fingers over her shoulder.

"They are nice. I like them," Gold said as he reentered the house, a childish grin breaking out across his face.

"Of course you'd say that," I scoffed. "They agreed with you."

Gold took me in his arms, letting out a long grumble that shook my chest. "I like you a lot more, though."

Playfully leaning back into his embrace, I made sure to twist my hips against his quickly growing erection. "Oh, I know just how much you like me, Gold."

It was pretty weird to transition from a meeting with the family to a flirting atmosphere, but around this dragon, I couldn't seem to help myself. Every moment alone with him was sensual torture.

Gold ground himself against me, and any of the awkwardness I'd felt earlier dissipated with the delicious feeling of his smooth chest against my own. This was no book cover man, but strong domineering dragon at my back.

With a crash, our teasing stopped in an instant, both Gold and I stilling our movements. The loud sound seemed to echo through the house, and I knew we both knew exactly where it had come from.

"There is no way he could move with broken legs and being tied to the bed," I whispered. "So what the hell is that?"

CHAPTER ELEVEN

We found the fae lying on the bed, still tied to the bed rails. His throat cut clean through, the man's eyes were open wide, staring blankly at the ceiling above him.

It dawned on me then my families warning couldn't have come any sooner.

"How?" I croaked, "There is . . . this is impossible."

Gold remained silent, his gaze locked on the man with a look I could only describe as mournful. I didn't think the dragon cared for the man, but the feeling was one that came with the pity of meaningless death. It was a bone-deep sadness that spoke of nothing but aching pity.

He had died tied to the bed, defenseless and beaten. He couldn't have defended himself if he had tried. He hadn't even been afforded the mercy of sleep, evident by his face being frozen in his final gasp of pain.

All of this happened under my roof — while I was home. In the span of the time it took me to open and close the barrier for my family.

I looked toward Gold as if he would offer some explanation, but his expression told me nothing.

All of our hope of tying the loose ends together flew out the window with the death of this fae. Hours of work re-brewing the same potions I was growing far too used to using was wasted.

It felt like a deathblow to our case.

"I had just checked on him." His gaze remained locked on the man. "I barely left him alone for ten minutes."

It was clear he felt guilty, even though he was by far the least to blame in all of this. If anyone should feel guilty, it was me, for allowing a breach in security like this even for a second. Everything in me wanted at that moment to take him upstairs and bury both of us under the covers and never see the light of day again.

"We had left him alone for hours at times," I told him, taking him in a comforting hug. "I don't think this was a matter of us not watching him closely enough."

Gold swallowed hard, his fierce amber-colored gaze meeting my own. "If that's true, then how am I supposed to protect you? If these people manage to sneak into the house and kill somebody in mere minutes without me even sensing them, then how would it even be possible?"

I didn't have the answer he wanted. I wish I could tell him everything was going to be okay and come up with some mystical plan, but now it seemed we were only left with one option.

"We have to leave. We are no longer safe here, if we ever were."

I don't think either of us was fully in the present as we took care of the fae's body. I tried not to think of what I was doing as we closed his body in the basement freezer, praying to the fates that he fit without a problem.

A lump caught in my throat at the thought that his family would never know what truly happened to him after this. It could have been true that he was evil and killing leagues of people without my knowledge, but I knew it wasn't true.

Anybody with a brain could put it together that the man was being pressured into working for these people. Between the meeting outside the shop and ending up near death on my lawn, he didn't stand any more of a chance at life that any person would in his place.

Gold made himself busy with the packing after that, working to stuff as much as we would need into a few bags while I contacted the necessary people. Lucky for us my family had ties with almost everybody in town, and there wasn't a family who didn't owe us some favor, so I could cross the body problem off our list with a single phone call.

Working with the local graveyard on quietly disposing of the fae in a respectful manner was as easy as that. Funnily enough, for some reason flexing my place as the daughter of one of the most powerful witch families in the states seemed to no longer bother me, when two weeks ago calling in a seedy favor like this would twist my stomach in knots for months.

I suppose it comes with the territory. You get involved with shady people, and slowly you become one of them. I could take small comfort in knowing I was at the very least embracing the path that would hopefully help me eradicate the people who caused this. I would do everything in my power to get revenge, both for myself and the fae, even if it turned me into a person I might once have balked at.

At the very least, I knew one thing in all of this. I wasn't alone. I might have enough pressure on my shoulders to rival the depths of the oceans, but I had people with me along the way. Gold and my family were enough to keep me afloat for now, and I would embrace that while I still had it.

Gold met me outside in his full dragon form, which was shocking to see out of the few battle scenes I had seen it in. Any other time I might be tempted to admire his shining scales, but I was hardly in the mood to do so. He had all of our luggage pinned to his back like he was some scaled minivan, tied tight with a rope I hadn't seen him pick up. To my chagrin he even had my broom, which I hadn't seen since the night we went to Faerie, tied to the top, ready to go at a moment's notice.

I had almost forgotten the thing, and just seeing it brought up memories of chasing this very dragon through the woods a few days before. I wouldn't get on that thing right now if somebody paid me money, but by the looks of it, Gold didn't have that in mind either.

Immediately upon spotting me, he preened, puffing out his giant chest as if he was trying to draw me in as a mate. I couldn't help a small smile at his antics, still pining after my attention even though the dragon had already mated me six ways to Sunday just this morning.

"Enough, you big oaf." I chuckled, walking up to run my hand over the smooth scales of his warm chest. "Am I supposed to ride you?"

The slits of his eyes narrowed and zeroed in directly down the front of my shirt. I gasped, covering myself as I feigned insult.

"You perv, you know what I meant," I scolded the dragon playfully.

The sudden change from the solemn mood from earlier was a welcome change. Being able to enjoy the next couple of days out with this man might be the only thing I could do to keep myself sane in all of this.

He made a short rattling noise that I for sure thought was his way of calling me a spoilsport before laying himself flat on the ground. It was a clear invitation to climb on top of his back, yet I stood there for a moment in hesitation.

The only other time I had ridden on this dragon was in his claws when we fled Faerie. I had never ridden atop his back before like he was some beast stead. I felt anticipation quickly rise as I realized I would be riding a dragon for the first time in my life.

If I was to climb on Gold, I would be one of the few dragon riders ever to exist. That was a feat in and of itself. Back in the old days the only people who could command dragons were kings. Since the people of Eerie were so secluded and proud, they had to truly respect the people they chose to allow so close to their vulnerable spots.

It resonated in me that he trusted me enough to allow me this. This wasn't just a one-way thing where I trusted him to keep me safe, but a joint belief in one another.

I held back my excited squeak as I rushed forward in a couple of paces, allowing my hands to run over his smooth side before attempting the climb. Trying to hoist myself up off of his smooth scales was nearly impossible because of the complete lack of grip, but somehow I managed to find purchase on the back of his muscled arm. From there it was one short slide to fit myself snuggly into the little cove between his head and neck spikes. It was such a perfect fit that I almost felt as if it was made just for me.

It felt nice, almost natural, like riding a horse but a bit more spread legs and stability. I will admit, only to myself, that the heat of his body against my lower regions provided an embarrassingly nice feeling.

"I have to say," I called over his shoulder once I had found the right place to settle, "I never thought I would ride a dragon."

He made a sound in response that was suspiciously close to a chuckle, and I might have kicked him if the sound hadn't sent vibrator powered vibrations right to my clit. It was a double edged sword, heat, and friction. If I had known it would feel like this, I might have made riding our new pastime a while ago.

My only warning before he took off was a firm shake, testing my stability, before he took a running leap forward. Even though I held on tight, the sheer force of his massive wings snapping out and pushing us into the air jolted me around hard, and I had to hug the closest neck spike to keep myself from jolting right out of my position.

My stomach flopped over itself as we smoothly settled right into an air current, gliding forward with each powerful to and fro of the dragon's wings. Despite the rattling of the luggage behind me, it was an oddly tranquil experience.

Gold made another rattling noise, catching my attention with a look over his shoulder as he implored me with his amber gaze. I knew what he was looking for, and I raised my thumbs in confirmation for him to open the portal.

I then watched as his entire body tensed for one long second, almost holding us still in the air as his magic shot out before us and tore a portal right into the sky. It took only a minute, and then we were barreling head-first right into the thick of it.

"Well, Eerie, here we come," I muttered.

I felt like the kid riding on Falcor at the end of *The Neverending Story*. Even after an hour of flying, I never once grew tired of this view. Eerie was a landscape painter's wet dream. From the back of a dragon, it looked exactly like a fantasy landscape stuck somewhere between the golden age and now filled to the brim with magical creatures.

Was it any wonder how miles and miles of rolling golden hills and beautiful mountain landscapes birthed dragons, griffons, gargoyles, and many other golden age creatures?

On this ride alone we had passed two other dragons and one griffon.

The little girl part of myself yearned to have Gold stop and let me admire the beautiful creatures in their natural forms. I didn't, of course, but I wanted to. I knew if I stopped Gold to admire another male he would most likely consider tossing me to the fields below.

We had only passed one town, a tiny circle of what looked to be farmhouses and a school. It seemed impossible how few houses we were passing throughout the whole flight, but I did remember learning in school Eerie was the least populated of the three worlds. That and the names of the seven kingdoms this land was split into were the only things we had ever learned about it, which was a real shame.

Right now, we were passing through the foot of the mountains that no doubt belonged to the Stone King, a gargoyle whose name I had forgotten since then. He was one of the seven kings we spent like a week on in school back in the day. It had always amused me how little time we spent learning about things outside of Earth and its histories when we could have been further educated on places like this.

I'm just saying. It would have come in handy. Now I would have to ask Gold more about this place while we were here. No doubt he would have very interesting tales to tell about the land he'd terrorized not too long ago.

It was no replacement for education, but it would be a hell of a lot more fun to hear about.

A short time later, a much larger town came into view. It was positioned at the top of a hill with brilliant red flags alerting anyone in a ten-mile radius of its existence, and I felt a tremor of excitement to see my first proper Eerie town finally. Immediately upon spotting it Gold dove, falling in line with another couple of dragons as we headed for a large patch of grass near the entry path.

He had barely touched foot on the ground before I flung myself off with the excitement of a kid on Christmas. My legs gave out almost immediately, and I fell forward onto my hands and knees with an audible huff. I hadn't thought only a couple hours of riding could mess up my muscles that bad, but I guess you couldn't predict how you would react to flying on a dragon for half a day.

I was too excited to care, though. I was setting foot in my first ever Eerie town, the one place I had been wanting to see since I was a little girl. I had thought I would never get around to it, always so busy with work, but here I was with a sexy ass dragon at my hip.

It reminded me of small towns during autumn festivals — bright reds and oranges, bustling people, bright signs pointing people towards the market districts. This was no city like New York or stylized markets like Fae villages, but a true old-timey town.

Catching me mid admiration, Gold huffed and knocked my butt with his snout before trudging past me in the direction of the main road without warning.

"You're an ass!" I growled as I barely caught myself before tumbling face forward onto the ground.

Others in the town turned to watch as I chased after the dragon, who seemed to be doing his best to remain a few steps ahead of me as he stormed into town. Fortunately for me, his pace didn't last long, because as soon as we passed the first male, he immediately reappeared back at my side, looking like a territorial wolf.

I hid my smirk behind my hand, amused by Gold's possessive display. I half expected him to flash back into his human form and declare me his right in the middle of town. It was unfortunate he couldn't because of our luggage strapped to his back, mostly because I would have found that display incredibly delightful.

What can I say? I was just one of those women more impressed by a he-man than a wine-and-dine kind of man — blame it on my kinks.

At least now that he'd slowed down, I could admire my surroundings a bit better.

One thing I noticed right off the bat was that there were no artificial light sources. There were no signs of modern technology at all apart from a bit of modern plumbing in the form of fountains and public use water area. It was an odd sight, since even Faerie was equipped with every luxury modern technology had to offer. Now that I thought about it, there were no cars or cellphones in sight either.

It was hard to fathom a world that didn't work without even one person walking around with some form of technology on them.

Of course, here I was walking next to a dragon and brushing shoulders with people who turned into giant fantasy beasts, and the only thing I found odd was there were no cellphones or gas fumes. I had to laugh at the ridiculousness of it.

Despite this, everyone seemed to be getting along just fine. It wasn't as if they were wearing *Farmville* clothing, either. Most people had on some simpler version of normal fashion throughout the three worlds. Some even bore finer brighter clothing that drew the eye to them from across entire pavilions.

I could barely remember the clothes Gold had arrived on Earth in, but it wasn't hard to picture him wearing one of the black leather coats and loose black trousers some of the men seemed to be rocking. The style was non-flashy biker meets mid-century pirate, and if I were to see it on Gold, I would no doubt be handing over any booty I had on sight.

"What are we doing here?" I finally asked as we entered a calmer section of the town, patting his head to get his attention.

Gold jerked his head to a large building in the middle of the town, clearly a town hall of some sort. As we neared it, I noticed that the stone building was decorated with intricate carvings of the many creatures of Eerie tangled around the doors, which were large enough to fit giants, and curling around every edge of the walls. It reminded me, funnily enough, of the gargoyles and the more common building decor of the old Victorian ages.

I suppose that this might be exactly where they got the inspiration. It was no secret that many people had accidentally traveled between the three worlds without knowing back in the day.

If I remember, my teacher described the events by explaining that the magic tying everything in the universe together had a very close bond between the three magically dense lands. It was a matter of magical gravitation and not mystical events. Almost like gravity or wormholes, but a bit easier to comprehend.

For all we knew, there could be hundreds of worlds with intelligent beings that just never connected to ours through the portals. That, or we just never knew if they did.

Gold turned and nudged me forwards up the stone steps, falling behind me as we entered the large building. The first thing I noticed was the grand marble floors and bookshelves lining the walls leading to a raised area in the back filled with row after row of tables. People bustled back and forth between strategically placed desks overloaded with thick leather-bound books, while a few rolled around portable bookshelves to their designated areas.

Overall there had to be twenty people in the building besides us, and all of them looked to be of some importance.

Why would he bring me here? I was confused when we had entered the town but had brushed it off as him needing to contact somebody before going home. Now I was baffled as to why a man banned from this entire world would visit what was clearly a government building sheer hours after our arrival.

I might have considered asking him that very question, but I doubted I'd get many answers in his current form. Gold continued lightly pushing me forward, jerking his head towards the large table in the center of the room. One man sat waiting, his arms crossed before him as he watched us enter.

I took Gold's lead and walked over to sit at the table across from the man, immediately feeling awkward and wondering whether or not to introduce myself. Gold remained in his dragon form, clearly unconcerned. It only made me that much more nervous as I turned my full attention to the weary-looking man across the table.

He was incredibly handsome, despite his age and his clear lack of sleep. His hair was a salt-and-pepper mix that fell to his shoulders in a half-pulled-back Nordic look that accentuated his strong features. Normally I would balk at the idea of long hair on an older man, but the man could pull it off.

"I got your message last night," the man began tensely, addressing Gold directly, "and I have been granted the opportunity to appeal the seven kings' unanimous decision to ban you from Eerie."

Something about the man's words felt off to me right off the bat, something too similar to the beginnings of a storm. It wasn't quite deception, but something that rang a bit too close to that feeling. All of the hairs rose on my arms as my gaze darted around the room as if I wouldn't have already spotted some assassin hidden in the shadows by now.

Gold apparently felt it, too, because the scales on his neck rattled as he let out a long clicking hiss.

The man exhaled a breathy sigh in response to the clear aggression and moved to straighten the pile of paperwork before him. "You'll have to forgive me for this, Gold."

The doors flung open then, revealing the large menacing presence of what could only be labeled a gargoyle. Unlike the dragon-like representations back on Earth, Eerie gargoyles were nine-feet-tall stone men that were formed like the Adonis, only with a far larger loincloth and a wicked pair of wings.

The wings in question unfolded around the entering man to completely block off the only exit, nearly blotting out all of the natural light from the open doors.

All other men in the room dropped what they were doing to kneel before the man, muttering a chorus of *my king*. I was on the edge of my seat, eyes wide and magic flaring as I tried to make sense of the new arrival. Slowly but surely, as no one made any move towards one another, it began to click in my mind just who the man was.

The Stone King of the Mountain Kingdom.

It had to be, unless the Mountain Kingdom bowed to some other gargoyle king. I felt both excited and fearful at seeing the man only a few feet away, some of my mood being tainted by Gold's clear fury.

Even though Gold's hackles were standing near on end, he didn't move to attack the man, but he didn't back down, either. Instead, the dragon stared at the king, eyes ablaze with the familiar look of betrayal.

"I thought I told you never to show your face in my kingdom ever again," the gargoyle growled, eating up the distance between us with giant steps.

Gold responded to the approach with a baring of his teeth, and I could feel in the pit of my belly just how bad this would go if one of them made the wrong move. If I allowed them to have their little standoff, it might result in a bloodshed nobody in this room needed right that moment.

I hastily stood, moving between the two as if the angry stone man and hissing dragon were no more than two angry children. "Hold on, hold on. I don't know what this is, but we didn't come here for a fight."

The Stone King's steps faltered, and he looked upon me with his pale white eyes. It was like being looked down on by a statue, cold and unfeeling. If any emotion was stirred upon seeing me, he did not show it.

"I wasn't planning on fighting." His voice sounded like the crunch of gravel. "I wouldn't come here just to fight that dragon. It's no place for a king to involve himself with the squabbles of foolish criminals."

Gold growled, but I maintained my position firmly between the two. Oddly enough, I believed the gargoyle. If he had wanted a fight, he wouldn't have cornered us in what was clearly an important library of sorts. It would cause far too much damage and might endanger civilians. However, I wasn't going to lower my guard even for a second until I figured out what his purpose for this intimation was.

"So then why are you here? People who aren't looking for a fight don't come crashing in the front doors of a town hall with their wings spread like you're trying to keep anyone inside from escaping."

The hint of a smile played at the corner of his stone mouth, the first sign of real emotion. "Good question, witch. One I will answer in due time. However, I feel I must introduce myself properly before then. I am Zeal Ironbind, otherwise known as the Stone King of the kingdom your friend is asking entry to." He accompanied his words with a subtle incline of his head, a gesture I assumed to be a royal greeting.

My shoulders relaxed slightly, reacting to the subtle release in tension everyone in the room seemed to experience at his words. It was clear that we were safe for now. No malice or trickery radiated from the male.

He was still a giant-ass gargoyle standing between us and the exit, though, so even though I pulled my magic back in, my defenses remained up. "If all you insist on is a greeting, then I'd be happy to comply. I am Storm Carlisle, a potions witch from the Earth town Witches-Brew Cove. Now that you know who I am, I'd like to hear your answers, if you don't mind."

It was no way to speak to a king, but the man didn't seem to mind at all. In fact, he seemed satisfied with my introduction. "Yes, well it would be better if we all took a seat then.

This might take a minute," he said with a sweep of his hand towards the table.

I hesitated for only a second, but after an exasperated look from the first man we had met, I decided not to argue and sat with Gold back in our original seats, feeling safer with his large presence behind me. The gargoyle was too large to fit in the human-sized chairs at the table and instead squatted next to the first man. Somehow he made the position look regal.

"Shortly after your call to Eerie, Giovanni Moore contacted me about your request to return to Eerie," Zeal said to Gold once we had all settled, inferring to the man who had remained nameless until now. "At first I considered denying your request completely, but when I heard you were protecting you mate, I couldn't in good conscience turn both you and your female away."

So this was the man Gold had been talking to earlier today. I supposed it made sense he would try and get in contact with a politician of some sort, but I hadn't expected it to be somebody with the power to contact the king in such a short time.

The plot only thickened for my dragon, it seemed.

"He's not going to shift into his human form," Giovanni informed the king after he appeared to wait for Gold's response. "He doesn't trust us enough to leave either himself or his female unguarded."

"I wish I could say I was surprised," Zeal said with a teeth-baring smile. "It should be enough to talk to you though, Storm. After all, you are the reason why I am here. If Gold wants to remain a spectator, he can. He's used to not involving himself with anybody but himself anyway."

I could tell it was a dig at Gold, but nobody appeared to react, not even Gold himself, who hadn't stopped fuming at my side. I knew just by looking at the dragon it would be smarter not to defend him like I wanted to and get this over with as fast as humanly, or witchly, possible.

"All right then," I agreed on a defeated sigh. "Fill me in on what you need."

The Stone King plucked a stack of paper off the top of the other man's pile, giving it a glance before sliding it over to me with a snap of his wrist. "After I heard your reasoning for escaping to my kingdom, I realized your situation closely mirrors that of my own. You see, we have been having problems with the woman your mate asked for information on, the Earth goddess Eris."

He allowed me a moment to look over the papers, and what I saw in them made my breath catch. They were reports on attacks in several towns, unidentifiable creatures that could only be described as *changed* versions of what they once had been ruthlessly raiding the smaller towns along the edges of The Mountain Kingdom, and all through the surrounding areas.

The descriptions of the monsters reminded me of the pixie, though I hadn't thought it was changed much from what a pixie normally was. Pixies were already described as terrifying incarnates of fear itself, at least to an adult's eyes, so not much had changed there. However, the entire report gave off the same feeling as the attack by the pixie.

Out of nowhere, in the dusk, summoned by a fae portal, it checked off all the bases for my own attack.

Only, one thing stood out. It was clearly stated that some were native creatures to Eerie, just turned into a grotesque monster of what they once were. If that were true, it would mean that Eris had upgraded her monster army to creatures of other worlds.

"By the fates," I muttered under my breath. "I had no idea it extended this far."

"It's been going on for a while. Those are just the recent reports," he told me. "It's a growing concern among my people as the year has gone by. While my people can defend themselves quite easily, the sheer number of attacks is a problem. Without some sort of protection above my current guard system, I risk more of my people becoming the casualties of these attacks."

I could grasp the direness of the situation, but why he was showing me this was confusing. I was no strategist, nor whatever a defense builder was called. I could barely protect my own home on Earth.

If I was right, what he was asking for was so far above my skill level it genuinely baffled me how he would ever think I could help him.

"You think I can somehow help with this?"

He nodded sincerely, and his companion continued his proposal for him. "When Gold called me to ask for a favor, he told me about your wards. While not one hundred percent effective, we believe they can be of help protecting at least the towns."

"My wards?" I hadn't meant for the words to come out as disbelieving as they did. "They require an immense amount of magic to summon, and I can't imagine being able even to cover one of your towns by myself. Even with help, it might take a week just to be able to summon a single one."

Giovanni nodded reservedly. "Yes, I comprehend that. While Eerie is more shut out from the other worlds than we'd like, we do understand that witch magic is powerful, yet limited. This is why we only want you to cover one of the towns, my own. In the process, you will be teaching our magically inclined people the process so they can replicate it themselves for the other towns."

They wanted me to teach novices how to summon a highly difficult witch spell? I had never been a teacher and had never planned to be. The only person I had ever taught anything had been Jessica, and that was potions work.

A ward of this size was a whole different ballpark. I would

be guiding people I hadn't known for a day through one of the most volatile magic practices a person could get into. It wwasn't that they'd blow their hands off or anything, but one small mistake and it could potentially permanently lock themselves in an impenetrable bubble of magic for days.

If it weren't for the stakes of our situation I would never think to involve myself with work of this size.

"What if they can't replicate it?"

Zeal sucked in air between his teeth, leaning back in his chair. "Then we forget it. You will have fulfilled your side of the bargain, and you won't have to continue doing any more work if you don't wish to. If, and only if, it doesn't work, I would hope we could convince you to at least help with our capital afterward. It is where our people would go to if anything more serious were to arise from this. However, that would be up to you."

I considered the offer for a moment, glancing back at Gold to see what his reaction was. He looked beyond pissed, which confused me. The offer was open and shut, help ward one town while teaching some people how to replicate it, no strings attached. Nobody would owe anyone a favor.

Considering we were getting repaid by a whole world allowing a formerly banned criminal back into the world of Eerie, I didn't see how Gold would find anything to be mad about.

It was clear whatever decision I made would have to be fi nal. Say yes and stay while angering the dragon and help a town, or leave a town defenseless and retreat to Earth.

To me, the decision was obvious, anger or not.

"It's a deal." I reached across the table to extend my hand to the men. "Consider me your newly hired witch."

CHAPTER TWELVE

The flight to Gold's cavern, hidden deep in the mountains, was quiet and tense. Since I'd accepted the king's offer and set up a schedule for working on the barriers, Gold had completely shut himself off from not only me but the world itself.

When we had left the town, I thought leaving him to stew for a while would help him get over whatever it was he was choosing to be mad about, only it didn't seem to help at all. After landing at the mouth of the cavern hidden in the crack on the side of the mossy mountainside, he reaffirmed his anger by wasting no time shrugging me right off his back and onto the grassy floor of the cave.

I tried to ignore it, not wanting to snap at him while he was already upset, but he was getting on my last nerve. Choosing to try and be the bigger person, I brushed past him and walked further into the cave, trying to distract myself with my surroundings instead of dwelling. If I focused on admiring my new lover's home, I might not focus on how flaming mad he was making me.

At least, that was where my mind was at.

Torches lit on the walls as I passed, revealing that the area we stood in was a large grassy clearing that narrowed into the mouth of a smaller cave. Tiny white flowers had bloomed in the center of the path, giving the area a soft and elegant aura.

It was beautiful and scenic, which was a bit of a surprise. Maybe I was bigoted, but I had expected the entrance to a dragon's lair to have like jagged rocks and bones spiking out to ward off intruders.

"How did you find this place?" I asked him as I spun to get a full view.

Gold said nothing, despite having shifted back into his human form. Instead, he grabbed two of the suitcases off the top of the stack he had placed on the ground and stormed off into the dark of the cave, lighting torches as he passed. It was a move fit for a high school teen dying to get the lead role in an edgy adaptation of *The Shrek Musical*. Or something like that.

What a dick.

Clenching my jaw, I stormed after him, hating that his foul attitude was spoiling the wonder of observing Gold's home for the first time. I had been anticipating finally exploring something that belonged to Gold. To think I had thought the whole ride here it would be the perfect bonding experience for the two of us, but here we were at odds with each other.

The worst part was, he didn't even have anything to be mad about. We should be ecstatic that we had the blessing of the king to hide in his kingdom, considering all it costs is a couple of rounds of barrier magic.

It was practically nothing in the scheme of things, and yet here he was acting like a pouty teenager.

I caught up with him just as we entered the main hall, catching his arm as he tossed the bags onto a large raw wood table. His jaw clenched, and he pulled his wrist from my grasp easily, but I wasn't going to allow him to slip away again.

I darted in front of him, making sure I was in his direct line of sight so he couldn't avoid my assessing gaze. He still looked furious, even more so now, his eyes glinting with yellow sparks of anger.

"Why are you mad at me?"

He took a moment to answer, clearly thinking through a thousand different thoughts at once. "The whole point of coming out here was to protect you." His voice was clipped, and I could tell he was tightly leashing his words. "How am I supposed to do that when you are out there working off what should be my punishment?"

So he was angry about the job. I can't say I was surprised, but it was confusing. If he had such a problem with it, there were a thousand ways to work around it that didn't have anything to do with pouting and storming away like this.

Nothing about this couldn't be talked over in minutes, so why did he have such an issue with it?

"You can come with me!" I offered. "And even if you don't, I don't know why you are so insistent that I'm going to be unprotected out there. I'm going to be surrounded by people hell-bent on protecting me because I am going to help their people."

"I don't care if every knight in the kingdom is protecting you. It is my job to look out for you." His voice was like a whip of fury turned on me with full force.

"Then why don't you come with me? You went into the town to talk to that man. I don't see why you can't accompany me while I work!"

This only appeared to make him that much angrier.

"Don't even speak of that traitor lord mayor. Need I remind you his last parting words to me were him apologizing for betraying me to his king!" he hissed. "Even if they allow me to accompany you, I would be driven out by the townsfolk. It couldn't be more clear from what happened today that the only reason I am even standing here and not in shackles is because of your presence."

I had seen the faces on the people in the town myself after they had realized just who we were, and I knew he wasn't over exaggerating. Many people hated Gold in that town alone. Not just the leaders, either, but most of the adult population.

It made sense they'd know who he was and what he'd done, considering he lived not far from the town, but I hardly thought he could have angered them all to that degree.

Even though I knew he had a past that he wasn't ashamed to admit, it angered me to see so many people against the man I knew Gold to be. Gold might have been a thief and a fool, but not once talking to anyone who knew him did I hear one thing that would justify that level of hatred.

"Gold, this is the only way they are going to allow you to remain here. If all it takes is a week or so of spell work, then why worry about it?"

"Why worry about it? I worry about it because you shouldn't have to!" He was growing more and more exasperated, his body showing more signs of going reptilian by the second. "That was my problem to solve. Not yours."

"Oh and I'm just supposed to sit back and relax while you do all the work?" I scoffed, and in a fit of anger, I shoved at his chest hard enough to make him stumble. I didn't want to hurt him, but at that moment I couldn't think of any other way to show him how furious I was at him. "Fuck that. If I want to do something for my fucking mate, then I can, and there is nothing you can do about it."

Those might have been the wrong words to use, because his skin flared into a burnished gold, the color of his dragon. Power flared and poured from his body, a barely leashed danger that was directly leveled on me.

"Do you see this?" The hint of a hiss clung to his words, the sign of his dragon coming forth. His arms widened to encompass all of the room, packed to the brim with ancient art and piles of gold and jewels.

"This is all mine. Everything in this room is mine." His voice was soft, yet dangerously firm. Ever so slowly, he moved closer to me with prowling steps until we were toe to toe. "Including you."

"You can't just decide what I do and don't do." I tried reasoning, the earlier defiance draining as I saw just how dark his eyes were growing. "Despite what I am to you, I am my own person. I am doing this for you."

His hand darted up to catch in the hair at the back of my neck just before I managed to take a step back, holding me firmly in place. His body moved forward to press against mine, and despite the anger clearly overtaking him, I could feel his hard length pressing into my soft stomach. It sent a primal shiver through me, awakening an instinct I hadn't known I possessed until now.

Every part of me screamed in awareness of this man, much larger and stronger than I. The anger only helped fuel the jolt of arousal that ran through my body at the sudden realization I was very much at his mercy now.

"I could lock you up." His breath rasped against the skin of my neck as he lowered his head and pressed his elongated fangs against my neck. "Tie you to my bed with the finest silks I have collected. I would make sure you couldn't do anything but lie there and beg for mercy as I made sure you were so pleasured you couldn't move."

Breath hitched in my throat at the mental image of his large body over me as he had his wicked way with me. I didn't want to be swayed by this caveman mentality, but I couldn't deny the rush of wetness between my legs at the thought of being tied down by this man. The witch within me demanded the dragon pay for thinking it would be that easy to keep me, but the woman within me wanted nothing more than to submit.

This new attitude had to be the dragon taking the place of the man in his angered state. The suspicion was only confirmed by eyes staring deep into mine as if they could eat me alive without ever laying a hand on me. They were not of a man, but of a beast.

"You wouldn't dare." My voice was weak and warbling, betraying the words meant to be strong-willed. "I would burn you alive."

His other hand shot out to snatch both of my wrists in one hand in a lightning-fast movement, holding them in place as he released my hair and pulled out a scrap of material I hadn't seen him grab. I gasped, trying to yank from his grasp, but failing miserably as his grip only seemed to grow firmer.

In a matter of seconds, he had my arms firmly pressed behind my back, still held firmly by his unrelenting grip.

"You forget yourself, little witch," he purred. "Your fire would do nothing other than heat us both. If you have the energy to even summon a candle flame in a few hours, it would mean I haven't fucked you hard enough."

I let out an angry growl, bringing one knee up to try and connect with his groin, but he only batted it away as if it were nothing more than a fly. In response, he spun me around roughly, taking me firmly in his arms. We now faced a mirror propped against the far wall. The two of us were interlocked in the reflection, him looking like a darkened shadow with glowing amber eyes looming behind my wild form.

I looked like a mouse caught in the claws of a cat.

"What are you going to do exactly, spank me?" I laughed harshly, feeling angered despite my arousal. "I'll have you know I'm a grown-ass witch, and I don't just bend over for dragons throwing a temper tantrum—"

My words were cut off as he promptly lifted me out of the air, and in a couple of brisk paces firmly placed me down on my stomach on a medium-sized side table. I immediately moved to push myself up, but despite my outraged cry, his firm hand held me steadily down against the table.

"Gold, I swear to the fates I will kill you if you don't let me go!"

He ignored my threats, leaning down to yank off my shoes

with one hand before moving his other free hand to the waistband of my leggings and tearing them off of me. It was somehow cold and robotic and yet wild and aggressive at the same time.

I screeched in anger, "Those pants were twenty bucks!"

Again, with that silence that reminded me of a stalking predator, I felt him loop an unseen fabric around one kicking leg, securing it to the table leg before mirroring his work with the other. My legs were now spread almost completely, baring my pantie-covered ass to the cool air. I attempted yanking my legs out of their binds, but a firm smack on my ass shocked every single thought of escape out of my head.

"Did you just fucking spank me?"

"You were acting like a spoiled little girl," he growled, reappearing at my back to reach around me and grip the edges of the table.

Any momentary confusion was erased as he dragged the table back from the wall and, with me still on it, moved the entire thing with myself atop it to sit directly in front of the mirror. Now closer, I could see him better and could watch in anticipation as he reached around once more to press me flat against the smooth wood of the desk.

I attempted to push against his grip once more, but another harsh slap against my ass held me in place. I gasped, feeling my ass warm from the stinging pain, and his satisfied gaze met mine in our reflection.

I had never even tried spanking, knowing I would despise the feeling of being punished, and yet the tantalizing warmth and tingle his palm left against my sore ass held an appeal like no other. I was hot, fuming, pissed, and wet beyond belief.

And he knew it.

"I'm not going to bind your hands," he murmured as he slid his rough palm against the hot skin where he struck me, "because I want you to know that if you really wanted to, you could stop me."

I bared my teeth at him. "You think I want to be bent over and tied to a goddamn table?"

Gold's hand dipped between my legs, sliding over the embarrassingly damp center of my underwear. "I think you more than want it, little witch. You're weeping for it."

Any reply I had was stopped by the moan that tore from me as he pushed the thin cloth aside to plunge two fingers inside of me without warning. I pulled against my restraints, overwhelmed by the sudden fullness in my core, but he only pulled my head up once more to stare directly at myself in the mirror.

"Watch yourself," he demanded as he bent over and locked his teeth around my throat. "Don't look away, or I will punish you by tanning your hide until you can't sit for days."

His fingers twisted and fluttered in my core, playing me like an instrument he had learned to wield over the course of a century. I couldn't stop myself from clenching around his rough fingers dancing with the most sensitive part of myself, my pussy begging for more than the two thick fingers plundering deep within me.

I watched helplessly as my face contorted in pleasure, cheeks growing flushed and my eyes glittering in the torchlight. I felt naughty, knowing that he not only could watch my reactions but could see every inch of my needful self on display all at once. He watched me with hungry eyes, licking his lips slowly as he brought me closer and closer, like a wolf sensing his prey was wounded and close to giving in.

He spared me no mercy, no fanciful tricks. It was just his hands and eyes on my body, dangling me over that shameful cliff, waiting for me to cave in. And I did—all at once. He didn't even allow me to look away as he took me over the edge in an embarrassingly short amount of time.

My eyes fluttered shut as I rode the waves of my orgasm, rocking my hips back against his hand to extend every fleeting pulse uncaring of how wanton I must look. In a flash, his fingers left me, and a harsh hand came down right on the spot he had hit before, my hips shooting up away as the pain shocked me out of my fervor.

"Asshole!" I whimpered even though the pain heightened the afterglow of my pleasure.

Another hard spank sent me flat against the desk once more. I pushed back in a fury at being manhandled so thoroughly, only managing to lever my hips up just enough for him to use the opportunity to grip my hips and plunge himself into me in one smooth thrust. There were no romantic words, not heated exchanges. This was a wild beast taking his pleasure out on his woman all at once in wild abandon.

There was no pain, apart from his spanking and hard thrusts, but a primal possession that pleased something within myself so deep I felt my mind start to drift as it overloaded in ecstasy. Everything started going fuzzy as the feeling of his hard cock pounding deep within me stirred my pleasure once more. I knew how I must look, being ravaged by this large dragon and no longer putting up the pretense of a fight, yet I didn't care.

His claws dug into my waist, holding me in place as each hard thrust knocked us forward into the table. Any pain I felt at the hard contact was erased by a long hard plunge that took my mind from any worldly discomforts. The mirror in front of us shook with each push, blurring the image of the two of us as the heat within us both began to rise.

I gripped at his shoulders, holding on for dear life as he became more and more wild, snarling and growling into the flesh of my neck. No human male could hope to achieve the speed or sheer power at which this dragon dominated me with, and I knew no other man could compare with this ferocity.

"Please!" I mewled, feeling myself climbing toward an orgasm I knew would shake me to the core. "Gold, more!"

His hand flew to the back of my hair, yanking my head up to connect gazes in the mirror. "Look at that. Look at you begging for my cock. You're mine, little witch, and there is no use denying it."

"I'm yours!" I echoed him mindlessly, digging my claws into his shoulders, urging him for more hard thrusts. At that moment, I might have said anything to make him continue.

He grinned over my shoulder, his fangs glowing a brilliant white. He looked like a savage, and I knew that the Gold who was with me now was little better than one. I was playing with the dragon now, and he had me right where he wanted me.

I was tied underneath him where no one could hear me scream.

"Come for me," he growled. "Come all over my cock and claim me as yours. Prove to me you're mine."

As if on command, I fell apart. My entire body melted into a pool of pleasure, going limp against the table as my body spasmed with each hard pull of my orgasm washing over me. In the reflection of the mirror, I could almost see my soul leave my body as the pleasure took me to places I had never hoped to reach before.

Gold's thrusts turned jerky and hard as he chased his pleasure. Gaze meeting mine in the mirror, he buried his fangs in the base of my neck, stifling his groan, as he poured himself within me. He didn't stop thrusting until every drop of essence was drained from within him, and we both lay against each other, riding the last throes of our combined pleasure.

His fangs left my neck long enough to speak in a voice

barely above a whisper. "And I am yours, little witch."

Our breathing was ragged — each harsh exhale of his stinging against the sensitive skin of my neck. The place where he'd bit me stung in pain, and yet each throb sent slow pulses of pleasure right to my core where we were still connected.

The only other sound in the cave was the slight breeze from the wind whistling in from the entrance, which I could hardly hear over the roaring pulse in my throat. I felt like I'd narrowly avoided a heart attack, my heart was pounding so hard.

We stayed like that, still together yet now resting in the afterglow of our passion. The feeling of his warm chest against my back through our still partially clothed bodies almost surpassed the pleasure from the sex itself.

"I can't make you stay here," he whispered against my throat, "but I'm not happy about this."

My heart melted at the vulnerability in his voice. He was baring himself to me now, after me baring myself to him. I could almost feel the poetry in the making.

I knew this whole episode happened because he was trying to get me to stay in any way he could. Now that we both had blown off the steam from our long day, we both were able to embrace the truth.

I would have to go, even if he couldn't, and that hurt him more than anything.

Despite the hurt in my heart for my dragon, I laughed it off breathily, choosing to avoid what would surely be a long conversation. "Lucky for you, I don't think I can go anywhere until at least tomorrow morning."

He didn't laugh, but I could feel his smile against my flushed skin. "Then for tonight, I will make sure that you can't go anywhere without remembering just what happens to little witches who try to escape me."

I felt him slice the binding around my legs, moving to catch me as my weak legs collapsed beneath me. "Well then, I hope the sun never rises again."

With a dark chuckle, he began to stalk toward what I assumed to be his bedroom, capturing my lips with his as our passions stirred anew.

CHAPTER THIRTEEN

The next few days progressed rather quickly. Gold had been moody ever since he released me to do my work in the village, but I tried not to take it to heart. I still managed to cheer him up in the meantime by pulling him into his bed each night for a renewed bout of passion.

For the first few nights after arriving back at the cave, I would find him perched on the edge of the cliff, anxiously staring out in the direction of the town waiting for me to arrive. He would turn on his heel and storm in once he finally spotted me, but just seeing him there made my heart tighten at the cuteness of his antics.

He had been thoughtful as well, laying out meals for me and drawing up baths for days when I was more drained than ever before. A long day of attempting to teach novice spell casters how to do witch magic was tedious. I found myself enjoying it more and more as time passed since I knew each day brought more and more positive results when it came to their ability to summon wards.

In all honesty, it was more than promising. Because of the strong bond with magic all of Eerie had, almost everybody was capable of accessing magic strong enough almost to match that of a novice witch on Earth. On the other hand, it seemed that just being here made my magic stronger. Just summoning the barrier magic took half the time it normally would, and that was without the help of my students.

I hadn't been anticipating going into town on my own the first time I hopped on my broom to fly out alone, but to my surprise, the few members of town that greeted me upon arrival seemed to be anxiously awaiting me. Even the farmers that passed looked at me with respect I had never garnered before in my life.

I was working with a group of no more than ten or so magic wielders of different origins. Some were dragons, one was a griffin, and one was a half-breed of sorts I had yet to identify. It was a mish-mash crowd, but one with surprising talent when it came to magic and learning.

Magic wasn't necessarily wielded only by witches, but it was a surprise to see so many non-witch magic wielders in one area. That is, it was surprising to see so many natural magic wielders, instead of the races bred with their magically gifted powers like my fire. Typically the chances of someone being capable of accessing any natural magic were about one in a hundred thousand, so these people had to have been rounded up from the surrounding towns as fast as possible.

Once I had all of the students capable of summoning the beginnings of the first ward, I dismissed them to practice, giving them time to stretch their legs before we did anything more taxing. The work was grueling on the magic reserves, but beneficial when it came to summoning any useful spells.

In the meantime, I excused myself to catch some fresh air away from the bustling crowds of the town, needing some space in order to collect myself after hours of work. At home, I could typically isolate myself in the back of my shop, or go out on hunts for ingredients when I felt overwhelmed like this, but there wasn't any time or freedom for that now.

My best hope of calming down was to hide from people for as long as I could out in the shadows of the town, which is why I was currently hiding out on the edge of town, in what had to be one of the only quiet areas in this time of day.

I had the town at my back and the forest to my front, with me standing alone in between the two. Being alone like this was rare for me recently, which was an odd realization. Before I met Gold, I would go entire weeks without seeing anyone besides my coworker, and now it seemed I always had at least one person at my side at all times.

What was odd was it didn't seem to bother me as much as I thought it would. Sure, I needed to unplug and take a breather, but I found myself liking being a part of a more socially active lifestyle like this.

It was like the longer I spent out here in this world, the less I found myself anticipating returning to the lonesome existence I had back on Earth.

A flash of a shadow in the distant woods caught my eye, drawing my attention from my mind to chase the figure in the tree line. At this distance, nothing could be made out but darkness swimming between the trunks of the trees. It gave away nothing, concealing anything that might be watching from deep within the woods.

Even without seeing them, I knew someone was there, watching me.

I hated the spike of fear that shot through me. I didn't want to be frightened of whatever it was that was pursuing me, and yet the feeling seemed to haunt me at the worst times. At that moment I regretted not forcing Gold to come with me. I would feel a lot safer with him at my side in moments like these.

Sure, I had more than a fighting chance finding a way out of whatever might come my way, but dealing with all of this alone would be a nightmare. Truthfully, he had been here with me since the moment everything began, appearing out of nowhere like a prince saving his damsel in distress.

It embarrassed me to think just how different I was then, a witch too scared to get out of her car and protect herself. If that were me now, I'd charge right into the fight with my fire blazing.

Okay, that was a lie. I would still panic as I did then, but my point is that now I am not afraid to defend myself.

"They hide during the daytime."

I almost jumped out of my skin at the sudden appearance of the huge man at my side. Giovanni Moore looked far different standing in the bright light of the afternoon than he did when we had met him in the town hall. For one thing, he was enormous, not rivaling the Stone King, but definitely in a category of his own.

It wasn't just in height, either. The man's arms looked strong enough to snap a tree trunk in half. It was honestly impressive to see a man of his age in as great a shape as he was, and I had to wonder just what he was.

My guess would be a griffin—half lion, half eagle, 100 percent beast.

"The creatures that the king talked about a few days ago?" I asked, trying to play off obvious jitters after being scared out of my pants.

He nodded. "Exactly. We have gotten many reports of people getting attacked by those things in the woods. More every day. I thought I'd tell you, since you seemed to be staring out into the trees as though beast would hop out and get you any second."

He was only partially right. "Do you think it's safe for me to travel by broom then?"

"More than safe. Air travel seems to be the only safe way to get around Eerie anymore," he stated grimly, and I could hear the edge of stress grating at his voice. "Even the oceans of late have been infested with Eris' abominations. The dragon king who rules over them has been having a hard time keeping them away from his towns."

The man was tense, more so than when I had met him a few days before. My guess would have to be that the new flood of bad news concerning the creatures in the woods was getting to him. I didn't envy his position of power. Just seeing the man trying desperately to keep his lone town together was enough to scare me away from any power lust hiding in the back of my mind.

The man before me was a walking talking representation of the difficulties that responsibility for a mass amount of people made for a person.

"Are some of my students going to help with those problems across all of the seven kingdoms? I hope the wards end up helping all of Eerie, and not just the Mountain Kingdom."

Giovanni looked pleased with my concern for his people. "Yes, at least one of your students is going to be assigned to each kingdom, where they will help protect the main cities until the seven kings can find a way to stop Eris in her tracks."

Ten or so of my students spread over an entire world putting up wards seemed like a bit of an off-the-wall plan, but I was hardly the authority in this. It was my job to teach them and teach them well, and that was it.

"The seven kings," I mused. "I almost forgot there were seven of them. In school I loved learning about the seven kingdoms of Eerie. The Wildling King was always my favorite to learn about."

His belt of laughter was loud enough to disturb the surrounding grass, "The Wildling King? You mean the king your people call Bigfoot?"

"What?" I asked, defensively. "You can't blame me for being interested. He's a being with the ability to travel between worlds at will, as long as where he travels to is a part of the wild. Do you have any idea how many humans lost their mind learning that not only was he real, but he lived in a world filled with every other creature of mid-century lore?"

Who wouldn't be interested in something like that?

He looked at me for a long moment, watching me with a calculated amusement. "You know, you're a lot different than

I thought you'd be."

That wasn't the first time I had gotten that from someone, but I was curious as to why he thought it. "How so?"

"Everyone who knew anything about Gold had thought his mate would be somebody like himself. A thief, con artist, somebody like that," he mused. "I think everyone will be shocked to learn that his mate is a witch like yourself."

"And what kind of witch would that be?"

"Considerate. Strong-willed. With morals." He paused as if considering the right words to say. "The kind of person not afraid to put herself at risk to protect a town full of people and keep her mate out of trouble."

I knew what he was getting at. He thought Gold would be with someone that could match his former personality before he met me. As much as I hated for the man I knew to be seen as no better than his past, I knew the judgment had to come from somewhere. Being a better person didn't mean he had righted all the wrongs he caused.

Even if I could overlook them, it was a lot different for the people he had wronged in his life. No matter if I defended him of not,

Gold would have to fix his reputation with the people of Eerie himself.

"What exactly did he do?"

The man's face fell into a cool mask, staring blankly out into the trees. "Your mate was quite the handful for a long time. He never hurt anyone, not physically, but he did his best to cause chaos everywhere he went. Stealing, drinking" — his gaze flicked to me for the barest moment — "sleeping with other people's wives."

"You've got to be kidding me?" My lip curled in disgust at the thought.

He held up his hands defensively. "To be fair, almost all of the women were either open about their relationships outside of their husbands or were in unhappy matings. Besides, there was only a handful of them. It may not make it all better morally, but he wasn't going out trying to hurt people's relationships. Unfortunately, the angry husbands took it upon themselves to play it that way to the public."

I'd be lying if I said I was completely fine with the revelation, but if I was going to overlook his criminal past it would be hypocritical of me not to overlook that.

"Is that all? Somehow I don't think that's enough to get a person kicked out of a whole world," I said sarcastically, trying to hide the annoyance my twinge of jealousy stirred in my tone.

Giovanni shook his head, the amused look returning. "Well, he stole the crown right off of the head of the King of the Forest, another dragon. I don't know if you know this, but stealing from another dragon is considered a pretty high crime. Put that on top of the dragon being a king, and you have a capital offense. So, that on top of his preexisting record and his alliance with the Thieves Guild, and you have a punishment of deportation or death. He chose deportation."

"Understandable."

"Quite."

Given the same options, I would 100 percent choose the same, even if I couldn't think of living without being able to go back to my hometown. It was one thing to move away from the place you were born and raised — another never to be able to see it again. I supposed that was the difference between Gold and me. I had a close tie with my family and community, and he didn't.

It wasn't the first time I realized we were two very different people tied together by fate. Not that it mattered. I wouldn't want to date a man just like me anyway.

I didn't have anything more to say to the man, and neither did he to me, so we both stood quietly together, gazing out into the dark woods. It was a comforting quiet, both of us off in our minds, absorbed in our thoughts. It wasn't until one of my students approached to say that the group was finished for the day that I even realized I was still there.

Due to the little zone-out session, I was going to be late getting back to the cave. If I didn't rush, Gold might tie me to that table again, which almost made me want to be late just to do a round two of that heated night.

"Storm." Giovanni's voice made me still, and I stopped climbing on my broom just long enough to turn towards him.

The man stood alone in the center of the main road, waiting for me to give him my attention. None of the students or townsfolk were out on the streets at this time, leaving us along in the quiet of the late afternoon.

"The people of Eerie owe you. We all owe you." He spoke earnestly. "I hope you can change Gold for the better, because having both of you on our side might help us all in the long run. Unlike the other leaders, I have always seen something hidden in that dragon, and I think you might be the woman to bring that out of him."

I nodded, giving him a brief smile. "After these last couple of days, I can say I definitely won't be against you. If there's anything you ever need after all of this, ask for me in Witches-Brew Cove on Earth."

"I hope I never have to," he replied cryptically.

With a sad smile, he turned on his heels and left, retreating into the town.

It was one of those days. Gold was moody, the class had finished early, and I was bored. No matter what I seemed to do, I couldn't seem to pull the dragon out of his funk. This time, it wasn't from the classes or me, but something else seeming to plague his mind. Not even fooling around could bring him to the present.

Sensing the only way to make him better was to leave him alone, I made sure to give him his space and allow him the distance he needed to work through his thoughts.

In the meantime, it gave me ample time to explore his home.

It was surprisingly roomy and well-lit for a home made completely of stone, and I didn't feel at all caged in walking through the enormous beautifully carved cave system. The entire thing had been made to accommodate his dragon's gigantic form with some wing room, so every room felt like the size of a cathedral. I felt small standing in the midst of it all.

He had at least ten rooms, one being a living room with a couch the size of a king-size bed and with several scattered items of furniture around a large roaring hearth and a surprisingly modern kitchen, excluding electric items. He also had a bathroom with a pool-sized claw-foot tub, a small library, at least four bedrooms including his own, and one room empty but for an atrocious pile of designer clothing.

That last part didn't surprise me in the slightest.

However, what I was most drawn to was the room at the very end of the cave.

His hoard room.

The largest room in his cave, the size of a school gymnasium, was packed from floor to ceiling with gold and valuables. Riches dripped from open chests and poured off of every available counter in the room. Piles of just shining silver jewelry glinted with the rubies and sapphires they were decorated with. There were only a few walking spaces that extended to the center of the room, which led me to believe the only way to traverse the rest was to climb the pile of riches.

Statues peeked out from where they were hidden in piles of expensive cloth, and paintings were scattered over the large walls. In my life, I could never have imagined such wealth accumulated in one place.

"I see my treasure found my treasures," Gold purred as he slinked into the room just after me, having escaped my notice till then.

"That was" — I sighed — "the single worst come on I have ever heard in my life."

Gold threw his head back in a long laugh, clutching at his sides. "Well, I'm glad you said so. I'll have to get better at them."

His laughter was contagious, and I couldn't help my small smile as I turned away to look back at his staggering pile of wealth. "Where did you get all of this? Is all of this stolen, or do you commission some of this yourself?"

For the sake of the art, I hoped he did. Artists got fucked over enough as it was. They didn't need a dragon coming to ruin their livelihoods.

"Depends. Some of it I earned, some I found, some I stole," he answered, tracing a finger over a golden goblet atop a desk to my right. "I didn't always steal. In fact, I only stole for the sake of knowing whether or not I could the majority of the time."

"So it was just to prove how good you were." A statement, not a question. I knew that was exactly why he did it.

"Again, I said the majority of the time. Sometimes I stole because I genuinely wanted the thing I was taking." He stopped to point at a painting in a glass case on the wall. "Like that. It was previously owned by a temperamental demon who tended to destroy everything he owned. I couldn't allow him to destroy something so beautiful, so I took it. I'm sure the artist is happy in whatever afterlife he dwells in."

I made a laugh that was more blowing air out through my nose. "Well then, if you didn't always steal these things, how did you find some of these things?"

"Well, I've never told anyone this, but I always preferred adventuring over my other avenues of work," he explained with an embarrassed look. "With Eerie being as old as it is and home to some of the more extravagant species, you can't go a few feet without running into some ancient treasure buried by our ancestors for their hoards. Now and then I go on quests or expeditions if a tale catches my ear, and from there I can find some of the treasures hidden from the worlds."

I turned my disbelieving look on him, but he didn't appear to be playing with me in the slightest. "So you're a treasure hunter?"

His cheeks grew red in an adorable blush. "Yes, well everybody has a hobby."

"Oh, I'm not trying to tease you, Gold." I walked over to wrap my arms around his torso and give him a playful squeeze. "I think it's cute and pretty awesome. If Earth hadn't been combed over for any penny left by our ancestors, I would consider it, too."

"Somehow I can't picture you as an adventurer. You are definitely the sexy reclusive librarian the adventurer would come to seeking information on long-buried treasures." His eyes glazed over as he pictured it, clearly stirring with the beginnings of arousal. "If I were that adventurer, I would definitely try to seduce out any kind of secret knowledge you may be hiding in your cozy little library."

"Hey, I'll have you know my sister is the librarian. I am the sexy potions shop owner, remember?" I scolded him with a hard slap at his shoulder. "However, even if I were that librarian, you would have to work very hard to get anything out of me. Carlilses don't give up secrets so easily."

I could picture it now, like a vision from an old '80s love novel. He'd bust in shirtless, hair blowing in the non-existent wind. He'd spy me from afar, prowling across the quiet library floor to take me in his arms. I'd refuse to give up the information on some old king's hidden treasure-filled grotto, and he'd torture it out of me with his sensual punishments.

His arms snaked around my torso to pull me flush to his body. "I guess I'm in luck you aren't the librarian then, because I don't have to go on any more adventures to find my boon. You're already right here where you belong, as my most valuable treasure."

"I change my mind. That was the corniest line."

He grinned. "I try my best."

Even though I was perfectly happy within his arms just then, ready to give in to whatever he had planned with the hardness at my hip, something about his words still confused me. "Why did you choose to join the Thieves Guild then? If you like exploring, then why even feel the need? What even is it?"

He let out a long sad sigh, as if it wasn't a topic he wanted to get into. I understood it, partially. I wouldn't want to spill details of my troubled past to a person so fresh in a relationship, but I was too curious to avoid the question.

I wanted to know about him, from him. Not from everybody else in the town. I had already told him everything about myself, so why couldn't I ask about him?

"My entire family has been a part of it at some point. The Thieves Guild is just a group of thieves who work together and live by a code, so, naturally, my family would gravitate towards it. It was inevitable that I joined my blood on their never-ending conquest for wealth." He shrugged nonchalantly. "Truthfully, I had a talent for it, and the wild soul to go with it. I wasn't quite the charmer you know now back then, so I took what I had and ran with it for as long as I could."

So the infamous guild was essentially a less threatening mafia, good to know. Even better to know the tidbit about his family. I had a feeling any details I got about them would be few and far between, so I'd take the information as it came.

As far as Gold's involvement, I wasn't too shocked. I had

already gotten an earful from when Giovanni had told me about some of his conquests from his youth back in town, so I already knew a great deal of the worst of it. I had seen it myself on the day we met when this very same dragon saved me with a stolen car at his back and an equally stolen police badge on his hip.

"You know, when I was younger I use to be a bit of a trouble maker myself," I purred, pulling him closer to grind myself against his growing erection.

"Oh, really?"

"Yes, really." I laughed. "It was no Thieves Guild worthy conquest, but I did prank quite a few unsuspecting members of Witches-Brew Cove in my past. Plus I did vandalize that one ex-boyfriend's car. I was a true menace to society."

His eyes twinkled with bright amusement. "I'm sure he deserved it."

"He did. He lied and told everyone he slept with my little sister after he broke up with me. She was fourteen, and he was seventeen." Even now I felt anger rise at the memory. "Luckily nobody believed it, and it sure as fuck didn't happen. I should have busted the bastard's kneecaps."

Gold made an annoyed sound, his lip curling in disgust. "A boy with less honor than a common fool. Next time you see him, tell me, and I will do it for you."

"It happened years ago. The boy is now a man with a steady family." I shrugged, not caring about it in the slightest. "My guess is that he was going through a rough time and took it out on my family and me. It's no excuse, and I sure as fuck don't forgive him, but I can understand. Besides, it was his dad's vintage Camaro, so it wasn't like he wasn't punished by the fates anyway."

His brows lifted. "Is that so? Your fates are odd creatures, indeed."

"They aren't that bad. After all, they placed you on that

road on that night. Without them, we might not have ever met."

"I never thought about how odd that was. I suppose I should thank them for bringing us together, then." His smile was positively wolfish, giving my ass a teasing slap. "What better way than for us to do exactly what fated mates are intended to do?"

I made a noise of protest, but his hands had already slid around to cup my thighs and yank me up in his arms. I had no choice but to lean into him or fall to the stone wood floor.

"Well, who am I to deny fate?" I replied heatedly, sliding my arms around his neck and meeting him halfway in a clash of lips and tongue.

The entire night passed in a blur of tangled limbs and various hard surfaces until Gold had dropped me onto the bed and promptly passed out. The sun was already beginning to peek in through the holes that served as windows on the cave walls of his bedroom illuminating us both in a soft pink glow.

I was exhausted, overused, and more sated than I had ever been in my life. I played with the waves of his hair, loving the soft pleasing moan my touch elicited from the dragon. It was so calming I could almost ignore the unsettled feeling growing in the pit of my stomach with every second that passed.

CHAPTER FOURTEEN

I awoke the next day to the sound of male laughter booming through the halls.

Groaning, I rolled over to cover my head with the pillow and block out the assaulting noise, only to pause once I realized that it was more than just Gold's laughter. Two distinct voices, audible yet too distorted to make out, drifted in on the wind of the morning, alerting me to the other man's presence.

I tried rolling over and telling myself if he was laughing, there was no reason to wake myself up and check it out, but my curiosity got the better of me. Getting up out of the comfort of my bed was almost too much to bear, but I somehow managed to get up and hunt down the sounds begrudgingly. Sure enough, it didn't take long to find the pair of men chatting loudly in the large room Gold designated to be the living room. Gold was splayed out on the large leather couch, feet kicked up without a care in the world, talking to a man in the corner I had never seen before.

The man could have been Gold's fraternal twin, the resemblance was so close, in features if not in hair or eye color. He had the same sort of sexy Vlad the Impaler vibes with the heavy brow and roman looks, only instead of dark hair like Gold he had long pale white hair and these spooky crystal blue eyes. He looked like an elf wet dream, straight out of a bestselling fantasy novel, and just as slender.

Where Gold looked like he could rip a tree trunk in half, this man was the picture of suave elegance, able to blend in with the highest of society.

"I didn't realize we were expecting company," I sleepily greeted the two as I placed myself in the armchair opposite of Gold.

At my appearance, Gold sat up with a wide smile, looking happier than ever now that I had arrived. I returned the smile with a small one of my own. After last night, just the sight of the man should have been enough to make me blush, which was something I was trying to avoid in front of our new guest.

"This is my brother, Silver," Gold explained, waving a hand towards the man. "His visit was a surprise, so I'm just as shocked as you are. It's not often I get to see this useless pirate."

Silver and Gold, how fitting. Whoever named these two must have been thumbing through the wrong baby names book. Again, I had no place to talk, though. My mother had named her girls Storm, Terry, and Valentine.

Even so, it was quite the shock to see Gold had any family whatsoever. I had thought that he was one of those lonesome travelers with a family long in the past. He had briefly mentioned his family when explaining the Thieves Guild, but I had gotten the impression they were long gone from how he had spoken about them.

I suppose that might have been a big leap to make. After all, my great-grandmother used to say *to assume is to make an ass out of you and me.*

Silver rolled his eyes. "Our mother named us after the colors of our dragons, in case you were wondering."

A surprised laugh bubbled up at his words. "How could you tell?" I asked.

"Most people are curious," he answered plainly. "It's not the most creative names, I'll say, but our mother was trying at the time."

"I can't say I've met many other Silvers or Golds, so it is definitely original." I extended a hand, which he took with a polite smile. "I'm Storm Carlisle, by the way. It's a pleasure to meet you."

"I know who you are. My brother told me all about you the minute I stepped foot in this wretched cave," he said with an exaggerated groan. "He's quite proud of his new mate. He probably told me three times about you burning that mayor's garden to the ground in Faerie."

"I like this place," Gold grumbled in response to his brother's insult of the home he was so proud of.

"Yes, well, of course, you would, brother," Silver drawled sarcastically. "It's a perfect fit for a caveman recluse like yourself."

The brotherly teasing had to be some of the cutest stuff I had seen in a long while. It was clear from the lack of tension between the two that their brotherly rivalry didn't extend any further than playground insults, and it reminded me of my relationship with my sisters.

Gold gave him what must be the Eerie equivalent of the middle finger. "At least I have a place, Silver. Not everyone can stay at their older rich mistress's houses. Some people like to be grounded."

That struck a nerve, if the brother's suddenly angry expression was anything to judge by.

"She was only three hundred," Silver snapped. "Which for a gargoyle is in their middle adult stage, and I'll have you know she was my only older lover."

My eyebrows nearly shot into my hairline at the thought of this elegant man having a female gargoyle lover. I had only seen one gargoyle myself, the Stone King the other day, and he had been almost nine feet tall with wings. The image of the dragon in the arms of a gargoyle woman was an . . . interesting picture.

"That's not why I'm here anyway." Silver now had an annoyed snap to his tone, apparently done with the teasing. "As

I was telling you before your mate arrived, I'm here on business."

Gold tensed, any humor draining from him all at once. Whatever the two had been talking about was clearly not something Gold wanted to entertain.

"What kind of business?" I couldn't help but ask.

Gold stared at his brother for a long moment before letting out a long, defeated sigh. "He wants to bring me back into the Thieves Guild, and I already told him I wasn't going back. I have a mate now, so I can't go around on petty thieving missions and abandon our fresh relationship. Besides, I am barely allowed in Eerie as it is."

Silver didn't look angered by his brother's words, just disappointed.

"I can see that," Silver murmured. "It's a shame, though. You were the best of the best. I'd love to have you back on my team."

Gold didn't look convinced by his brothers placating words. "Sorry, brother, but I have much bigger problems. I take it you have heard about the problems in town?"

Silver's face closed off, but not before I could see the look of recognition cross his face. "You aren't talking about Eris are you?"

He didn't just know about the creatures. He knew exactly who we were talking about. I didn't know if the name was commonplace in Ecric as of right now, but I hadn't heard anyone but the king and Giovanni even mention the goddess.

I straightened in my seat, intrigued. "You know of her?"

"Yeah, I know of her." Silver's lip curled. "Wretched goddess. Just plain evil. You don't know fear until you've come face to face with her monsters."

"Wait, you've met her?" I asked, growing more and more invested by the second. If he had met her himself, he knew more than any of us. Not a single person I knew had talked to the woman directly, not even the king.

"Her directly? No, but I've seen her"—a shiver of disgust followed the statement—"in the forest. Some of the other members of the guild and I were going to confront her for slaughtering our people out there, but things went wrong. Once we got close, it was like . . . a person's worst nightmare. If you were there, you would have known why we didn't."

I had seen some of the glimpses of the monsters in the woods on my flights, so I knew full well what he was talking about, but I had to press. "What did you see?"

"She bred evil. She was like . . . I can't explain it. On the outside, she looked like a pale, stick thin, sickly little girl. Only the closer you got, the more you could see she was just wrong. Everything about her was off, and that was only her looks." He swallowed hard, eyes going glassy. "Those things she surrounded herself with . . . they were like walking corpses, only somehow still alive and breathing."

Just like the pixie. The glimpses in the woods must not have done justice to the beast's horror, because I had not been able to see what he was describing. Eris was another thing entirely. The description of her was new and necessary information, even if it wasn't particularly helpful.

"What happened after you saw her?"

"I turned the party around," he said with an elegant sniff, "and went right back to the guild. I'm no idiot, you see. I know death when I see it, and that thing, whatever she is, is death incarnate. Since then we've been doing the best we can to keep her out of our territory, but it's only a matter of time until we have to move."

"Has anyone been killed?" Gold asked.

"Two new recruits in Eerie, but a whole crew in Faerie," Silver answered with a solemn nod. "We've pulled all of the guild members out of Faerie entirely. It's overrun over there. No one's safe, at least in the Summer Kingdom. There's still a base in the Dark Woods, but it's not looking promising."

"I had no idea this spread that far," Gold muttered, sounding disturbed by the news. "The only reason Storm and I are in on this is because a while ago she got into some trouble with the fae in the Summer Kingdom. We later found out the woman in question orchestrated it."

Silver laughed without humor. "Well, if Eris went out of her way to have something sicced on your mate, then you're in it for the long haul."

Gold grinned wryly. "Trust me, I know. I'd drag myself naked through the thorn fields of Faerie for this woman though, so I don't mind it."

Gold's disturbing yet oddly heartwarming confession aside, I was put off by his brother's words. If his brother was so insistent Eris was bad news, then that didn't bode well for either of us.

I had known a while ago the woman was dangerous, but not quite to the degree Silver insisted she was.

My pensiveness must have shown, because Silver quickly added, "If it makes you feel any better, their presence in Eerie has lessened as of late. Since they were discovered, the seven kings have been hunting them down and eradicating them from the kingdom," he said blithely. "Unfortunately, Faerie's governments are so weak I'm afraid they will just spill over there because of it. That just means more corrupted fae creatures on an already exhausted population, which means everyone over there is going to need a lot more silver if they hope to kill them."

The mention of Faerie reminded me of my sister, who very well still could be in that realm. The ball of worry that had been building since she ran away to that kingdom only seemed to grow the longer we went without even a mirror call. For all I knew, she could have been pixie food by now.

I just hoped she was handling all of this well. Now I worried the reason we hadn't heard from her was that she was caught in some trouble.

Sensing the room had gone quiet. I looked up to see Gold had gone still, looking blankly in the direction of his treasure room. His face shifted between emotions, clearly caught in a maelstrom of thoughts.

After a long moment, he finally turned to address Silver. "Thank you for coming over, Silver. I missed your company. You're welcome to come back any time, but I'm afraid I just realized I have something to do. Storm can accompany you out."

With his clipped parting words, Gold pushed up to his feet, giving me the barest of smiles before disappearing out the doors. Silver and I both stared in his direction, confused by his sudden disappearance.

Well, that had come from nowhere. We shared a bewildered look, Silver giving me a shrug as he stood to follow his brother out. Neither of us had picked up on Gold's antsy mood until now, so his fervor to have Silver leave left both of us at odds.

"Well, I see that was my brother's not so subtle way of telling me it's time for me to go," he said with a dry laugh.

Giving him an apologetic smile, I stood to follow him. "I'll escort you out."

Silver nodded agreeably, though his gaze strayed to where his brother had disappeared to. I could tell how concerned he was the entire walk to the entrance, practically feeling the tangible waves of stress rolling off the dragon's body.

He held himself like a carefree king, walking with a couldn't-care-less swagger, yet it was clear from a single look in his eyes he was suffering. Whether it was the worry from his brother or the things the dragon had seen in the woods those few days ago, it was clear everything was weighing on him.

Unable to hold back from comforting the man, I laid a comforting hand on his arm once we reached the natural light of the outside. "I'm sorry about your dead," I said earnestly.

He looked down at where my hand rested, blue eyes still alight with the storm of his worries, and yet they seemed to soften the barest amount. It was a small comfort, that was for sure, but from what I could see, it was appreciated.

"Thank you. I never thought I would get apologies for dead thieves, but I'm sure wherever they are, they are happy about it."

A lump rose in my throat, making it hard to swallow. "Most people have, at one point, been thieves, from kings to common folk. I don't think someone deserves death just for that."

"No. No, they don't." Silver fixated on the world outside, looking out over the green landscape with a sad look. "I hope I get to see you again, Storm. I think you and I will be friends in the future."

With a final nod, he strode away, shifting seamlessly into the form of a brilliant silver dragon and walking right off the edge of the cliff. I sadly watched as he flew away, his lithe dragon form dancing through the treetops below.

It took more energy than I cared to admit to tear my gaze from the sight and head back inside, but at this moment, it was my duty to care for the dragon within.

I found Gold in our bedroom, sitting on the bed waiting for me. He had a long shining sword cradled gently in both hands, partially unsheathed as he admired it. He looked to be lost in memory, eyes flicking back and forth as if he was watching a movie only he could see.

"This sword belonged to a witch slayer, back in the seventeen hundreds, around the time of your Salem Witch Trials," he said as I entered, only slightly startling me.

Stepping forward cautiously, I stopped to stand just before him. He held the sword like a trophy — attachment shone in his eyes as he admired the blade. I didn't reply to his greeting, sensing he wasn't able to hear me as he was too lost in his thoughts.

"Vicious bastard, and to think he was only a human," he scoffed angrily. "He not only killed hundreds of witches but every kind of other folk he could. It's said he was only ever stopped because he accidentally fell through a portal into our world and was slaughtered almost immediately trying to kill a powerful dragon in his lair. Just goes to show that being strong doesn't mean you're smart."

The irony didn't escape me that a man who had killed so many of my kin by that blade was killed by one of Gold's by a twist of his unfortunate fate, and by the same fate, that very same blade now belonged to him. It would be the perfect Grimm's fairy tale.

"Why are you showing it to me?" I asked curiously.

"My brother reminded me of it when he mentioned the silver." He held the blade up for me to see. "This sword just happens to be silver. Not only that, but it could kill almost every living creature known to the three worlds. Excluding ghosts and the like. It's powerful, but not that powerful."

He unsheathed the sword fully, holding it to the light to show the deeply carved runes in the perfect shining blade. It was so pristine it almost looked like glass. It was so perfect it almost distracted you from the fact the sword had been wielded in the hands of evil.

"My people kept it in the hands of royal families for hundreds of years, keeping it safe because they recognized its power. That is until I stole it on one of my missions long ago." With one final glance, he sheathed it fully and extended it to me. "I want you to have it."

"What? No," I sputtered, shocked that he would even think

to give it to me. "It's yours. This belongs to one of Eerie's people, not myself. I can't just—"

He shot up and pressed the sword flatly into my chest, raising one finger to my lips to hush me. "This sword was forged to kill your people. I think it's the perfect sword to wield to defend them."

His words shook something inside me, and I shakily reached up to grasp the sword in both of my hands. Even in my awkward grip, it fit like a dream, the weight of the sword almost seeming made for me.

Something in me clicked just then, and the power of the sword rushed into my body. It sent a tingling trail up my arms just holding it, and I knew it had been the fates themselves who placed the blade in my hands.

"I will cherish it," I whispered in awe.

A wide smile split his face. "I thought you would. When Silver reminded me about the silver, it was the first thing that came to mind. It may not be Excalibur, but I think everyone and their mother is tired of that old legend by now."

Gold reached toward the table and pulled out a weapon's belt, taking the sword from my hand and securing it and its sheath to it before setting it aside on the table.

I smiled coyly, the tension of the day melting from me at the sight of the dragon acting so husband-like. "Wow, so I get to meet your brother and get a brand-new sword all in one day? You're going to spoil me."

Gold grunted, looking sheepish as he took me in with a long weary gaze. "You were spoiled long before I met you, little witch."

His words were so bashful yet playful that they sparked a hidden naughtiness within me that begged to pounce on him then and there. There were many ways I could think to reward him for such delectable behavior, but only one stood out to me then.

I reached down to toy with the waistband of my leggings, teasingly pushing them down off my hips. "You know I still want to use that bathtub I saw hidden in your bathroom. After last night, I think I really need to relax my muscles."

It took all of two seconds for his eyes to blaze a glowing amber. "I think I know other ways to relax you."

I dodged his arm as he reached out to snatch me, reaching down to toss the discarded leggings in his face. "You'll have to catch me first!"

With a delighted shriek, I darted from the room. The low growls of my mate followed me as we enjoyed the last few moments of the day before we were split apart by the cruel fates of having to go to work.

CHAPTER FIFTEEN

"I did it!" the elf mage cried, dancing in place as she cele-brated her first-ever successful ward spell.

The other students danced around the elf girl, clapping and cheering along with her as the last of the ward erupted up-wards to complete the barrier around the town. A glowing blue dome materialized overhead, covering the whole town with a pulsing translucent magical field.

It was magnificent.

"That's it? The ward is complete?" another cried, and the whole group turned to look at me for confirmation.

"That's it," I confirmed, smiling proudly at my students. "The ward is up and running, strong as it could ever be."

The group erupted into a buzz, engulfing me briefly in a flurry of hugs and excited handshakes. It was odd to see such a mismatched group of people differing in races and ages all so happy in that one moment. It was like everything, but our success faded to the background as they rejoiced.

After almost two weeks of non-stop effort, my work was finally finished. It almost seemed too good to be true. The small group I had nursed for the past few weeks had sucked up everything I taught them like sponges, so eager to protect their towns that they stayed up most nights practicing before I arrived to teach another lesson.

For some reason, it made me feel inadequate. Even though I had devoted my time and energy these last few weeks to help these towns, I couldn't help but feel guilty about how I had to be talked into helping the very people applauding me for my *good deeds*. I often found myself looking at their grateful faces wondering if they knew the only reason I was helping was that their king had dangled Gold's and my fate in their hands.

As I basked in their praise, I found myself wanting it to be because I had chosen out of my goodwill to help them. Never before in my life had I felt the need to be giving like this. My answer to the *if you found a million dollars would you donate it or keep it* was always to keep it. Even my shop wasn't completely selfless.

I did it for a living, with a side of helping people. Sure, I didn't need the money, but I if I truly cared about it, I wouldn't have been able to drop it as easy as I did. The question was, had I ever really cared about it?

I suppose it helped my conscience slightly that the classes were a wild success, with every single student able to manipulate their magic to mimic my witch magic. Their barrier turned out to be one of the strongest I had seen in my life, thanks to the plentiful wild magic of Eerie. It would be more than strong enough to hold off the brunt of Eris' force without problem.

The success was all thanks to how well I had gotten along with all of my students, however. They didn't care who I was or what trouble I would bring, they just wanted to learn from someone who could help them, and so they had.

To my surprise, most of the inhabitants of Eerie had been more than happy to embrace me as one of their own since I had decided to help them. I had expected some backlash, being an out-of-worlder come to enforce a strange magical barrier, but there was none. In fact, I had gotten more welcome offers to have dinner at people's houses and free drinks at the tavern than I ever had on Earth.

Never in my life had I felt so okay with being who I was, not feeling the need to hide the oddities of my nature. If my fire just happened to slip one day, they laughed and teased me, telling me I'd have to pay in full if I accidentally caused a village fire.

The longer I stayed here, the more I fell in love with this magical, though outdated world. It held a charm unmatched by the outside world. Its people, its community . . . I wished I could stay here forever and learn more about them.

"Excellent job everybody," I congratulated them, returning each of their hugs with one of my own. "Looks like we're done here."

I watched with a sort of melancholy happiness as the group slowly began to dissipate, all heading their own ways away from the barrier as I stayed there staring after the group. A couple turned to invite me to come with them to take a drink to celebrate, but even though I would like nothing more, I turned them down.

I had promised Gold I would come home as soon as my work ended here, and I didn't want to disappoint the man by showing up late to whatever sex party he had been planning all day. Since the classes were a success, I could now convince him to come down here with me at any time, so it didn't matter if I missed this one outing.

If I had my way, there would be many more, and not only in this town. I was looking forward to convincing Gold to travel all over this kingdom the minute his leash was off.

I waved the last couple goodbye, turning to head up to the town hall once I was completely on my own. I wanted to be the first one to inform Giovanni of the barrier, even though I knew he had probably already gotten wind of it himself from one of the many guards I had seen poking around my group at all times.

Even now, I was being followed by a gargoyle who darted between alleyways. He must have thought that because his skin was a near match to the shadows you wouldn't be able to see the eight-foot-tall giant playing mission impossible in the shadows around you. It didn't bother me much. In truth, I was happy with the fact that at least one other person was keeping their eye on me in the middle of all of the turmoil around town.

Plus, who wouldn't want to watch a giant beast dance around in the dark like he was invisible? I'd pay money to see that.

The town hall was empty that day, except for Giovanni positioned at the head table surrounded by the oh-so-familiar mountain of paperwork he had collected around him at all times. He waved one hand at me in greeting once I entered, not looking up from the paper he was heavily invested in.

"You'll be happy to know that every single one of my students was a wild success," I chirped, almost skipping to meet him by the table.

"I am," he grumbled, pushing away his work to focus on me. "It's a major relief to not only me but surely for the king, once he receives my word. I have already sent a message to him to declare Gold to be officially renamed a rightful citizen of Eerie."

That was a relief. I had thought it would take a bit more negotiating for that to happen, but they appeared to want to rush this process as fast as I did. It was almost too easy. That's when I noticed his mood.

The man looked tired and worn out, a look I should be used to seeing on the perpetually stressed man, but one I didn't like seeing at this moment.

He should be ecstatic, cheering with his people at the success of the barriers to help protect his people from Eris' creatures, but he wasn't. Instead, he somehow looked worse than ever. He was somehow even more drained than he ever had been before.

"What's wrong?" I asked, my gloating tone leaving me in

place of concern.

Giovanni's hand rose to his brow, massaging the bridge of his nose. "Nothing is wrong. Your job is done. You can return to your dragon."

He was lying to me. I could see it all over his brooding face. It was the same look Gold gave me when I told him I was still going to work in town, only without all of the pent up sexual tension, of course.

"Don't lie to me, Giovanni. You know you can talk to me if you have a problem. I've worked with not only you but your people long enough for you to at least trust me with that," I told him, cocking a hip on his desk to show him I wasn't going anywhere until he gave in and gave up the information.

The exasperated look he gave me was cold enough to freeze me in place, but I didn't miss the small flicker of relief that crossed his face once he realized I was staying to listen. "I am happy the classes were a success, but at the same time it is a bit disappointing."

Disappointing how? Had I somehow not done enough? I had worked every day for weeks trying to teach novices how to do a master spell, and he thought it was disappointing? I ought to hex the fucker.

I waited for him to say more but was too impatient to allow him the time to think over his next words. "How so?"

"It's disappointing because that means your work with Ee-ric is finished." He sighed and paced irritably over to one of the large windows. "If I'm to be honest, when you first came here, I didn't want to extend the offer to have you work with my people at all, but the Stone King convinced me that even if we were allowing a known criminal back in our lands it would be useful to gain knowledge of outside magic. Since then I have come to the realization you are far more helpful than I ever could have imagined."

His flattery was nice and all, but I was confused as to where he was headed with the conversation. "So, you're upset because I am useful?"

He rolled his eyes. "No, I am angry because you could be far more useful to us than teaching some wards. I recognize you are no teacher for your kind, but your power is clear. Working with the wild magic of Eerie is beyond difficult, and yet somehow you managed to not only harness it yourself but teach others how to do so."

It hadn't seemed difficult when my students or I had been working with it. In fact, it flowed through me easier than any other world's magic I had sampled. Here, the magic was so smooth I could conjure even master spells with ease.

Though, now that I thought about it, I had been alone in that. Almost all of my students had trouble leashing Eerie's magic, but I had thought it was that way with every novice. Back on Earth, I had almost equal difficulty early on.

"I had thought it was powerful, but nothing like that," I said in disbelief. "I had seen some struggling, but nothing too shocking for people new to the craft."

"Well, your students aren't quite new at it, you see. They had just never successfully wielded magic and were labeled that way," he informed me. "You see, that's the reason why we don't have witches and other magical folk flocking to our lands to take advantage of our magic. It's because of how difficult it is to wield. Yet, you manage to control it without even the slightest of struggles and simultaneously teach those previously incapable at the same time. We've only ever had one other magic wielder do that in the past."

That couldn't be correct. I hadn't done anything special in my teaching methods, nor did I know any tricks when dealing with difficult magic. I had just done that I always did with magic. Unless they just never had a competent witch on their roster, I was bewildered as to how they had rarely been able to leash the magic of their lands before.

Perhaps that was just it though. Perhaps I just approached it in a way other witches hadn't. It wasn't anything new to have outliers in any field when it comes to different approaches, so perhaps that was it. I just thought in a different way that made me different from other witches.

It wasn't that I was better, just that I thought differently. The signs had been there all along, now that I thought about it. My potions always had their unique twists, the potion being as strong as it was. Even my fire was different from my sisters.

Maybe I was more helpful than I thought.

"What are you trying to say with all of this?"

"I'm saying I want you to work with my people. I want you to use your knowledge to work with Eerie and help our people as a permanent ally." He paused to collect his thoughts. "I understand you have family and work on Earth, but you would be far more useful here. I'm not talking a full-time job, just joining us in helping Eerie build up its defenses against the growing forces in our shadows."

That was still a pretty big job to thrust on a person, but that was hardly the biggest issue I had with his invitation.

His offer would mean leaving my home. Moving here permanently and severing the roots I had planted there. In truth, I missed my family more than anything, but what Giovanni was offering was a life-changing opportunity. This was no hocus pocus and brewing potions for backaches and sicknesses, but working with kings and helping far more people than just brewing potions could accomplish.

Yet it was hard to imagine giving everything up for a life like that. I would need someone by my side to keep me grounded, but I didn't know that Gold would be the man for that. Gold was many things, including kind and adventurous, but was he the kind of man who would support me through this kind of a thing?

And could I give up being close to my family to take a risk like that?

On top of that, I would be leaving my shop behind and my home. However, it didn't feel like such a bad thing, the more I thought about it. For some reason, it felt like a door opening. I would be leaving the safety of my nest to do something I had learned I genuinely enjoyed doing, and not just because I had already invested in it.

If I stayed, there would be more students and more towns grateful for my help. I would be the helper of kings and kingdoms, not just my lonesome hometown.

I wanted to say yes and throw all of my cards in, but that slight seed of doubt held me back.

Was I good enough to say yes?

"Will you let me think about it?" I asked, my voice hollow as I was stuck in the storm of my self-doubt.

"Absolutely." He nodded. "Take your time. I'm sure it's a lot to throw on your plate, but I encourage you to settle on what feels right at the end of the day. Eerie will be waiting for you."

Numbly, I walked away, managing to make my way almost entirely out of town before I realized what I was doing. His words were echoing in my ears as if he had just spoken them. I looked back at the town, taking it all in once more.

I realized then that I wanted to stay here. To say yes. I wanted to explore this world and help in ways I never had back in Witches-Brew Cove.

Different buildings, different people, a better cause.

Yet, before I could turn back and say yes, I realized I still had unfinished business. I knew I needed to solve my problems before I jumped into something big like this. So for now, I was walking away, heading back to the cozy cave with my mate, knowing that I would come back eventually and cement my future.

Somewhere over the never-ending expanse of Eerie forest, the mirror in my back pocket began to vibrate, alerting me to a call. It had been so long since I received a mirror call, I had forgotten I even carried the thing. I knew before I even picked up who it was.

"You forgot to call me this week," Polly grumbled, sounding grumpy as ever. You would think a woman perpetually young and beautiful would be less grumpy than this old lady, but you'd be wrong. Apparently, women aged the same no matter how they looked.

"Hello to you, too, Polly."

Polly's face rippled into view on the clear silver surface, looking grouchier than ever in her too-perfect makeup. "Where are you? I only see the sky."

I held out the mirror for her to see the world around me as I cruised slowly above the trees on my broom. It was a sight I was growing used to seeing, but one I knew Polly would appreciate. She didn't like riding on the brooms any more than I did, but there was something to be said about the breathtaking heights you might never see otherwise.

Personally, I preferred riding on Gold to my broom, both in dragon form and otherwise, mostly because it could prove to be a wholly satisfying experience with the right friction.

Again, both in dragon form and otherwise.

"Didn't anyone teach you not to mirror and fly?" she prodded once she was satisfied knowing I was safe.

"Nope," I teased, before turning the mirror back to me. "What are you calling for, anyway? You normally give me at least three days after being late to a call."

She chewed on her bottom lip, clearly nervous over something. That visual didn't bode well. If Polly was nervous, it was something I had to be nervous about as well.

"Things are getting dicey in Faerie. Your sister called yesterday."

I was so startled I nearly came right off my broom. "Terry called? For real? I thought we weren't going to hear from her until she reappeared ten years later, like Carmin."

Polly laughed dryly, not surprising considering she was still sore over that. "Haha. She called late last night. It was as much of a surprise to us as it is to you."

I knew she was right about that. She wouldn't be calling otherwise.

"So, what did she want? Did she say anything specific?"

"Just that something drove her out of the Summer Kingdom. She's been in the Dark Woods for the last couple of months," Polly replied. "She was calling to say she was making her way home soon, in the next couple of days, but in the meantime she wanted me to tell you something, since she couldn't reach you in Eerie."

Why would Terry want to talk to me specifically? I knew she would try to call me if she ever reached out, but what would she have to say to me that was important enough for her to have Polly call me?

"What did she want to say?" I asked hesitantly.

"She said there are rumors in Faerie that the cultists have been gathering a large group of those monsters recently. She thought it was important to tell you that because she had caught wind of you being in trouble through one of our messages to her. Apparently, she believes something's brewing and it has something to do with Eris." Polly paused for a second, clearly thinking back over her words. "That is, she didn't mention Eris in specific. She just said the cultist."

I laughed nervously, trying not to appear as upset as I was at such heavy news. "Okay, well that was right to the point. I guess it was bad to hope she might just have wanted to message me about a hot guy she met."

"Yeah, well, it was a shock to us, too. I had thought there was no way she was collecting our messages from the post,"

Polly said without humor. "Apparently she's serious about it though because she reached out to us. If she didn't think it was important, I doubt she would have gone out of her way to have me tell you."

She wasn't wrong. It was a warning, if I've ever heard one. Terry always had a thing for sensing danger, and she probably wouldn't have jumped to the conclusion of calling me if she didn't think it had something to do with me.

It left a sour taste in my mouth and a sense of danger in the air.

"Oh, okay," I replied, swallowing the lump that rose in my throat. "Well, I mean, that's a lot to take in, but I suppose it was something I needed to hear. I'll tell Gold when I get back to the cave."

"Right . . . just be careful out there. Terry's going to be home in a few days, and I want you to be here when she arrives."

"Will do," I said with all the fake cheer of an upset youth. "I just finished my work in the village, so I have some free time to come visit you. I think it will be good to talk a few things out face to face."

Polly nodded. "Call me before you decide to head over, then. There's a reason you are over there, and I don't want you to risk it if we don't know it's safe."

"You're the one who asked me to be there!" I jokingly exclaimed.

"And I'm the one that's asking you to make sure it's safe before you do!"

"Fine," I said with my first genuine laugh, amused at how incapable of picking up on teasing she was. "I'll double-check everything before I leave. See you soon."

I ended the call with a final goodbye, feeling all of the excitement from earlier drain away on the wind with Terry's warning.

This whole situation just left an odd feeling in the air. I had gotten the feeling many times when spotting the creatures tangled among the brush in the forest below, but it was never as powerful as now.

It felt like something was sitting in the shadows and waiting for me to make a wrong move. I knew turning down that goddess had probably put me right on the top of her hit list, so going this long without hearing or seeing anything was only making the wait for her retaliation an agony.

It would come eventually, and I knew it would be when I was the least prepared for it, I just hadn't expected it to be right then.

I saw it the second I pulled up to the cave. The surrounding rocks leading into the hidden entrance were coated in filth and blood, trailing right down to the trees below the bloodied cliff. It looked like something had clawed its way right up from the depths of the forest.

From where I hovered in the air, the eerie silence of the windy cliff face was the only sound that could be heard. I tried to tell myself that was a good thing, Gold must have fought off whatever it was that climbed up to his cave, but I knew that was wrong. Gold would have flown to see me at the slightest sense of danger.

He wouldn't heal in the silence of his cave.

Fear grew in my heart, and it beat frantically in my chest as I forced myself to continue forward. Any other time I might have turned and run, but this was no ordinary situation. My mate could be in there, bleeding to death on the stone floor.

The scattered corpses of Eris' creatures littered the cave floor, their bodies illuminated in the low glow of the pre-lit torches. It looked like a scene in a modern horror movie, all blood and gore. The smell of the cave was putrid, the smell of festering meat. I might have gagged at the thick clinging stench if my fear hadn't stopped me from making any noise.

The further I stepped into the cave, the more I heard the sound of a chorus of animal grunts and squeals grow in volume in the bloodied halls.

I didn't want to go any further, but I couldn't seem to stop myself as I took step after step, growing closer and closer to the sounds.

One room was open, the treasure room, its contents scattered and spilled out into the dark hall. I knew without a doubt I would find what I was looking for in there.

Even with that knowledge, I hadn't fully been prepared for the sight I would see once I cloaked myself in magic and snuck into the room.

Silver was right. They were even more horrendous up close. Grotesque mockeries of what might have once been animals and sentient creatures littered the room, almost filling it with their swarm.

It sickened me to watch them in silence as they worked to destroy everything Gold had built. They swam in the piles of gold and destroyed the precious art on the walls. Years of beauty and collections were turned to ruin all at once.

What was worse might be the tangle of bodies massed in the center of the room. It was like those depictions of hell in old paintings, just a tangle of horrors and limbs. Some looked like animals, others like fae monsters — some with the heads of different animals, some with the heads of humanoid creatures.

What might have been bears with the limbs of a lion intertwined among pixies with eight haphazardly sewn on arms like a spider? Some were riddled with boils and growths, others with pristine pinned flesh that wasn't their own. The longer I looked, the worse they got, but the very worst piled at the top. Creatures of nightmare and childhood fear were positioned atop the creatures below, holding in their horrendous grasp a woman above all.

I knew without question who it was just by looking at her. Her beauty was ethereal, the goddess perched above the mountain of bodies she had collected on her terror-filled pilgrimage, dark wings fanning out around her like an invitation to come closer. I didn't dare even entertain the compulsion.

It was part of her pull, the dangerous symphony of beauty and the lure of chaos. The very reason for her being was to trick folk like me into her web only to kill me once I made the mistake of coming close.

Instead, I desperately looked around for any sign of Gold. Only he was nowhere to be seen—no golden dragon scales or signs of the man hidden among the bodies littering the room.

So where was he?

"I was waiting for you to arrive, witch."

CHAPTER SIXTEEN

My blood turned to ice in my veins, chased by a fiery panic at the fear of having been caught. Slowly, I inched my gaze back up to take in the woman whose black beady eyes now fixated on where I thought I had been concealed. My concealing magic must not work in the face of this goddess, yet I couldn't find the courage to move under the weight of those cold dead eyes.

She was worse than I had ever imagined, beautiful and wretched all at the same time. Bodies intertwined with her own, curling around her like a maelstrom of arms and legs.

Her voice was just as eerie, high pitched like a child, yet another harsh contrast to the environment surrounding her.

"Oh, come on," she cooed. "Don't you have something to say? I know you've been anticipating this meeting as much as I have."

Right, because I definitely hadn't turned down meeting her face to face multiple times. I definitely hadn't run to this other world in a bid to escape her at all.

Look at what good that did.

"I haven't been anticipating anything," I spat. "Where's Gold?"

She looked dissatisfied with my tone, her playful expression melting into one of mock sadness. Her aura was that of a pouting child mixed with the stomach-turning vileness of the evil surrounding her.

"Oh, that dragon? He escaped sadly." She pretended to sob. "He managed to weasel out of my grasp while that pesky little silver one distracted me."

Silver. Why had he been here? I'd thought for sure we wouldn't see him for a while after Gold had kicked him out.

Could she be lying? Trying to trick me into thinking she had his brother? But that didn't make any sense. Why would she lie about having Silver if she could say she had Gold? I had much more of an attachment to my mate than his brother, so it made no sense to claim Silver over Gold.

"Oh, but don't fret. We still have that one here," she continued, her voice sweeter than sugar. "Look, I'll show you."

She waved a clawed hand out to one of her minions, and from the shadows, they brought forth a bloodied familiar form. Even from this distance, I recognized Silver's pale hair and thin body, even though his face was swollen beyond recognition.

My stomach turned at the sight of the dragon, forcing me to swallow to avoid retching on the cave floor.

"What did you do to him?"

Her childish grin turned cold. "He's alive, isn't he? No need to sound so disgusted. I could have killed him, couldn't I?"

Just like her voice, her words were childish, though I didn't believe it for a second. Every aspect of her was a clever ploy to trick those unfamiliar with this brand of manipulation.

The look I gave her in response to her words was murderous. "Why didn't you, then? What do you want from me so bad that would make you do this?"

One clawed hand rose to her mouth, tracking a nail over her bottom lip. She looked hungry, staring at me like I was a snack she couldn't wait to snap up.

"Isn't it obvious?" She giggled. "I want you. That's why I sent that fae to go get you all those weeks ago. All of this has been for you."

Bile rose in my throat until it felt as if it was choking me, but I refused to allow her the satisfaction of knowing how deeply she got to me. "I'm not an idiot. I know you've been trying to get my attention. What I want to know is why. Why you've been attacking Eerie. Why you attacked my mate and his brother."

Her demeanor turned flippant as if my questions annoyed her. She didn't appear to like being questioned, but I wasn't going to stop just because I was near shaking in fear. If I was making her squirm, then I was turning her tricks around on her.

"Oh, those? Those are the first steps of my master plan." She stopped to point toward me. "One you are a part of, silly. Don't you realize how important you are? That potion may have been a silly marketing scheme, but it proves how powerful you could be if given the proper tools."

"It was a hallucinogen. That's all," I scoffed. "How the hell do you think that could have ever helped you?"

"It may have been that in the beginning, but under the right guidance, something like that could become a weapon." She rolled her eyes and pushed away from the tangle of bodies to stride closer to me. "Can't you see it? The horror something like that could cause? How useful that could be to the right person?"

I could. I could see exactly what my potion could do if corrupted to harm instead of pleasure. It could torture without ever touching someone. It was a conclusion I had already drawn long ago, and one that haunted my every waking thought.

Recognizing the disgusted look on my face, she threw her head back and cackled in delight. "You do! You understand, just like I thought you would!"

How could somebody be so happy about this? Gloat in the possibility of horrors beyond imagination?

"What would something like that accomplish? A war? Do

you seek pain that much? All that would accomplish is the deaths and torture of innocents."

Her look turned bewildered as if I was stupid for not coming to the conclusion already. "Do you forget who I am? I am Eris, goddess of strife and discord. I want to rule over the ashes and chaos that my army will leave in its wake. With your help, I want to take control of the three worlds and bring it to what it was always meant to be. A world of wild chaos."

She spoke the words like a prayer, awed at whatever horrid visions were flitting through her mind. Every word that fell from her mouth was embraced like a lover.

"You are out of your mind," I hissed. "Even if it were possible, I would never help someone like you."

She stilled, her body going tense with a cold fury. The full force of her empty black-eyed fury turned on me, freezing me where I stood. Those had been the wrong words to say to her at that moment.

Never once breaking my gaze, she stormed back to her pile of monsters, climbing atop them to look down on me as she strode dangerously close to the incapacitated Silver. Her mind looked to be racing to find the right words to reply, only to settle back into the disturbing calm I had first seen her in.

Her next words were as smooth as spiced honey. "You know, you aren't the first Carlisle I've had the pleasure of meeting."

Of all the things I had been expecting her to say, that wasn't it. Though that was probably why she chose them, to throw me off so she could manipulate me once more.

"What does that have to do with anything? Even if I believed you, there is no way you could convince me to join you by claiming my family might once have worked with you," I said sharply, not even considering her words for a moment.

If I allowed her to worm her way under my skin, I was done for. I couldn't allow myself to be vulnerable with her

209

having Silver in her grasp.

"No, no. It's true." She giggled, sliding one long talon-tipped finger over Silver's jaw. "I knew your father. Samuel. It was around the time I began to build my army."

It was smart bringing up my father. Everyone in the family knew he had contacts in life that weren't the most savory, but never once would I believe my father would have anything to do with this woman.

"Bullshit. He'd never willingly work with the likes of you," I spat.

She made a pouting face, claw nicking the pale skin of Silver's throat. The action had just the effect she wanted, sending my brain into a panicked fury.

"No. No, he wouldn't." Her thumb moved to catch the bead of crimson, pulling her fingertip up to taste the dragon's blood. "It was sad, really. All I wanted was for him to use his influence to help me win over a couple of witch families, but like you he denied me . . ." Her dead eyes flicked up to mine, a look of false sympathy crossing her face. "I didn't want to start that fire, but I had to send a message."

Her words were like a bucket of ice water.

The fire.

That was the night when half of my family had died.

She had to be lying. There was no way she was there. She had probably just learned about it and wanted to use it to sway me using fear. That had to be it.

"I don't believe you," I growled.

"You don't have to. Just ask your great-grandmother. Ask your aunt." She grinned. "Tell me why they just happen to know a ward powerful enough to stop a god."

The ward Aunt Carmin had dropped off that night. The one with the new steps, far fancier than any casual witch would know. My mind briefly recalled their faces when I had told them about Eris—fear, but no surprise.

They already knew.

They had been hiding the truth from me this whole time.

This woman. This goddess had been a part of my life this whole time, tearing my family apart from the beginning. If what she was saying was true, she was singlehandedly responsible for killing my parents. My grandparents. Polly's husband.

Eris hadn't just appeared two weeks ago. She had been in my life since the beginning. Images flashed in my mind, shadowy memories of her just out of sight—her outside my house before the mayor had shown up, her shape in the burning fire of my childhood home.

No matter how hard I tried to push the doubt from my mind, something within me knew it was true—all of it. This goddess had destroyed my family those years ago, and now she had her claws on the pulse of my family once more and was grinning down on me like a satisfied cat.

Was this what my father felt before he died? The stark fear of someone caught in a corner watching their loved ones in the palms of danger.

"Why?" My voice quaked with fury. "Why are you doing this? For power? Money? None of that will be worth anything with no one left to rule, and under your hand, there will be no one left."

She shrugged as if the answer was obvious. "Because I want to."

"That's it? You think you are going to tear down the three worlds because you want to?" My voice trembled with emotion, choked by the mourning of deaths turned murders. "You killed my family because you wanted to?"

Her lip curled in disgust, the first sign of her anger bleeding through the surface.

"Oh please, you think that's all I have going for me? Faerie is already practically falling into my hands as we speak. All it took was talking to the right people to start the crumbling of that weak world," she snarled. "It hasn't had a proper queen in centuries. I am giving you the opportunity to serve in my army before I begin crumbling the three worlds, starting with that husk of a kingdom, and you deny me? Your family was stupid to not side with me when I gave them the chance. What happened was their fault. Don't make the same mistake they did."

She gripped Silver's throat, constricting tighter and tighter around it as she spoke. "All of these civilizations are a thin coat of ice over the top of an ocean of chaos. I am just going to break that ice."

She was going to crush his throat, kill him right in front of me. The realization made my blood boil. "It will never work. Not by yourself. If you can't even manage to make a single witch side with you, you will fail as you always have."

"But I'm not by myself. Since your father, I have come a long, long way." She gestured toward the creatures around her. "Not only do I have connections in high places, but I have my beasts. I spent a long time corrupting them to be as strong as they are. By the time I'm finished, I will have enough to rip armies to shreds, dragons or not. The worlds will fall at my feet."

My focus was pulled once more to the creatures. Any one of them could be the textbook definition of a monster. It wasn't hard to imagine the horrors they could inflict, but what bothered me more was the horrors inflicted upon them.

Knowing that they suffered at the very hands of the person my own family had suffered at made a fearful sadness course through me. What they had gone through was far worse than my own family had, however. Because my family had died with the choice to deny her, but they were forced to obey her every command as a mere shell of what they had once been.

I refused to be like them. To cower at the feet of the woman who had hurt thousands. I would do what they couldn't.

"I don't care about your connections or your beasts. Nothing you are going to say will convince me. I will never join you," I declared, putting all of the righteous anger I felt for my family and those beasts behind my words.

It was a mistake.

Her lips parted over her teeth in a snarl. "Then I'm just going to have to find another way to convince you."

With a sickening meaty snap, her jaw opened wide, too wide for a normal human. The corners of her mouth split down the center, allowing both rows of yellowed jagged teeth to be bared as she snapped them down on Silver's throat. Silver awakened as her fangs tore into his jugular and buried themselves deep in his throat, and I watched as his eyes widened in fear.

I shrieked in rage, every ounce of pent up anger exploding forth at that moment. My fury was deep and feral, burning through my veins like wild magic. As I watched her tear into the throat of my mate's brother, I allowed my magic to fully unleash from my body for the first time in my life.

A power long concealed within me burst forth, burning through my chest and arms. My fire took me then. I was consumed, my body replaced with flames the color of suns colliding. My hands found the sword at my waist, unsheathing it as we both were engulfed in flame.

In a flurry of fire and limbs, I burned through the line of monsters between the goddess and me, incinerating every creature upon contact.

The second I broke through the final guard, she ripped herself back from Silver, her gore-covered face morphing into a look of shock. It took a matter of seconds for me to appear before her, flaming like the mythical phoenix. For the first time, her face drained of all leftover humor and was replaced with the deadened look of someone realizing they were in danger. She turned, only for a moment, her back to me as she sought something in the crowd.

It was just the opening I needed.

With a grunt, I snapped my wrist, flinging the fiery sword right at her back. It missed as she shot away, somehow sensing the blade before it struck. I might have cursed myself for missing such an obvious shot, but in her panic to dodge the blade, she had released Silver, allowing him to fall back into the pile of writhing bodies. I hesitated only for a second, making sure the dragon didn't get caught in the burning bodies, then fell to the safety of the inner cave before charging forward toward where the goddess had disappeared in the fray.

I had to dive to avoid the clawing arms of one of her spider monsters, shoving a ball of pure flame into its gaping mouth and frying it before continuing on my pursuit of the woman. She tried to get past a wall of towering monsters, but they didn't part soon enough, and I took advantage of the moment and launched myself at her.

She tried in vain to bat me away as I fell on her, but I locked myself onto her back, struggling against her unbelievable strength to find her throat with my flaming hands. Wrapping them tightly around her throat, I watched as my flame began to burn over her whole body, melting the flesh around where I made contact.

It seemed too easy, the woman far weaker than her monsters. It took so little effort to cage her with my fire. She barely had the strength to resist as she burned under my grasp. Instead, she begged silently with pathetic cold dead eyes. Just as I thought it was over, and her eyes rolled back in her head, succumbing to her fate at my hands, I was ripped back from the woman by a large fleshy paw.

The creature had snuck up behind me, using my distraction to get a hold of me and fling me into the stone wall. I tried to brace before I hit, but the sheer strength with which I was thrown felt like I had shattered almost every bone in my left side.

This time the scream was not of fury or rage, but pain. It felt like my entire left side was engulfed in an inferno. My vision went double, then triple as everything seemed to enter a wind tunnel. The sound was robbed from my ears, the heat from my burning flames fizzling with the onslaught of agony. I couldn't focus, my brain in shambles as it rang in my skull.

Loud hissing screams echoed in my mind, and I barely focused enough to see large dark beasts pile into the room one after another. They tunneled through the fires, latching onto any and every creature they could as they tore through the mass of flaming bodies.

The flash of gold was enough to alert me as to who our new visitors were, and through my delirium, I had enough of a mind to recognize my mate.

He had arrived, with reinforcements.

Even if I failed at killing the goddess, we still had a fighting chance with our rescuers. Elation filled me, even as I lay broken on the stone floor of the cave, smoke filling my lungs and blurring my vision.

My joy may have come too soon, however, because my vision was suddenly crowded by the large dark figure of one of Eris' giant beasts. Its gaze locked onto me as it trudged slowly over to where I lay crumpled on the cave floor.

I couldn't defend myself with my magic anymore, any leftover energy diverting to keeping me breathing through my pain. I didn't even have my sword at my hip any longer. I was defenseless and vulnerable.

Panic overrode my adrenaline, and I tried clawing away towards where I knew my rescuers could see me, but its large paw latched onto my shattered ankle and dragged me right back. I tried looking for a weapon, anything to use against the beast, but my vision was still distorted with fire and shadows.

Just as it leaned down to take my torso in its meaty grip, a glint of something silvery drew my attention. Even though I was cornered and my leg was swollen beyond belief, the realization of what it was gave me enough energy to pull myself back just far enough to curl the stinging fingers of my intact hand around the hilt of the sword. Just as I managed to get a grip I was snatched right off the floor like a doll, my broken body limply complying.

I could barely make out its features in the light, but what did make itself obvious was its putrid smell and the sharp sizzle its slimy skin made as it burned through my shirt and stung on my skin. My brain screamed at me to escape, to try and struggle out of its grasp, yet I was held immobile by the immense pressure I could feel building around my shattered chest.

I could feel my ribs cracking even more under the force of the hideous creature's paw, my breaths growing even more labored as I locked gazes with the milky gray eyes of the beast. Its eyes showed no intelligence, no sign of anything human beneath an animal hunger burning deep within itself.

Despite that, I knew this was not what the creature had once been, that its very nature had been corrupted under the hands of the very goddess who tore my own world apart years before. Both it and I were victims of the same woman.

Whatever it had once been was long gone, replaced by the drooling vicious beast Eris had corrupted it to be. It was easy not to see it as anything more than that when looking at the tangle of other monsters. Yet, when forced to come face to face, you could see the exact tragedy that had created it.

Every creature here was a victim like so many others, and they weren't even left with the minds to comprehend that.

"I know you can't understand me, but I promise you I will do everything in my power to help stop the bitch that did this to you," I gasped through labored breaths, emotion and pain from my wounds choking my voice.

Mustering the last of my strength, I used every ounce of what was left of it in my body to heave the silver sword right through its gelatinous eye and into its skull.

It let out a warbled cry, grip slowly loosening as it brought us both crashing to the ground. I remained in its grip, trying to lessen the pain in my chest with shallow gasps as the world burned around both of us.

Dragon fire turned the world a burning orange, surrounding me and the creature whose life was seeping from its body in its eviscerating beauty.

"I'm sorry," I whispered into the fire.

Heavy mourning settled deep in my chest, the feeling so hollow I had to close my eyes and allow myself to bask in the pain of it.

It was a pain that came with the final throes of battle, a pain I would need to remember. Soon I would use it to burn every single person responsible for Eris' monstrosities to the ground.

I focused on the dancing fires around me as my world faded into the seductive pull of unconsciousness, my body succumbing to its wounds. My final thoughts before drifting off were of my dragon, of his smile and his warmth.

CHAPTER SEVENTEEN

I woke to a warm hand on my forehead, strong masculine fingers brushing the hair from my forehead. I was sure it was a dream. It felt far too nice to be a product of anything but my deepest dreams, yet there was one man who always seemed to be able to deliver that feeling to me.

"This is a nice change," I murmured into the quiet.

I opened my eyes to Gold's brilliant smile as he leaned close to me from where he stood beside where I lay. "I wouldn't say it's nice to have to nurse my mate back to life, but I can see what you mean."

I let out a small laugh, which turned into a weak cough. Gold helped me sit up and knocked on my back to help me through the fit, tucking me closer to his chest. It felt like I had tree sap coating my insides.

"That's our healer's salve. She had to coat your lungs with it to help heal the punctures from your ribs," Gold told me as he pulled my oversized shirt up to reveal the green coating on the skin of my midsection extending further up under the shirt.

It was familiar, all right. I had seen it several times before sealing Gold up. The stuff was more than powerful. Just a dab could heal a broken bone in hours.

Comforted by the knowledge that I was well taken care of, I moved onto the next topic crowding my mind. "Is your brother okay?"

"I'm just peachy, thanks for asking," Silver's familiar regal voice chirped.

I hadn't realized we weren't alone in the room, but now that I had my bearings and could look around, I could see I was surrounded by two other men in medical cots, both sporting a significant amount of bandages. One was Silver, and the other was a griffin I had seen guarding me on one of my many village outings.

I smiled politely at the guard before turning my attention back to Silver. "It's good to see you're alive. After what happened I had worried . . ."

Silver grinned wide, extended his hands in a *who'd have thunk it* gesture. It was so similar to something Gold would have done that I knew it had to be something passed between the brothers.

"It takes a lot more than getting my throat torn out to kill me, love." He laughed, gesturing toward his throat where a huge pink patch of flesh looked to be healing. "Thank the gods for dragon genetics."

I looked down at my own body, which looked worse for wear despite not feeling any pain. I knew when I had passed out that I had broken every rib I had along with every other bone on my left side, so the fact I was even sitting upright was a bit of a shock to me, even with the salve.

"How long was I out?"

"Twelve hours," Gold answered. "After we got you out of the cave, you were taken to the kingdom's best healer, which is why you are even awake right now."

"After you'd been chucked into a stone wall by a monster and then almost being squeezed to death, the king saw fit to rush your treatment. Though it might have also had something to do with my brother losing his mind and threatening to tear down buildings if you didn't get help immediately," Silver said teasingly.

Gold's arm snuck out to snap against the back of his brother's head, knocking him forward on his cot. Silver hit him right back, landing a sharp jab right in Gold's stomach with an audible thud.

I had to fight back a giggle at the two, amused by their brotherly antics.

Seeing the two together like this, I found it was hard not to realize the two were blood. My sisters and I are the same when we're together, even though we're all practically full-grown women.

"You were always the barbarian, Gold," Silver hissed after taking a hit to his sore ribs. "That's what I get for rescuing you."

I had almost forgotten how odd Silver's presence had been in the cave. After everything that happened, I hadn't even thought to ask why he had been there in Gold's place. I suppose I had thought Silver just happened to be in the wrong place at the wrong time.

"How did you get captured anyway? I heard some of it from the bitch, but not all," I asked him curiously.

Gold's eyes narrowed, and he focused his gaze on his brother, suspiciously. "Right. Why were you there? I know you were stupid and got captured trying to help me escape, but you shouldn't have been there at all."

Silver let out an awkward cough, looking anywhere but at us. "I was concerned for you, is that a crime? After all the problems happening recently, I didn't want you guys to not have some eyes on you. I just happened to be those eyes."

So he had been guarding us. How adorable.

"You were spying on me?" Gold growled, completely missing the point and straightening to crowd his brother.

Before any fight could break out between the two, they were interrupted by the arrival of a guest.

"Enough, it hardly matters who was spying on who," a familiar gravelly voice interjected.

We all turned to see the giant stony form of the Stone King

crowding into the small room, followed by Giovanni Moore, who wore his arm in a sling. I hadn't seen the Stone King since our first meeting a couple of weeks ago, so the shock of seeing his hulking form was just as fresh as the first time.

Silver moved to dart up and out of the room, but Gold's arm stopped him in his place. "He's not here to arrest you, Silver. Relax."

"Not today," Zeal said stonily, eyeing the dragon with a dry gaze, "but don't think because your brother and his mate are now out of the woods that you are, too."

The silence stretched between the two, until Giovanni finally interjected, "With all due respect, King Zeal, but after the fight, I doubt anyone is in the mood to argue. That goes for you, too, Silver. We're here for a reason."

Everyone in the room focused on me, making me squirm under the intensity of their gazes. It felt like I was sitting in the principal's office awaiting my punishment.

"So, what is it you came for then?" I asked impatiently.

Giovanni sharply inhaled, as if realizing he was the one who had to speak. "We need your answer on the offer I made you a few days ago. Gold has already agreed to work with us as long as you are with him, but that means we need your answer. Will you partner with us to help protect Eerie against those things that attacked you?"

Gold had agreed to — wait, what?

I looked to the dragon for confirmation, and he nodded in response.

The thief of Eerie had agreed to work with the crown? For me?

My heart warmed all at once, happiness exploding through me. Gold had agreed to work with the people he trusted least, for me. I was anxious and happy and relieved all at the same time.

Any worry I had before for the dragon not being stable

enough to help me through this process melted away as I threw my arms around his neck, hugging him for all he was worth.

"I thought you didn't want anything to do with the crown?" I breathlessly asked once I had pulled away.

He held up a finger, quieting me. "Whatever you thought was wrong. While I've spent my life rebelling against these kingdoms, I would reverse it all in seconds in order to be by my mate's side."

The look in his eyes was gleaming with love and adoration, every ounce of his commitment shining through onto me. It was such a compelling sight I found myself wrapping my arms around him once more to bring our faces closer to one another.

"If you guys even think about doing anything lovey-dovey while I'm in the room, I will not hesitate to end my own life right here and now," Silver groaned.

Gold gave his brother a wolfish smile over his shoulder. "That sounds like jealousy, brother."

Silver's eyes flashed in anger, yet once more just as he was about to launch himself off the bed, the Stone King let out a loud frustrated sigh.

"By the fates, can we just get an answer so we can go back to our work?"

Gold and Silver looked properly chastised, sobering at their king's words.

The king focused an unforgiving stare directly on me, "Storm Carlisle, I wouldn't offer you this position if I didn't think you could handle it. While I won't punish you if you disagree, I will be disappointed. You show promise working with my people, and I personally would like to give you the opportunity to work with them on your own terms."

I had already thought over what my answer would be a million times. It had been on my tongue from the start, only held back by my worries for my mate. Those all seemed to be so far gone now.

I now had much greater worries than the petty ones from the days before.

I had been face-to-face with a monster, had her in my grasp, and watched her escape. How could I turn away from this now, when people were in danger because I couldn't finish her off?

I didn't think it was my fault, but I felt like I would be doing a disservice to the woman I had become in that cave if I didn't say yes here and now. If I said yes, I would be working to help protect people from the same fate my own family had fallen victim to.

"Okay, I'll do it." The words fell from my lips like an oath. "Just give me whatever I need to sign, and I will."

"You look fine."

I fidgeted with the front of my jacket, jerking it this way and that until Gold's strong hands stilled my own. With a firm tug, he pulled me flush with his body, holding me against the broad expanse of his chest.

"If you don't relax, I'm going to have to make you relax," he purred in my ear.

His words sent a knowing shiver down my spine, and I half debated taking him up on the offer. If only we had the time to do so.

"You can't blame me for being nervous."

He let out an amused huff. "No, I definitely cannot. I've met your family myself, and I can't say I'm anticipating their reaction to your news."

I rested my chin on his chest, allowing myself a moment of comfort before pulling away. "Fine, I'll just put my big girl pants on and do it. It can't be any harder than the last month, after all."

"Good." He gave me a slight push right on my ass, making sure to let his hand linger for a second too long. "Let's get going before those crones croak from old age."

I grumbled under my breath, trudging forward toward the cabin I had spent the majority of my childhood inside of.

Polly and Carmin were waiting outside as if they had somehow known we were coming, which they probably did. I wouldn't doubt those two witches could tell when anyone a mile away walked on the property.

"Welcome home," Carmin said with a wave. "We've been waiting."

Called it.

"I don't doubt that." I laughed, stepping up onto the porch.

Polly watched both of us as we approached, giving us a warm smile. "Glad to see you two are both in one piece."

"Pleasure to see you, too," Gold greeted.

Polly looked between the two of us, seeming to implore us with just her gaze.

It was Carmin who finally voiced her question. "Well, we know you're here for a reason. You might as well get it out now and avoid the small talk."

Right to the point, just like her.

"I'm moving — to Eerie. I was offered a job, and I took it. I'm going to work for the seven kingdoms to help build the magical defenses there." The words spilled from my mouth all at once, as if saying them faster would make them any easier.

One of Polly's perfectly carved brows rose. "That's it? You got a job? Storm, you just barely escaped a battle with your life, and you think we'd somehow be angry you took a job?"

She sounded almost angry. I was taken aback by her reaction, not thinking she ever could have taken my declaration in that way.

"Well, not exactly. I didn't think you'd be angry, I just—"

"You just were nervous we wouldn't approve," Carmin explained, rolling her eyes. "Simple as that, Grandmother."

Polly's outraged look melted into one of exasperation, and she snorted. "My granddaughter runs a sex toy shop. If you think I wouldn't approve of you fighting for a kingdom, you're dead wrong."

"Hey, you said you didn't care about that!" Carmin cried.

"I don't, that's my point," Polly told her, turning back to redirect her attention on me. "It's your life, Storm. If it's what you want to do, then so be it. Just be careful."

I hadn't thought it would be that simple. I had thought for sure she would yell, or be angry, maybe even strike Gold with a lightning bolt, but none of that happened. Instead, she genuinely looked like she supported me.

I felt stupid for worrying, stupider for assuming she'd somehow look down on my choice. Polly had only ever been supportive of my ventures, and I had misjudged her.

"Of course, Polly," I insisted. "We both will."

Gold agreed, placing a protective arm across my waist, "I'll always be there to help keep an eye on her, so don't worry too much."

"Good. Knowing my great-granddaughter, she'll need all the help she can get," Polly said with a sigh. "Don't mistake my words for thinking she's weak, either, dragon. She's more than proven she's capable on her own."

Gold nodded in response before turning to remind me. "We can't stay long. Though I enjoy every moment spent with your family."

"Don't be a kiss-ass," Carmin drawled, tossing the stick she had been fiddling with at his head.

Gold batted it away with one hand, giving her a pinched look. It looked like there was no love lost between the two . . .

"Enough of that, Carmin," Polly said with a smack at her

granddaughter's head. "Just say goodbye like a normal person."

With that, all stood and exchanged our partings, with both Carmin and Polly giving us tight hugs. Gold looked uncomfortable at the attention but gave it back with gusto.

I don't think either of us wanted to leave, but we both knew our time here had to be short. We had barely made it a few steps before out of nowhere Valentine came barreling up the driveway, her pink hair wild around her head.

"Wait!" she called.

I paused just long enough for her to slam right into my side, enveloping me in a bone-crunching hug, "Thank the fates I didn't miss you!"

It had been so long since I had seen my sister in person that I had almost forgotten her scent. Bubblegum and daisies. The nostalgic scent of my flowery youngest sister.

"Hey, Val." I laughed, tightening our embrace. "I was wondering when you'd show up. It's bad enough I didn't get to see one sister — missing you would have been the worst."

"I know! That's why I wanted to be here. I just didn't expect it to be now," she said cheerily, her happiness clear in her smile.

I patted her on the head, mussing her perfect curls under my hand. "Well, it's good to see you, Val, even if I've got to make it brief."

Her face crumpled. "Aww, you're already leaving?"

Her disappointment was heartbreaking, but there was little I could do. "Yeah, I've got some traveling to do. I'm going to meet some kings."

She looked like she was somewhere between pouting and feeling happy for me. I knew how disappointed she must be to know I wasn't here to stay and chat, but it was clear she knew I was serious.

Val frowned, tucking herself further into my arms. "Well,

at least you know we will always support you, no matter where you are. Remember that," Valentine comforted.

"Good. Just don't get mad when I ask for some of that support." I laughed and laid one parting kiss on her forehead.

It felt like eons since I had any of my family members in my arms. After all of this, I had thought I might never be able to ever again. I pulled in deep breaths of her scent, memorizing it before pulling away and staring around us at the home I had grown up in.

It would always be the same glass cabin and graveyard of singed lightning rods. It pained me to say goodbye to it, for now, not knowing when I might come back to it. I had so much to do, and so little time for visits like this.

"So that's it, huh? You're off to fight in the seven kingdoms of Eerie all by yourself?" she asked in an awed whisper.

I looked over my shoulder to see Gold in full dragon form waiting beside a portal, amber eyes watching me wistfully. "I won't be alone. I've got Gold. Who could ask for a better guard?"

Her glossed mouth perked into a wry smile. "I suppose you're right. I can't wait to grow up and find a mate like yours."

"Hey!" I chided her, reaching a hand out to snatch her chin up. "Don't grow up for anyone but yourself. Live your life for you, not a man nor a woman. The rest will come later. Trust me."

She batted away my hand with a small chuff. "Yeesh, I got it. I didn't expect you to get all poetic on me."

I guess a lot changes when you go through as much as I have. I suppose my preachiness was a bit off-putting, now that I thought about it.

"Just remember what I said." I laughed, giving her a final little wave as I began to stride toward the portal. "Oh and don't forget to smack Terry for me while I'm gone."

"Got it!" she called, waving us off energetically.

Gold leaned down to offer me his back, but I dismissed the offer.

"I think I'll fly with you for this one," I told him, calling forth my broom with a snap of my fingers.

It materialized immediately, the broom feeling warm and familiar in my hand. In a complete shift of fate, I found myself missing the feel of it in my hands when I did not have it. If only the old me could have seen me now.

"Well, let's get going then. You and I have a lot of work to do." I stopped to turn and give him a wicked smile. "After we christen our new home, that is."

He teasingly tried to snap at the back of my broom, but I was already ten steps ahead of him, shooting right into the portal without a backward glance.

My life was about to get interesting.

EPILOGUE

"It's just as you said," Polly Carlisle said into the darkness of the kitchen.

Across the table, Carmin Carlisle fidgeted with a steaming potion she had procured from her niece's shop. Or now, ex-shop. With her a world away, it meant one less Carlisle helping Witches-Brew Cove.

"I told you that was why I left."

Polly sighed. "I know. I just had hoped it wasn't true."

"Everyone wants to think that they live in a world where things like this don't happen." Carmin's words were soft, yet firm.

Carmin had come to terms with what needed to happen years ago, after the visions she had seen in the fire that took her family's life. It was why she had disappeared for so long when she should have been at home with her family.

"It's not going to be easy," Polly murmured.

Carmin looked out into the dark woods beyond the window, the sky sparking to life with the beginnings of a storm. "No, it is not. Something big is coming, and not only to Witches-Brew Cove, Grandmother."

Polly sighed, low and distraught. "I realize that. It's just hard to rest easy knowing that so little of this is in our hands."

Carmin gave her a reassuring smile. "To be fair, I don't think resting easy is going to be an option for either of us. We have a lot of work ahead of us."

"Well, then I suppose we better prepare. Do you know who's next?"

Carmin's smile turned wicked, sliding her gaze out to the dark yard once more. "I think our second champion is just arriving."

YOU MAY ALSO ENJOY THE FOLLOWING FROM EXTASY BOOKS INC:

The Perils of Feeding Handsome Shadows
Ellise Valentine

Excerpt

I hadn't been expecting company so late into the night. Outside, the wind howled loudly, trees shaking with the force of it. The high winds of late fall were always the best for setting the atmosphere for the holidays up north, that is if you don't mind giant tree branches occasionally snapping off and hitting the house. That's what I had been half afraid happened when I heard the first knock.

Things always seemed to interrupt me in the middle of working. I was halfway through preparing the first round of dishes for my lonesome Thanksgiving, making a large surplus of food in preparation in case any of my lone wolf siblings showed up at the door. I knew they wouldn't, but I liked to hope.

The sudden sound shocked me right into the air, almost making me send my perfectly pressed pie crust to the ceiling. With a curse, I speedily dusted the flour off my hands and onto a stray dishtowel, hurrying toward my front door. Along the way, I tried in vain to fix myself up as much as possible before greeting my guest.

I already knew it wasn't going to be any of my family, since they had called long earlier to hand in their excuses as to why they couldn't come. Having a visitor was a bit out of the normal for me, so I checked through the peephole just in case I was being tricked into inviting in some sort of burglar or a serial killer.

Seeing nothing upon my first inspection, I slowly open my door just enough to get a small glimpse of the porch. The darkness of the night didn't help me as I scanned the path outside, but either way, I didn't see anything. Only the same untouched, quiet landscape I was used to seeing most of my days.

I almost dismissed the knocking, telling myself I was probably just hearing things, or maybe someone was pranking me. You'd be surprised how far kids would go to do silly stuff like that. Once a year, around Halloween, a group of teens would invariably travel two hours into the forest to mess around in a terribly haunted mansion just to win points with their peers. It was a tradition everyone around participated in at least once in their lives, and I had the scars to prove it.

It was only when I started to close the door that I spied a small dark figure huddled in the corner of my porch.

No bigger than a medium-sized dog, it stood in the shadow of the windowsill next to the door, shaking wildly. Its slitted yellow eyes glowed in the light of the door, watching me warily as it remained where it stood. The thing made no move to leave, or pounce — instead, it just recoiled and shook like a wounded animal.

I knew the general rules when it came to animals that strayed too close to civilization. Typically, if they were close to people, they were either wounded, starving and seeking anything edible that wouldn't put up a fight, or the type that wasn't afraid of us and more likely to just attack.

Since I had opened the door and it hadn't pounced, it was probably hungry. Biting my lip, I considered my options. I could leave the creature out in the cold and snow, or I could risk myself and go out and help it.

Damn that holiday spirit.

Making a quick trip to my kitchen, I return with a whole slab of roasted ham. I slowly eased the door open, and cautiously crouched down to extend the meat toward the creature.

"Hey, buddy. I have some food for you," I crooned, trying my best to radiate peaceful energy as I inched my way across the porch.

In the darkness under the windowsill, I couldn't make out even a single feature of the thing. It was like it melted right into the shadow. It could have been a gremlin, for all I knew.

When it moved into the light, I almost shot right back into the house. Instead of a physical form, the creature moved forward with smoky tendrils of grey mist, like a living cloud. At my slight start, it recoiled slightly, only to continue its forward momentum with renewed vigor once its gaze landed on the meat.

I had no idea what bravery I conjured to keep my shaking hand outstretched. Part of me was terrified of this mysterious creature and wanted to flee, and another didn't want to scare away the already skittish thing. Probably the only reason I stayed in place was the fact that if I turned and left it now, I would beat myself up for days knowing I left some poor creature hungry in the cold.

I had already sealed my fate when I went and grabbed the meat — a hunk of ham I was going to use for a soup later in the week. I would have to face it now, even if the thing was a demon ready to eat me whole.

The first tentative brush from one of its tendrils on the back of my hand made my entire body shiver. It was the most peculiar rush of warmth and energy, with just the barest amount of physical form to it. It was both there and not, solid and yet incorporeal at the same time.

The first touch was quickly joined by another, then another, until my entire hand was engulfed in warm writhing tentacles of smoke.

I could feel it tug at the meat in my hand, not removing it as it explored around my grip. My arm felt heavy, drooping with the heft of the creature attached to it. It seemed strange that something that looked like a storm cloud could even have weight, but that was far from the strangest thing about the situation.

It took less than a minute for the thing to finally pull away, falling back onto the porch and leaving me with an empty palm.

It even ate the bone.

"Hungry little thing, aren't you?" I huffed a small laugh, unable to help the tremble in my voice.

ABOUT THE AUTHOR

Ellise Valentine is a fan of epic fantasies, spicy romance, and everything fantastical. Always aiming to entertain with her words, she sometimes writes a good story to go along with them. Living in the magical state of Washington, she most commonly resides at home staring out a window and imagining the perfect plots to torture her readers with next.